Meant *for* You

SAMANTHA CHASE

sourcebooks
casablanca

Published by Sourcebooks Casablanca, an imprint of Sourcebooks, Inc.
P.O. Box 4410, Naperville, Illinois 60567-4410
(630) 961-3900
Fax: (630) 961-2168
www.sourcebooks.com

Printed and bound in Canada.
MBP 10 9 8 7 6 5 4 3 2 1

Prologue

"I DON'T LIKE THE SOUND OF THIS."

They never do, William Montgomery thought to himself. Why did everyone have to go and question his motives when all of his decisions in the last five years—in business *and* his personal life—had been raging successes? Thanks to his leadership, Montgomerys was a Fortune 500 company with more growth and expansion to come. And as for the family? Well, if it weren't for him, the whole Montgomery line might have come to an end. Yes, sir, William had gone on a one-man campaign to get this young generation to start falling in love and making families.

His own three sons had been more than pulling their weight in that department. At last count, William was the proud grandfather to four beautiful grandchildren, and he had high hopes of watching that number grow. He looked over at his brother, Robert, and frowned. "What is there not to like?" he asked.

Robert was younger than William by only a year and yet he always came across as being much older; he took life way too seriously and it didn't always bode well for his family. Just recently, Robert's second oldest son, James, had come back to North Carolina after over twelve years of living apart thanks to the discord between him and his father. William knew his brother loved his kids; he just didn't seem comfortable with really *knowing* them.

That was William's gift. He was a people watcher by nature, and over the years, he had honed his skills to a science. With just a little bit of time and knowledge of a particular person, he was able to figure out who would be a perfect match for them. It was easy with his own sons because he was with them all on a fairly regular basis. His niece and nephews? It was taking a little bit longer.

Luckily Ryder and James already knew the women they wanted to spend their lives with; William had just given them a push in the right direction. His eldest nephew, Zach, was a challenge; he was getting ready to head to Alaska on some sort of climbing expedition. If William didn't know better, he'd swear his nephew was doing it purposely, to avoid spending time with him. He chuckled. He'd get to him eventually.

"Summer is not cut out for the corporate world, William. Why would you even consider such a thing?"

He shrugged. "She's tried everything else. She's been moping around here between your house and ours for almost a month and seems to be a little lost. All I'm suggesting is that we give her a little guidance and see if perhaps she could find a place within the company."

"But why send her to Oregon? Zach will be furious!"

Of that, William had no doubt. "Oh, it doesn't take much to make your son furious these days. Eventually we'll figure out what exactly has him in a constant snit; in the meantime, I think Summer could be a great asset to his team."

Robert let out a mirthless laugh. "Have you met my daughter? William, Summer is flaky and flighty and doesn't know a damn thing about business. She paints, she dances, she sings. None of those things are going to be an asset anywhere within the company!"

William didn't care for his brother's description of Summer. Robert may have been her father, but William felt fairly protective of his niece. "Maybe she does those things because no one ever expected her to do anything more with her life. Seems to me you just wrote her off as a spoiled heiress who'd marry well and then be her husband's responsibility."

"That would make my life a hell of a lot easier," Robert said wearily. "Seriously, William, I don't see this as being her thing. She doesn't even know anyone in Oregon."

"Nonsense. She knows her own brother. She's visited the offices there before, so she's familiar with the staff. And then there's Ethan Reed."

Robert glared at him for a moment. "Ethan? Why would you mention Ethan?"

The urge to roll his eyes was strong, but William resisted. "Do you have a problem with him? He and Zach have been friends since they were ten years old. He's practically family."

"Yes, but Summer had a crush on him for the longest time. She was always trailing after him and Zach. I was relieved when the boys finally graduated and went off to school. I'm fairly certain she's over it."

"Did he ever do anything inappropriate?" William asked.

"No. He was always perfectly respectful. But he's much older than she is."

"Six years is hardly a lot these days." By the look on his brother's face, William realized he wasn't helping.

"All I'm saying is I'm sure you have nothing to worry about. He probably considers her a sister after all these years. And you said yourself Summer seems to be over her childhood crush. I was merely pointing out that she would have another friendly face in Oregon."

"Why can't we place her here? In North Carolina? Why send her to the West Coast?"

Why was his brother being so difficult? "She needs to feel like she's doing this on her own, without either of us hovering over her."

"Zach will hover."

William didn't doubt it for a second. "At first. Then he'll get annoyed and leave her to her own devices and move on. Plus, he's got the whole Denali thing coming up, so she'll actually have a chance to work on her own without any interference from any of us. It could be exactly what she needs to shine."

"Summer would shine in a room filled with thousand-watt bulbs," Robert said almost begrudgingly, unable to hide the pride in his voice.

That made William smile. It wasn't often that his brother had something positive to say. "She certainly does. Let's give her a chance to shine while showing her that we believe her to be a woman we take seriously. I think it would be the perfect thing for her confidence right now."

"I could kill the bastard who broke her heart."

William agreed, but he also knew whoever the man was, he wasn't Summer's true love. William had spent enough time with his brother's family to make quite a few observations. It was almost getting too easy. Soon he'd have to find another hobby, but for right now, he figuratively sharpened his Cupid's arrow and prepared it to take flight.

Chapter 1

"It's quiet; it's too damn quiet."

"No, it's peaceful. For the first time in over a month, I can hear myself think."

Zach Montgomery looked over at his friend Ethan and grimaced. "That's the problem. When Summer is in town, no one should be able to hear themselves think. I'm telling you, something is up."

"Why are you looking for trouble?" Ethan asked wearily. "For weeks you've been practically begging for a little peace and quiet, and now that you have it, you're bitching about it. Just be thankful, and long may it last."

While Zach knew Ethan had a point, it just wasn't sitting right with him. When his father had warned him his little sister was coming to Oregon to try her hand at the family business, Zach had been less than enthusiastic. It wasn't that there was anything wrong with Summer, per se; it was just that she was like a force of nature.

And not in a good way.

"Why would she go silent now?" Zach said as he paced his office. "Besides trying to work in every department we have here at Montgomerys and making everyone her new best friend—she's baked cookies for every department she's interned with, when she was in accounting she organized Sheila's baby shower, in human resources she taught Margaret's daughter how to tap dance, and in legal she dog-sat for Mark—and in the midst of it all, she has been particularly vocal about this whole Denali thing. I leave in less than thirty-six hours and she goes missing? She's up to something." He looked to his best friend and company vice president and waited for his agreement. "Right? She has to be up to something."

Ethan shrugged. "Personally, I'm just enjoying the quiet." The truth, however, was that Ethan was worried about Summer's whereabouts, maybe even more so than Zach. Summer had been a distraction since she arrived on the West Coast. The first time he had seen her step off the elevator, Ethan was lost. When had Zach's little sister grown up into such a vibrant and sexy woman? It had been a shock for him to see that the girl he had grown up with wasn't a little girl anymore. She wasn't a nuisance anymore, and the more time he spent with her and got to know her, the more intrigued he became. He had come to expect to see her around, talk to her. Hear her laugh.

See her smile.

Oh, man; he had it bad. A quick glance at Zach and he was relieved his friend was too busy staring out at the city skyline to notice what was probably a goofy look on Ethan's face. He'd gotten pretty damn good at hiding his feelings for Summer; hell, he had to. If Zach or any of the multitude of Montgomery males found out Ethan had a serious thing for Summer, he'd be screwed.

And beaten to a bloody pulp for sure.

Not something he was looking to see happen.

So he hid his feelings, brushed her off, and generally tried to make her feel like she was just a friend, a coworker. She was far from it. Summer had a light about her, an energy that was impossible to ignore. Sometimes all she had to do was walk into a room for him to feel it. He wanted to embrace it and engage in conversation with her. Unfortunately, there was always one of her brothers or cousins or uncles around waiting with the stink eye whenever he let his guard down. It was pretty exhausting to keep up with them all.

So right now? Yeah, he was happy to have a little peace and quiet and a chance just to be himself without having to watch how he spoke or looked or hovered whenever Summer Montgomery was in the room. He'd take whatever he could get in that department until she moved on to whatever adventure she wanted to take on next.

"Why won't she answer her phone?" Zach snapped, effectively pulling Ethan out of his own introspection.

"Maybe you just finally succeeded in pissing her off." Ethan sighed. Honestly, dealing with this family was enough to make him thankful to be an only child. One minute Zach was complaining about having his sister around and the next he was complaining because she wasn't around.

"What's that supposed to mean?"

Ethan stood and walked toward the large picture window to stand beside Zach. "Listen," he began, placing a hand on his friend's shoulder. "You have been less than hospitable since your sister got here. You've let her know on a daily basis that you're not taking her interest in the company seriously because you think she's just going to move on whenever the mood strikes."

"Well?" Zach said with a hint of annoyance. "It's true! She's been...what? She's been a photographer, a yoga instructor, a New York City tour guide…then there was her whole dog-walking business. I mean, Summer has a short attention span, Ethan. She's wasting my time and the company's time by coming here and trying to play in the business world like some sort of corporate Barbie."

"That's just cold, Zach, even for you."

"Look, you've known my sister almost as long as you've known me. Am I exaggerating any of this?" Ethan shook his head. "Summer is a free spirit; hell, my mother must have known it at birth because she gave her the perfect name for her nature. She's an amazingly talented and creative woman; she just needs to channel her energy someplace else and leave me the hell alone."

"Isn't that what she's doing?" Ethan reminded.

"No. She's being a pain in my ass right now. I wouldn't listen to her constant harping on me about the climb and how I am being irresponsible and—"

"Well, she kind of has a point there."

Zach rolled his eyes. "Not you too," he said, sighing irritably. "We've been over this. I got the doctor's clearance."

"And that doesn't mean squat and you know it," Ethan replied. "I've known you for far too long, man. I know when you're not one hundred percent on your game, and you're not. You're still limping from the last trip."

"It was a broken leg, Ethan. It wasn't a big deal."

"It is when it's not fully healed. You need to be thinking a little more responsibly. This isn't an easy trip. You need to be in top physical condition, and you're not."

"It's a limp and it's not going to be a problem."

"Zach…"

"Can we get back to the subject at hand? Summer and how she's off pouting somewhere and probably hoping I'll cancel my plans because I'll have to look for her. Well, it won't work; I'm not buying into it."

"You can't have it both ways," Ethan muttered as he turned to walk away.

"Excuse me?" Zach said, his gaze honing in on his friend.

Throwing up his hands in frustration, Ethan turned back around. "I can't keep saying it; you say you don't want her here, so she's not here and now you're ticked off. Make up your damn mind, Zach!"

Ethan was right; Zach knew it and yet it didn't help to put his mind at ease. Stepping away from the window, he went and sat back down at his desk, resting his head in his hands. "I swear she's like a miniature hurricane; she swoops in, wreaks havoc, and then moves on. I just wish she'd answer my damn calls so at least I'd know she's all right before I leave for Denali."

"Have you asked around the office? Maybe she mentioned to someone she was going someplace."

Zach looked up and considered Ethan's words. "I hadn't thought of that. She's so chatty that I'm sure she had to say something to someone." He immediately reached for his phone and called his assistant into the room. While he waited, he returned his attention to Ethan. "Gabriella knows everything that goes on in this building; if she doesn't know where Summer is, we're screwed."

"We?" Ethan said with a laugh. "Sorry, bro; your sister, your problem."

"Don't give me that," Zach said dismissively. "You

and I both know you're practically family and I'm sure that, deep down, you're a little bit worried about her yourself.

More than you know.

Luckily he didn't have to respond because Zach's assistant came into the room. Gabriella Martine looked like she'd stepped right off the pages of Italian *Vogue*. She was tall and slim with just enough curves to grab a man's attention. Ethan had always admired her beauty, but not in a way that made him want to act on it. Gabriella had jet-black hair, crystal-blue eyes, and a cool, distant disposition.

Ethan seemed to prefer the type with blond hair, dark eyes, fair skin, and a chatty nature.

Summer Montgomery.

He was so screwed.

"You wanted to see me, Mr. Montgomery?" Gabriella said in her usual cool, clipped voice.

"Have you heard from Summer?" Zach asked, leaning forward at his desk.

His assistant looked at him oddly. "Is there something wrong?" she asked.

"I can't get her on the phone, and I wanted to talk to her before I leave tomorrow night."

"I last spoke with your sister yesterday before she left. She needed help with some travel arrangements." She looked curiously between Zach and Ethan. "It didn't seem like a big deal."

"Travel arrangements?" Zach yelled, coming to his feet. "What? Was she planning on going back to North Carolina without saying a damn word to me? Why didn't you tell me?" he demanded.

Gabriella seemed to shrink back momentarily at his outburst. Ethan was about to intervene, but Gabriella composed herself quickly. "She's not moving back to North Carolina; she was making plans to get away for the weekend with...a guest."

"A guest?" Zach repeated, completely stupefied. "Who the hell is this *guest*?" He turned to Ethan. "Did you know about this? Did you know that Summer was dating someone?"

Ethan was too stunned to speak. Summer was dating someone? When the hell had that happened? How did he not know? Wracking his brain, he tried to remember if he had seen Summer with anyone but came up empty. And pissed. And insanely jealous. Feeling Zach's intense scrutiny yet again, Ethan shook his head and turned away.

"Where are they going?" Zach asked his assistant, who was slowly walking backward to the office door. She stopped at her boss's question.

"She...she booked a weekend getaway—one of the hot springs resorts."

Zach cursed under his breath. "It's just like her; leave it to Summer to drop a bombshell like this right before I have to leave."

Gabriella took a step back toward the center of the room. "No disrespect, sir, but Summer didn't drop a bombshell; she simply did as you requested. She left. She knew the two of you were going to keep fighting if you left for that...that climb you're doing," she said with just a hint of disapproval and then cleared her throat at Zach's arched brow. "So she decided not to add to your stress before you left. If you ask me, she was trying to help you."

Coming around his desk, Zach stalked his assistant until she began to back away again. "Help me? *Help me!*" he barked. "How is going off for a weekend with some man none of us knows helping me? This little stunt hasn't decreased my stress; it's added to it! Get her on the phone! *Now!*"

"No."

Both Zach and Ethan froze in place at the one softly spoken word from Gabriella. "Excuse me?" Zach said with a hint of a snarl.

"I said no. This is not a business problem; it is obviously a family problem. In my opinion, Summer did the only thing she could. She didn't agree with what you're about to do and neither do..." She stopped. "If you want to argue with her or yell at her, you'll have to do it on your own." She looked at her watch. "I'm going to lunch." She spun on her ridiculously high stiletto heels and left the room, closing the door quietly behind her.

The two men stared at one another, completely dumbfounded. "What the hell just happened here?" Zach asked. "She has never spoken back to me like that! What is going on with all the women in this place?" He raked a hand through his hair. "This is all Summer's doing. Gabriella never gave me any trouble until now. Until Summer."

"Dude," Ethan interrupted, "you have got to stop blaming your sister for everything. You are clearly starting to lose it. I think you are officially done here. Go home, finish packing for the trip. I'll wrap things up around the office, and I'll meet you at the airport tomorrow night. Trust me; you're not going to get anything done here. Just...go home."

"Dammit, Ethan, how am I supposed to get ready to leave when Summer's out there with some…guy no one knows? I'm supposed to be looking out for her, and she totally took off with a stranger!"

"Okay, dramatic much?" Ethan said sarcastically, hoping to defuse the situation. "Just because you didn't know anything about this guy doesn't mean there's anything wrong with him."

"She's been here for a month, Ethan. The first week she was here she didn't leave my sight. So she's known this guy for a few weeks. Tops. I don't like it. Maybe I need to find that spa and talk to her." Turning and scanning the room for his keys, he spotted them and continued to think out loud. "What if it's that creep who ruined her life in New York? What if he's come here and is trying to win her back? Maybe she'll believe all of the crap he'll try to sell her about how sorry he is and how it will never happen again. Right. Like that would be the truth," he spat.

Ethan stopped him before he could walk out of the office. "Zach, get a grip. You are getting ready to do this climb. You need to focus." He knew he was going to regret his next words, but he couldn't stop them if he tried. "I'll go; I'll get the information from Gabriella and go try to talk some sense into Summer."

"You're climbing too, Ethan. You don't need to be chasing my sister up and down the coast."

"You got a better idea?"

Defeat washed over Zach. "No. But if anyone's going to go, it should be me. Summer's my responsibility."

"And this climb has been something you've been looking forward to for a year."

"And you haven't?"

Ethan shrugged. "It's going to be great, sure. But I'm just along for the ride. I don't have any illusions of making it to the top. That's all you, buddy. I'll be happy if I make it to the midway point."

Zach shook his head. "What's the point in that? You should be right there with me! How cool would it be to stand at the summit and look down at the world around us?" He grabbed Ethan by the shoulders. "Can't you just see it? This will be our best adventure yet!" When Ethan didn't respond, Zach removed his hands. "You used to want to do all the same things I did; what's happened to you?"

Taking a step back, Ethan shrugged again. "Nothing's happened to me; I just don't get the rush out of it anymore the way you do. You wanted to do this and I think that's great. I'm going to be there with you just like always. If I make it to the top, great; if not, I'll live."

"Lame. Totally lame."

"Now you see why it's better for me to go after Summer; you need to get your head on straight. That's what's important. I'll take the drive, find her, and talk to her and make sure this guy's on the up-and-up, and I'll meet you tomorrow night. I promise."

Zach took a minute to think. "Just make sure you do, man. She could be anywhere in the damn state. Those resorts are scattered everywhere. I don't want to do this without you."

Ethan smiled. "I wouldn't miss it for the world."

—ᴧᴧ—

It took every ounce of willpower Ethan possessed to be patient while Zach got his things together and left the office. He didn't let out a complete breath until the elevator doors closed, and even then, it was a full five minutes before he let himself relax. He checked his watch and noted that Gabriella should be back from lunch any minute. He'd always had an easy working relationship with her, so Ethan figured it wouldn't be hard to get the information he needed about where Summer had gone.

And with whom.

Could Zach be right? Could her creepy ex-boyfriend be here, trying to woo her back? Summer hadn't said much about what the guy was like other than how he had devastated her, and that was enough to make Ethan want to kill the bastard. While he wanted to believe Summer was stronger than that—that she wouldn't fall for this guy's excuses and promises—he couldn't be one hundred percent certain. For as long as Ethan had known her, he didn't really know her on that level. He'd hate like hell to have to kick this guy's ass and send him packing and risk Summer being angry with him because of it.

With his fists clenched at his side, he paced. Where the hell was Gabriella? Back and forth, back and forth, until he began to feel like an Edgar Allan Poe character, slowly going insane while listening to the clock ticking on the wall. There were dozens of things Ethan needed to do in order to be ready to head for Denali with Zach the following day; this little detour was certainly not going to help him in any way, shape, or form. Unfortunately, he was putting Zach's needs first, so his friend could have more time to focus.

Then he heard a desk drawer close and the sounds of Gabriella getting settled back in at her desk. With a fortifying breath, Ethan pasted his most relaxed and charming smile on his face and walked out to the reception area. At Gabriella's anxious expression and quick look around, Ethan knew exactly how to play this. "No worries, I sent him home."

She visibly relaxed. "Oh, okay."

Ethan walked over and sat himself down on the corner of her desk. "Between you and me, I couldn't stand him another minute longer. It's bad enough I'll have to travel with him and all. Hopefully he'll take the next twenty-four hours to chill out."

"One can only hope," she said coolly, organizing papers on her desk.

"He just has a lot on his mind and, you know Zach; he likes to control everything and everybody. I know he's just concerned about Summer, but he needs to realize how crazy he comes off sometimes."

"Try all the time."

Ethan hid a smirk. "Well, believe me, I've known them both for so long, this is nothing new. I don't think Zach can help feeling responsible for Summer. And Summer? She just likes to push his buttons. And she's good at it." Gabriella barely shrugged. "Still, you can't blame Zach for being upset. I mean, he has so much on his plate right now…the least she could have done is told him where she was going."

Gabriella sighed wearily. "I know what you're doing, Ethan," she finally said. "It's one thing for me to step in when you and Zach are snapping at one another; it's really quite different when it's Zach and Summer."

He was confused. "Why?"

"They're family. The two of you are the top

executives here at Montgomerys; it is beneficial and sometimes necessary for me to step in and send you each to your own corners until things cool down. The way I see it, this is a *private* family matter. They need to work it out for themselves. It's none of my business."

He hated when people threw solid logic at him. "But it's going to affect Zach on this climb. Is that what you want? For him to be so distracted that he makes a stupid mistake and hurts himself or another member of his team? All I'm asking for is the name of the town she went to, Gabriella. That's it. Please. For Zach's safety."

She glared at him. "Low blow, Ethan."

Knowing he just about had her, he leaned in closer. "I'm going on the climb too. Zach's the leader. I need to know I've done everything humanly possible to make sure his head is on straight." He paused and gauged her reaction. "Please, Gabriella. If you won't do it for him, do it for me. I just want to make sure Summer's all right."

She sighed. "Fine. She's going to Burns. There's a resort there where you camp in a giant tepee not too far from the hot springs. She was supposed to leave today but I'm not sure what time."

"Thank you!" he said before jumping from her desk and heading to his office. Using the office phone, he tried calling Summer. It went right to voice mail. He did a quick mental checklist and realized he could delegate the rest of his work to the junior execs and be out of here within thirty minutes. First, he'd swing by Summer's place just in case she hadn't left yet. Then, if by chance he missed her, he'd stop by his own place and grab a few things before making the five-hour drive south. Tepee camping? Leave it to Summer to do something so outrageous. Most of her family wouldn't be caught dead in anything less than a five-star hotel.

This family was going to be the death of him.

With any luck he'd catch her before she left, and all of this could be cleared up before he had to meet this mystery guest and fight the urge to strangle him. This was so not what he needed today. Before Ethan could talk himself out of what he had clearly gotten himself into, he called an emergency meeting and did his best to wrap up all the loose ends around the office before packing up and heading over to Summer's.

He wasn't sure what he was hoping to accomplish with all of this. Obviously it was going to put Zach's mind at ease, but in the process Ethan was torturing himself. For the last month, Ethan had done his best to keep his distance from Summer and make sure he was never alone with her. By going after her like this, he was certainly tempting fate.

What would he actually do or say when he found her? What was he going to say to this mystery guest of hers that wasn't going to result in charges being pressed against him and missing the flight to Denali? Summer Montgomery had done nothing but tie him up in knots for the better part of twenty years; he should be used to it by now.

But somehow, the image of a teenage Summer and the woman she had grown into brought to mind two very different kinds of knots. Back then, it had been a fleeting feeling—more of a whimsical wish. Now? He was drawn to her as a man, with all of the feelings that went with it. If it weren't for his friendship with Zach and his closeness to the entire Montgomery family, Ethan would have acted on his feelings for Summer as soon as she became an adult.

He was too loyal.

He was too afraid to rock the boat.

He was totally screwed.

Chapter 2

WHAT WAS SHE THINKING? SURE, SUMMER WAS always up for a new adventure, but maybe she should have given this one a little more thought. The fact that it was going to piss off her brother was certainly a perk though. The soothing voice of her GPS informed her she had another sixty miles to go. "I should have just flown," Summer mumbled to herself. "Road trips are all fine and good, but this is a little more than I was looking for."

She didn't mind driving; she even found it to be relaxing. Looking over at her sleeping travel companion, she felt a twinge of envy.

"Note to self, get some sleep over the weekend."

It was one thing to say it and quite another to actually accomplish it. It seemed like months since Summer had gotten a good night's sleep—one of the downsides of having your life turned upside down and being unsure of what to do next.

Her family had always been a blessing though, and when her father and Uncle William had suggested this temporary move to the West Coast, Summer had figured, why not? What did she have to lose?

Nothing.

That was the problem.

For all of the traveling, exciting jobs, and constant stream of activities in her life, Summer Montgomery had nothing to show for it. No permanent home, no career to call her own, and no one to love her. Well, except her family, but they didn't count. Not in the way she meant. She wanted a man in her life. She wanted someone who was hopelessly in love with her and brought out the type of passion you only read about in a good romance novel.

She thought she had at least found part of that with Alex. He had swept her off her feet—literally—while she had been out walking her clients' dogs. He had started walking with her in the park after their initial meeting and had talked about his love of dogs and how he wasn't allowed to have pets in his building. Summer had actually felt bad for him and found it sweet that he had wanted to spend time with her—and the dogs. He was attentive and romantic and said all the right things, but they were all a lie. It had been crushing to find out that he was actually a married man with a wife and two kids living in Chicago. There had never been a question about why he was always traveling; his job dictated it. What she hadn't known was that she was the pit stop, not the other way around.

The thought of being the other woman made her want to retch. That was so not who she was—not who she had ever wanted to be—and yet, here she was. It hadn't taken long to pack up her New York apartment and head home to her family in North Carolina, but after a month there, she had grown restless. It must have been obvious to everyone, because when her father and uncle had sat her down, it seemed like they had everything worked out. They must have been working on it for some time to have had all of the details already in place for her, including a new condo in Portland.

The West Coast was definitely a pleasant change of pace for her, but she had yet to fully make the connection. It was as if she knew that this too would be temporary and so she held herself back. It would have been different if her brother hadn't welcomed her with barely veiled hostility.

Typical Zach.

It wasn't that she was expecting some kind of grand gesture from him or a welcoming committee, but it would have been nice for him to at least smile in her direction once in a while or tell her that he was happy she was there. It wasn't normally Summer's MO to run away from a challenge, but at this particular point in her life, she needed a little more TLC and a lot less…well, of whatever you'd call it that Zach was always spewing in her direction.

All of the employees at Montgomerys had welcomed her with open arms and warm smiles. Even Ethan.

She sighed at the image of how pleased he had looked when she arrived. It was almost as if he had been waiting for her. All of her girly parts melted on sight. And if it weren't for Ethan running interference between her and Zach, she probably would have left by now. Music played softly in the car; maybe the love song channel wasn't the best choice, but it certainly fit her mood. Someday she'd have what all of these songs were talking about: love, passion, and someone who wanted only her.

Not her plus a wife and kids.

Damn Alex.

A soft snore beside her brought a smile to Summer's face. To be able to sleep that soundly, that deeply, was to be envied. Maybe this weekend getaway would help her achieve at least a small amount of peace. While not really a fan of roughing it, the thought of sleeping in a tepee with a private hot tub seemed to be just the sort of thing for her. She knew she could be a bit eccentric and quirky. No one in her family would even consider camping like this. Good. They weren't invited.

She was making good time now that she was out of the city limits and let out a sigh of relief when the GPS stated it was only another thirty miles to go. Either she was going really fast or she had seriously lost track of the time. It didn't matter; she was almost there and it would be a blessed relief to get out of the car and stretch her legs.

One more glance at her companion and she whispered, "Just you, me, hot tubs, hot springs, and the stars in the sky. It sounds perfect."

A weekend away from everyone and everything was exactly what she needed to perhaps gain a little perspective on her life. Who knew? Maybe by the time she got back to Portland, she'd have a sense of direction and finally be able to put this miserable chapter of her life behind her and move forward.

With a renewed sense of purpose, she pressed down on the gas and smiled. "Welcome to the first day of the rest of your life, Summer. Hopefully."

One of the many perks of working for a multibillion-dollar corporation was having the use of the company plane at your disposal. Ethan didn't know why he hadn't thought of it earlier; he was already pressed for time, so why drive almost five hours each way when he could make it a forty-five-minute flight? He didn't feel bad about using the plane—after all, this was Montgomery business. Personal business, yes, but Montgomery business nonetheless.

He wasn't sure if he was relieved or annoyed when he went around to Summer's place and found her gone. It might have saved him some time and energy if she'd been there, but now he had a little extra time to think about what exactly he was going to say to her. The idea of sounding like one of her brothers didn't sit right with him. For starters, Ethan didn't want Summer to think of him that way. Then there was the fact that he had never been on board with how patronizing Zach, Ryder, and James had always been to Summer. She was the baby of the family and the only girl, but it was like they did their best to keep her out of their little inner circle. For all intents and purposes, Summer was an only child with three siblings. He didn't want to be lumped in with that.

He could present himself purely as her friend, someone who was just looking out for her, but he had a feeling she'd see right through that as well. There was no way to deny that he was there primarily on her brother's behalf. Although Ethan was many things, he wasn't a liar. So maybe it was best to play that particular role to the hilt. It was safe; it was expected. Summer wouldn't question it at all. Meanwhile, he'd get a chance to have some time with her without prying eyes and reassure himself that she was really okay.

Though she didn't talk specifics about why she had left New York, Ethan was shrewd enough to know she hadn't left happily. Maybe it was a job issue, or maybe it was one of those times where Summer had grown restless and just wanted to move on. Neither of those would be a surprise, but he had noticed an underlying sadness in her, making him consider the idea that it was something more. People broke up all the time without having to move to another state to get over it. He would have expected Summer to have a big enough support network of friends who would make her want to stay in New York. If it *were* because of a breakup, just what had this guy done?

The thought filled him with rage. How could any man hurt her? Didn't the jackass realize how fortunate he was to be with a woman who was so full of life and love and laughter? Ethan had dated a lot of women in his life and none of them came close to the level of vivacity Summer had without even trying. Any man who would willingly walk away from her was a fool. Ethan had searched for a woman who was just as amazing as Summer, and it was damn near impossible. If he had been allowed the opportunity even to consider a relationship with her, he would grab it with both hands and most likely never let go.

Whoa…hold on there, he chided himself as he felt the plane begin its descent to the runway. *Where the hell had that thought come from?* While Ethan knew there would be issues on many, many levels if he had a relationship with Summer, was he even considering it being a permanent one? Well, that would solve any issues with the Montgomery males wanting to castrate him if the relationship ended, but getting married and settling down was something he had never really given thought to.

Haven't you? a little voice inside asked. *You never thought about settling down because you aren't allowed*

to settle down with the one woman you really want.
"Oh, shut up," he muttered and then rolled his eyes at
the ridiculousness of his current predicament. He was
flying to the middle of nowhere to chase after a woman
he wanted but couldn't have, all in the name of helping out a friend. *Sucker*, the little voice mocked, and
unfortunately, Ethan agreed. "And a glutton for punish-
ment, apparently."

Distracting himself with the view out the window,
Ethan did his best to push thoughts of settling down
aside and finally try to come up with what he was going
to say when he actually found Summer. He had no idea
when she had gotten on the road, so for all he knew, he
might arrive before she did. Wouldn't that be a kick in
the pants? Racing to get there only to end up having to
sit around and wait? That would be his luck.

Although Gabriella hadn't divulged the actual name
of the resort, Ethan had gone online to research the area
and discovered there were only three to choose from. He
had arranged for a rental car to be waiting for him at the
airport, and the GPS on his phone was loaded up with
all of his destination options so he could make the most
efficient use of his time. He probably could have pushed
a little harder for the information, but he had a feeling he
had already done enough to tick Zach's assistant off. If
he didn't watch himself, he'd find himself going on his
own lunch and coffee runs or ending up with an endless
line of inefficient temps to help him on upcoming projects. Gabriella was scary good at her job, and he needed
to remember to treat her with respect. Even Zach knew
to tread lightly with her most days.

Until today.

Ethan shrugged. Not his problem. Zach would have to work it out with her when he got back from Denali. Right now Ethan had his own problems to deal with. He already had to smooth things out between Zach and his sister; he wasn't going to get sucked into a tussle between Zach and his assistant.

A guy could only do so much.

When the plane finally came to a halt, Ethan collected his few belongings—his phone and wallet, a jacket, and a pair of sunglasses—and made his way to talk to the pilot. "I wish I could give you a more accurate time that I'll be back. Unfortunately, I'm not one hundred percent sure where my final destination is going to be."

"Not a problem, Mr. Reed. I've actually made arrangements to take care of some maintenance while we're here, so I'm good for several hours."

With a wave and a word of thanks, Ethan made his way through the airport to the rental car agency. Though he'd called ahead, on such short notice, he was unsure that he'd get a vehicle of his liking, but right now beggars couldn't be choosers. Cursing the slow process, he waited his turn, and when he finally got to the counter, his worst fears were confirmed.

"Seriously?" he snapped at the kid behind the desk as he took a step back to indicate his size. "There is no way I can fit into a compact car!" He was so going to give Zach hell for this.

"I'm sorry, sir; there's nothing else available. If you'd like, I can direct you to one of the other agencies and maybe they…"

Ethan held up a hand and shut him down. "I'm on a serious time crunch here," he said. "Just give me what you've got." With any luck, Summer would be at the first stop he went to and his time crammed into the tiny car would be blessedly short. Signing the necessary paperwork and snatching the keys, Ethan stormed out into the parking lot, cursing Zach the entire time.

On some level, he knew he should be equally annoyed with Summer for all of this, but it was far easier to direct his anger toward Zach. He didn't allow himself to show any emotion where she was concerned; he'd had a lot of practice.

Any hopes of the car being larger than what he thought were dashed as he walked up to the tiny, white two-door vehicle. Ethan sent a prayer heavenward and unlocked the door before bending his body in a way that did not feel the least bit natural. Even with the seat back as far as it could go, he felt crammed in. He got himself situated as best as he could, pulled up the GPS, and did his best to remember that he was doing a good thing. He was keeping harmony between a brother and a sister.

Both of whom he loved.

Just in very different ways.

—⁓—

Everything felt different. Summer had gotten herself settled into her tepee and felt a sense of giddiness at the experience. The furnishings were sparse and she didn't consider it a problem. The weather was unseasonably warm, so once she changed into more comfortable clothes, she opened the large flap to let in the fresh air.

"What to do first?" she said as she stepped outside and looked around the property. "I could go for a swim in the springs or I could just crash right here and relax."

She tapped a finger to her chin while considering the options. It didn't take long for Summer to realize she was far too keyed up to just plop down and relax anywhere. Glancing back into the tepee, she noticed her traveling companion had decided to relax on the padded pallet on the floor. What Summer wouldn't give to be able to do that herself.

"Yoga it is," she muttered, knowing thirty minutes of it would put her mind and body at ease. Then she'd be able to fully enjoy not only the hot tub in the middle of her makeshift room, but also the outdoor springs, if she decided to take the walk down there.

Being well-prepared was something Summer excelled at. Walking across the space, she pulled her yoga mat from her supplies and decided to set it up right outside her little temporary abode. Getting into position, she took a deep breath and then slowly let it out.

Is anybody watching?

I wonder if it's going to rain while I'm here.

I know I brought my own food, but what if I want to go out to eat?

Do these pants make my ankles look fat?

Relaxing her pose, she huffed with frustration. "Okay, clearly I am not in a good place yet." Doing her best to clear her mind, she once again got into position and took several deep breaths. Relief hit her when she actually began to hear the sounds of nature and not the voices in her own head. Bending over slowly, she touched the ground and held the pose. Working from her toes up, she felt her muscles begin to relax. Once she had gotten through several basic stretching poses, Summer stood tall and breathed in deeply and finally felt herself reaching the level of peace she had been seeking for over a month.

Unwilling to break the inner peace she had going on, she moved into a series of lunges. She was feeling the burn and scolded herself for taking such a long break since she'd last worked out. From there, she moved into a downward facing dog before deciding she was ready to be off her feet and go to some of her favorite floor poses.

Inversions were always a favorite for her, and it didn't take long for her to twist and bend until she was completely folded in half in a plow pose. One of Summer's yoga instructors had told her this pose would help her sleep. She had never found it to be true but was still hopeful. "I could stay like this for hours," she said softly, listening to the sounds around her. Birds chirping…water flowing…breezes blowing…car doors slamming. Wait, car doors slamming? What the…?

It wasn't often that Summer made special requests when she stayed at places away from home. This was one of the few times she had. She had asked for a campsite far away from where the general public or other guests were staying. From what she was told, this was sort of a VIP tepee and ensured her privacy. Her eyes were closed, her breathing deep, but there was no mistaking the sound of a car or the footsteps quickly coming her way.

And that's how Ethan found her. Bent in half in a way he didn't think normal humans could be. He nearly tripped over his own two feet and his tongue at the sight of Summer's perfect body folded completely in half.

Without breaking her pose, she said, "Hey, Ethan. What are you doing here?"

Chapter 3

CLEARLY HE WAS BEING PUNISHED FOR SOMETHING HE must have done in a previous life. It was the only explanation Ethan could think of for how he found himself in the current situation. "Uh…"

Summer gracefully unfolded herself and ended up in a sitting position before rising to her feet and heading into the tepee. She emerged a moment later with a bottle of water in her hands. "So?" she prompted.

"What? Oh, right," Ethan stammered. "Your brother was a bit frantic when he couldn't get you on the phone. We leave tomorrow night for the climb, and he was flipping out wondering where you were."

She arched one perfectly manicured brow at him. "Really?"

Ethan nodded.

"Well then, tell me this, Ethan," she said as she slowly walked toward him. "If Zach was so bent out of shape, why is it that *you're* here and not him?" She stopped just inches from him with a smirk on her face and her hands on her hips.

The temperature seemed to climb at least another ten degrees, because suddenly Ethan was sweating. "Well, he had a lot of things to take care of before we left. You know, we'll be gone for a couple of weeks."

Summer nodded. "And you don't have a lot of things to take care of, is that it?"

Why isn't she dressed more appropriately? he wondered. Skintight yoga pants and an equally snug tank top left little to the imagination. What was she doing… bending all over the place dressed like this? Where was the guy she was supposedly here with? "I…um, I didn't have as much to handle as Zach, so I said I'd come and check on you."

Disbelief marked Summer's face. "You know, Ethan, I really thought you were different." Spinning around, she walked back into the tepee. If it had a door, she would have slammed it. Dropping a canvas flap just seemed like a waste of time and far less impactful a way to drive a point home. He followed her into the tepee regardless, and his hand on her shoulder almost made her scream as he spun her to face him.

"What is that supposed to mean?"

Summer brushed his hand aside and moved to put some space between them. "I expected you at least to be honest with me. Zach isn't here because he doesn't want to be here. He's hoping I've packed my bags and booked a flight back east. I know it; you know it. It's not that he's curious about where I am; he's mad because he's not in control of where I am. Big, tough Zach Montgomery pitched a hissy fit and so he sent his little minion out to check on me. Big surprise." She had hoped to come off sounding mean and confident, but in the end it just sounded mean, and she immediately regretted her words. Especially after seeing the look on Ethan's face.

He took a menacing step toward her. "Let's get one thing straight, Summer. I am nobody's minion. Yes, your brother was upset, and yes, partly because he wasn't in control, but my being here isn't because he sent me. I thought it would be better all around if I came and talked to you rather than Zach coming and screaming at you. My mistake."

Ethan didn't mean to make such a hasty exit, but he was seriously ticked off. Was that really how she saw him? As her brother's minion? What the hell was a minion anyway? He stalked to the ridiculous excuse for a rental car and was about to get in when he heard footsteps behind him. Dropping his chin to his chest, Ethan silently counted to ten and waited for what he was sure was going to be a very angry rant.

"Zach's been yelling at me for over a month and you haven't done anything to stop him," she said quietly. "Why now?"

The yelling he could have handled. But this? This quiet plea coming out of nowhere was nearly his undoing. Turning slowly, he faced her. He could just tell her the truth: he was tired of Zach bullying her around. He was trying to protect her. He was trying to keep the peace between them.

"Zach needs to have his head on straight for this climb. He's leading our team, and none of us has done something this extreme before. I can't have him climbing while he's freaking out about where you are and who you're with." The look of devastation on Summer's face nearly had him recanting his words. And yet… "Which brings me to another point of contention. Who are you here with? Who's the guy?"

"What are you talking about?" Luckily Summer recovered quickly from Ethan's disappointing admission. She stiffened her spine, crossed her arms, and prayed he'd be on his way shortly.

"We were told you booked this place for you and a guest. Where is he?"

Summer wracked her brain trying to figure out what Ethan was talking about when it hit her. Bless Gabriella's devious little heart! She almost wanted to laugh out loud, but she held it together just to keep Ethan on his toes for a little bit longer. "I don't think that's any of your concern, Ethan. You can go back and report in to my brother that I am safe and sound at the hot springs and I'll be reporting for duty back in the office Monday morning. Not that I'm needed. Zach made it clear that he wanted me to take a break while he was gone. I guess he doesn't trust me not to get into any trouble. But like it or not, I'm still going to go in and at least review some of the things I've learned so far. I think I'm supposed to be in the marketing department when he gets back."

They stood facing one another for what seemed like aeons. Finally, Ethan took a step closer. "Look, Summer, I've got to get a flight back to Portland and get myself packed and ready to go. Just let me meet this guy so I can tell Zach he's on the up-and-up, okay?"

She shrugged. "No can do."

Rage was beginning to build inside him. None of this was damn fair. He was a good friend, a hard worker, and dammit, he deserved to have something go his way for once. The Montgomery siblings were seriously messing with his life right now, and his patience was at an end. He closed the distance between the two of them until Summer had to tilt her head back to look up into his face. "I'm not playing games; I came here for a reason. I don't want to be here any more than you want me to be here. So bring this guy out and I'll be on my way. Now, Summer."

"I would, Ethan, I really would, except…"

"Except what?" he snapped.

"I didn't come here with a man. My companion is… female." She purposely put a little sass in her statement and loved the way Ethan's jaw worked like he wanted to say something but didn't quite know what. Who knew teasing Ethan Reed could be this much fun?

"You're…you're here with a…with a…woman?" He understood that girls went on weekend getaways all the time just for fun, but something in the way Summer announced it had him doubting that theory. He knew she dated men; he'd met many of them over the years. Was this why she'd been so out of sorts lately? "So…" He tried to sound casual, but somehow his words came out more like a croak. "So I would still like to meet her."

Actually, he wouldn't. Hell, it was almost as bad as her being here with a guy because now he'd have all sorts of erotic girl-on-girl images in his head starring Summer Montgomery. Yup, he was definitely being punished for something he did in a former life.

Without a word, Summer turned and walked back to the tepee. Ethan had no choice but to follow. He felt sick to his stomach as he scrambled to figure out how he was going to graciously meet this mystery female and then explain everything to Zach. *Hey, Zach. Things went great. As it turned out, Summer wasn't away with a boyfriend; apparently she's decided to give up on men and is now spending the weekend with her new girlfriend.* Yeah, that's going to go over well. There was no doubt the messenger was definitely going to be shot.

He almost wished someone would shoot him right now.

Walking into the tepee, he was momentarily distracted by the space. To say it was tall would be an understatement, but that wasn't the most impressive thing about it. In the center of the space was a large private hot spring, with a king-sized pallet on one side and a small sitting area on the other. It was rustic, for sure, but incredibly inventive. As outlandish as Summer was known to be, this place seemed a little too far-out even for her.

When he finally returned his attention to her, she was sitting on the corner of the bed. Now there was an image that was bound to mess with him more than all of the others. Ethan cleared his throat and tried to sound more in control than he had moments ago. "So? Where is she?"

"You're looking at her."

Brows furrowed, Ethan looked from the bed, to Summer, and back again before scanning the room. "Excuse me?"

"I said you're looking at her. Come closer."

This was both everything he ever wanted and feared all rolled into one. Summer beckoning him toward a bed? He was about to weep with gratitude. Then he remembered why he was here. Summer. Zach. The mystery guest. There was no one on the bed beside her. What was she playing at? All he saw was Summer and some sort of lump beside her. A pillow? A sweater? He took another step forward. *What the…?*

"Ethan, I'd like you to meet Maylene. My dog." At the sound of her name, the tiny dog lifted her head.

"She's a pug and she's only three months old." Summer turned and scratched the puppy behind the ears before leaning down and kissing her. "Say hello to Ethan," she said in a voice most people normally reserved for talking to babies.

"So you made a reservation for you…and your dog?" he asked, confusion lacing his tone.

Summer nodded. "No one said I was going away with a man, did they?"

Now he felt like an idiot. All Gabriella had said was Summer had made reservations for herself and a guest. He and Zach had jumped the gun on who they thought the guest was. Running a hand through his dark hair, he looked at Summer with a lopsided grin. "I guess you must be feeling pretty smug right about now."

"You would be correct."

There was no way to make a graceful exit, so Ethan just decided to own the blunder and be on his way. "Okay; we screwed up. I'm sure we'll all get a big laugh out of this when we get back." Summer stood and began walking toward him even as he was walking backward toward the exit. "So…um, I'll tell Zach you're fine and he has nothing to worry about. And you have a…a… dog. When…when did you get her?" he asked, struggling for something to say that wouldn't make him sound as foolish as he felt.

"About two weeks ago," she said simply. "I was feeling a little homesick and lonely, and it was obvious my brother was tired of entertaining me, so I decided to get a dog. I did a little research, found a breeder, and when I went, I took one look at her and knew she was meant for me."

I know the feeling, he thought. "Well, that's...that's great. She seems...cute." *For crying out loud, Ethan. You had better social skills when you were thirteen!* "I'm sorry for busting in on you like this. We really were just concerned about you."

"We?" she asked with just a hint of playfulness.

"Yeah. We. I...I hope you have a good weekend, Summer. I'll see you when we get back."

"Ethan?" she called out to him as he turned to walk away. He turned around and faced her again. "I don't have a good feeling about this. I know Zach thinks I'm just being ridiculous, but I'm not. His leg isn't healed all the way yet. He's being stubborn and impulsive. I know I'm not a doctor, but I am a trained yoga instructor, and I know a lot more about the human body than Zach thinks."

"Look, I agree with you," Ethan admitted. "I think he's being hasty too. But because the climbing season is so short, Zach's afraid that if he doesn't do this climb now, he's going to have to wait another year before he has the opportunity."

"That's the stupidest reason in the world to go on a climb like this! He's not ready for it physically. And besides that, the weather isn't very predictable...well... things can go wrong in the blink of an eye. Please. I really don't want you to go." Both her eyes and her voice were pleading with him.

"Me?" he asked gruffly.

Summer blushed. "Well, you and Zach. It's too dangerous." She walked up to him and placed one small hand on his arm. "Promise me you won't go, that you'll talk to Zach and convince him to postpone the climb. I know it will be another year before he can do it and he's been planning this for a long time, but it's just not safe for him."

In the twenty years they had known one another, they had never touched, not even in the most casual of manners. The feel of her hand on him had Ethan teetering on the edge of control. He looked down at her hand and then to her face. Her dark eyes looked up at him filled with worry, and he slowly felt himself drowning in them. It was sensory overload and he wasn't sure he'd be able to survive it.

"Summer," he began carefully, "I know you're worried. This is a little out of our usual scope of adventure, but your brother and I have trained really hard for this. I know that Zach isn't in his usual top shape with his leg and all, but he's managed to get a doctor's approval and talked to the expedition company about it. The guides are fine with the medical reports and confident that the weather won't be an issue. They're the experts and we have to trust them. You should trust them too."

"Even experienced climbers get lost or hurt or even killed on climbs like this," she said somberly. "I'm begging you, Ethan, as a friend. Please reconsider."

"Is that why you took off without telling anyone?" he asked. "So that Zach would have to come after you and you could make him postpone his trip?" He hated even asking the question but knew that he desperately needed her answer.

"No," she said without hesitation. "I left because I couldn't bear to watch the two of you leave. If anything happens…" She broke off as the first tear fell. "Dammit," she muttered and turned away, but Ethan surprisingly turned her around and forced her to look up at him.

"Hey," he said, holding her chin. "Nothing is going to happen. We're going to go, we're going to be ridiculously cold, and we're going to feel like we're standing on top of the world, take some pictures, and come home. When we get back, you're going to wish we were away longer."

Summer shook her head fiercely. "No. He shouldn't be doing this, Ethan. Zach is going to hurt himself and possibly others because he's not ready for something of this level. Don't go on this climb. Please," she cried.

Right now he wanted to give her exactly what she wanted; hell, he'd agree to anything if it meant she'd stop crying. "Summer." Her name came out as a plea and before he could stop himself, he pulled her into his embrace. "Please don't cry."

"Then promise me you won't go," she cried into his shirt. "I've never asked anything of you, Ethan. Please. Please do this for me. If you don't go, Zach won't go, and I'll know that you're both safe."

"I can't do that, princess," he said softly, using the nickname he had always called her when they were kids. She looked up at him, her eyes shining. "Everything is set. We can't back out because you think something *might* go wrong. There's a chance that we could get hurt at any given time, Summer. We all take risks every day. There are no guarantees in this life. Sometimes, you have to take a risk."

Summer continued to stare up at him as he spoke. *Ethan's right*, she thought. There were no guarantees. She had taken many risks in her life, not like climbing one of the tallest mountains in the world, but to her, they were huge. Could she possibly do that again?

"Most people go through life too scared to take a risk," he continued. "I don't want to have any regrets and neither does Zach. We committed to this and we're going to see it through. Tell me that you understand. Would you be able to live with yourself if you never took any risks?"

She seemed to instantly sober up. Her eyes became clearer, and she shifted against him. "You're right, Ethan," she said quietly. "Everyone needs to take risks."

He nodded, seemingly happy that he had comforted her and that she finally seemed to come to accept what he and Zach were going to do. "Exactly. I'm glad you agree."

"Oh, I do," she said right before she stood up on her toes, wrapped her arms around Ethan's neck, and pressed her lips to his. Summer felt a moment of panic when Ethan seemed to stiffen against her, but then in an instant, everything changed. His arms banded around her, pulling her as close as she could possibly get against him. He was warm and solid and everything she had ever imagined he would be.

In her wildest dreams, she had never imagined Ethan Reed kissing her like this. Summer had hoped to surprise him with her kiss and then have a perfectly pleasant experience to remember. But this? What was happening right now? Pleasant didn't even begin to describe it. Ethan kissed her like his life depended on it. His tongue lightly traced her lower lip and when she dared to open up for him, he swept inside and completely took control. She may have whimpered; she may have moaned. All

Summer knew at that moment was that never in her life had she been kissed like this, had never felt like this. Needy, anxious, and yes, completely and utterly turned on. *Wow*.

Everything in Ethan honed in on the woman in his arms. A man could only take so much temptation. Besides, Summer had kissed him first, so he felt like he wasn't doing anything wrong. How could kissing her be wrong when everything about it felt so incredibly right? She fit perfectly in his arms; her lips felt incredibly soft against his. And the way her curvy little body fit against his? Well, perfect didn't even begin to describe it.

Summer raked her fingers through Ethan's dark hair, and before she could question what she was about to do, she did her best to pull him back toward the bed. If he was going to give an entire speech on the importance of taking risks, then he should be prepared to follow through. For too many years she had wanted to take this particular risk, but there had never been the time or the opportunity. It was as if heaven itself had dropped Ethan Reed in her lap today. All that was missing was a big red bow around him. She smiled at the image.

It didn't take much prompting to get Ethan to move, and once the back of Summer's legs hit the bed, Ethan gently guided her down until she was on her back. He was stretched out beside her and still he didn't break the kiss. *Oh my,* she thought as his hands suddenly got in on the action. Gently, one large hand caressed her from knee to hip to rib cage to cheek. Summer wanted to push his hands a little back in the opposite direction. Luckily, Ethan seemed to read her mind and slowly, ever so slowly, he began the journey back down, until he cupped one breast in his hand and gently kneaded it.

At that point, he moved his mouth from hers and let it follow the path of his hand. Summer arched beside him, pushing herself further into his hand, and almost cried out when he replaced that hand with his mouth. His name came out on a sigh, and with just a little bit of twisting, she had him on top of her. The puppy let out a whine at being disturbed and jumped down to her makeshift bed on the floor.

Ethan could not believe his good fortune; having Summer wrapped so intimately around him was better than anything he had ever fantasized about. The feel of her curves beneath his hands, the softness of her skin, and the soft purrs of delight she made when he discovered new places to touch her had him ready to take things to a place he never thought he'd get the opportunity to go to.

Everything was perfect: her response to him, the way they fit together, the setting... Ethan couldn't ask for more. A vibration in his pocket stopped him cold. At first he thought it was just his body's response to Summer, but then he realized it was his phone, and he quickly jumped off her and rolled to the other side of the bed as he pulled the phone from his pocket and cursed.

Zach.

Dammit.

He was torn between what to do: answer the phone and completely kill the moment or ignore it and roll Summer back under him to finish what they started. "You better answer that," she said softly at his side, and Ethan didn't have to face her to know disappointment was written all over her face. With nothing else to do, he touched the screen and accepted the call.

"Yeah."

"Well? Did you find her? I heard you took the jet. Is everything all right?"

"Everything is fine. Summer is fine. She's here at a hot springs resort for the weekend."

"Who's the guy? Do I need to fly down there too?"

Ethan let out a mirthless laugh. "No, you don't need to fly down here. She isn't here with a guy."

"What? But Gabriella said—"

"She said 'guest.' You and I just took that to mean a guy."

"I don't get it. Then who's there with her?"

"Maylene," he said as a small smile crossed his face with a glance at the tiny sleeping dog.

"Maylene? Who the hell is Maylene? She's not…? I mean, Summer's not…?"

"Relax, Zach. Maylene is her new puppy. A pug. Pretty damn cute, if you ask me."

"Seriously? My sister got a dog?" Zach cursed. "She's barely able to take care of herself and now she thinks she's responsible enough to take care of a dog? A puppy, no less! With my luck, she'll get tired of it and *I'll* be stuck with the damn thing!"

"What the hell is the matter with you?" Ethan finally snapped. "I don't know why you suddenly think all kinds of crap gets dumped in your lap and it all comes from your sister, but it's bullshit!" Standing, Ethan strode from the tepee and away from Summer's soft gasp of surprise. When he was a safe distance away, he spoke again. "Ever since she showed up here, you've had it out for her, and you've been blaming her for every little thing that's gone wrong. You and I both know it's not the case, so what is your problem?"

Zach was silent for a long moment. "First Gabriella argued with me and now you. And both times because of Summer. Tell me again how I'm wrong?"

Ethan wanted to growl with frustration. "Fine, in those two instances, yes, but all the rest? No way. Summer is very different from you, but that doesn't make her the enemy. It's time you stopped treating her like it."

"She won't settle on a career, she won't settle into a place to live, she takes these ridiculous jobs and—"

"And what? She's doing all of the things she always dreamed of? How is that different from the way you keep trying out all of these extreme sports? The way I see it, she may be going from job to job, and some of them seem a little out of the ordinary, but none of them are life-threatening like what you're doing."

"Whose side are you on?" Zach said with deadly calm.

"It's not about sides, dammit, and I'm tired of having to choose one! The two of you are more alike than you realize. She's the female version of you, only with less of a death wish! You need to back off a little bit and think about that."

"She's a pain, Ethan. She's trying to tell me not to go on this climb, and why? Because she *thinks* my leg isn't strong enough! She even accused me of paying the doctor to give me the clearance letter. Is that logical to you?"

"So? You tell her every day not to do far less dangerous things—don't join the gym unless it's your gym, don't go to the Chinese place on Fifth because you don't like it, don't buy a car unless you pick it out… Is *that* logical to you? You try to micromanage her entire life. She's asking you not to do one thing—*one thing!*—and you're acting as if she's committing some sort of mortal sin. You may not believe it, but she is concerned about your well-being."

Zach sighed. "I never thought of it that way. It's just…she's so young and to me she seems irresponsible. I mean, take today for instance: She just up and took off without telling anyone!"

"She removed herself from an upsetting environment. There's a difference."

"Why are you defending her so much?" Zach asked suspiciously. "You've never defended her like this."

Crap. "I'm only playing mediator here," he said, trying to sound diplomatic. "You're my friend and she's my friend, and I'm trying to make this difficult situation a little less…volatile. You need to have a clear head to go on this trip, and she needs to know you're going to be okay." Ethan looked over his shoulder and saw Summer standing in the makeshift doorway of the tepee. He smiled. He wanted to go to her, hold her, kiss her…but he needed to finish dealing with her brother first.

"I will. Nothing's going to happen, right? I know there's a slight possibility that my leg will give me problems, but I think I know my own body better than she does. I promise to sit and talk with her when we get back."

"Good," Ethan said with a sigh of relief.

"Speaking of which, when are you heading back?"

"Soon. I told the crew I'd call when I was on my way back to the airport. They were going to do some routine maintenance on the plane, so I want to make sure they'll actually be ready for me when I get there."

"Was that necessary?" Zach asked. "Why couldn't they wait until they were back in Portland?"

Ethan shrugged. "No idea. I didn't question it because it seemed like a good way to spend the time rather than twiddling their thumbs while I was trying to find your sister."

"Is she really all right?" Zach said, and for the first time, it was actual concern lacing his voice, not annoyance.

"She's fine. She's worried. Hell, I'm sure she's not the only one who is. She's just the only one who was outspoken about it."

"I'm sure. Okay, look, I appreciate you going there and getting things under control. I'm sorry to have made you waste a day chasing Summer down. Get back here and get yourself ready so we can leave tomorrow and go with clear heads."

Ethan wasn't sure he'd be able to leave with a clear head, not tomorrow and certainly not today, but rather than share that observation, he told Zach he'd see him tomorrow and hung up. His first instinct was to head back into the tepee, but he knew where that would lead, and as much as he wanted it, Ethan also knew it wouldn't be beneficial to anyone in the long run. "Dammit," he cursed and searched his phone for the pilot's number and called him instead.

~~~

Summer wasn't sure what she'd expected, but this certainly wasn't it. Pacing the space around her, she patiently waited as Ethan got on another call. When she had left Portland this morning, she honestly didn't think anyone would come looking for her. She wasn't a fool; she had seen all of her brother's missed calls and knew he was chomping at the bit to talk to her. She just hadn't been ready to talk to him yet.

Finding Ethan standing fewer than ten feet away from her while she was doing yoga? Yeah, big surprise. And seeing he was concerned about her, and not just concerned on her brother's behalf, had been a little eye-opening.

And then there was the kiss.

Oh Lord, how the man could kiss!

Even now, some ten minutes later, her body was still happily vibrating from the encounter. For so many years, she had taken Ethan's indifference to her and lived with it. She didn't like it, but there didn't seem to be anything she could do about it. How could he have treated her with such detachment for so many years and then kiss her like that? It didn't make sense. Summer wasn't naïve where men were concerned, but there was definitely something about Ethan's kiss that was anything but casual.

Was he really attracted to her? Why hadn't he acted on it before? Was it because of her family? It wouldn't come as a surprise if Ethan had been reluctant to approach her because of her brothers (and father and cousins and so on). Most of her life, Summer had had to deal with being from a predominantly male family who enjoyed intimidating any guy she ever brought home. Was it any wonder she'd moved away at eighteen?

Risking a glance outside, Summer saw that Ethan was off the phone, but he didn't seem inclined to hurry back inside to continue what had been interrupted. *That can't be good*, she thought. Was he regretting it? Had she somehow disappointed him? That was a depressing thought. Turning away, she shook her head. "No," she muttered and returned to her pacing. "No, this is totally not because of me. If he's hesitating, it's because of his own issues." Summer had always been a confident woman, and she wasn't going to change now.

"Hey," Ethan said from right behind her.

What is he, a ninja? she thought, spinning around to face him. "Hey, yourself. Everything go okay with Zach?" Ethan gave her the abbreviated version of his conversation with her brother. "So...what? Now he's fine? Is he seriously just realizing how much of a jackass he's been to me in the last month?"

Ethan chuckled. "Baby steps," he said. "I can only hope that when we get back, he'll be true to his word and actually take some time to figure out why he's so hard on you."

When we get back. Summer sighed. "So you're still going?" she said sadly.

He stepped in close and put his hands on her shoulders. "We have to. I told you already."

Just as quickly as he had touched her, Summer pulled away. "Obviously there's nothing I can do to change your mind so...you should just go." It nearly killed her to say those words. What she really wanted to do was pull him back to the bed with her so they could finish what they'd started and to hell with the stupid climb. If anything happened, at least she'd have the memory of this time with Ethan.

But she wasn't the kind of woman who could do sex without giving her heart, and clearly, if he had truly ever felt anything for her, he would have acted on it before now. It was probably just the emotionally charged circumstances and the fact that she had initiated the kiss. He probably kissed all of his former lovers like that. The thought made her ill.

"Summer," he began, but she was entirely focused on petting the sleeping pup. Ethan waited to see if she would acknowledge him, and after a few minutes, he decided he was tired of waiting. "Please don't be mad. I wish I could give you a guarantee that you have nothing to worry about, but I can't." He looked at his watch. "I have to head back to the airport. The plane should be back together by the time I get there, and I have a lot to do back home."

Alarm prickled down her spine. "Why is the plane apart?"

"It's not as bad as it sounds. The crew was just doing some general maintenance. There was a small oil leak and they were taking care of it. It will be ready by the time I get there. Nothing to worry about." *Smooth*, he thought to himself. Give her something else to freak out about. He waited for her to try to stop him with rantings and ravings about how unsafe it could be, but she merely shrugged.

"So go," she said. As she made her way across the space, she stopped and forced a smile to her face. "Have a safe trip, Ethan," she said with a cheeriness she didn't feel and made her way back to her yoga spot.

He called her name one more time and was surprised

when she actually stopped in her tracks. "I wish things could be different. You and I both know that what happened here…it would complicate things. Too many things. I'd have your entire family chasing me down to kill me."

Looking over her shoulder, Summer gave him a sad smile. "That's the thing, Ethan; there's no one here. No one would ever have to know."

What was she saying? His mind raced. Was she giving him the okay to have one night, one night where he wasn't her brother's best friend and he didn't have to worry about angry Montgomerys vowing to do him bodily harm? It was almost too good to imagine. He was about to take a step toward her, but his conscience got the better of him. "You deserve better than that, Summer. You deserve someone who can give you more than one night. You're better than being someone's dirty little secret."

If anything, her expression grew even sadder. "It wouldn't be the first time," she said quietly. "Goodbye, Ethan."

Ethan wasn't sure how long he stood there, stupefied by the exchange. If Zach hadn't called, they would both have been naked and out of breath and he'd be looking forward to round two right about now. *Dammit.* He looked down at his watch again and cursed. He needed to get on the road, but he knew this wasn't finished. Time might not be on his side right now, but eventually, he and Summer were going to have to discuss what could have happened here and what they were going to do about it.

Maybe what they were going to do was more of what they had already done, but without the threat of her family.

A man could only hope.

Chapter 4

"WHAT DO YOU MEAN WE CAN'T LEAVE?" ETHAN snapped. He stared from the airport mechanic to his pilot, Mark. "You told me on the phone we were good."

The pilot looked a little uneasy. "At that point, I thought we were. It was a small leak. We had to call out for a part and the last I checked, everything was getting put back together. The wrong part was sent and unfortunately, I can't get another one until tomorrow morning. They're sending it overnight, but I'm afraid the earliest I'll have it here is ten a.m. You'll be in the air by eleven, but it's the best I can do. Sorry." The mechanic did seem sincere, but that didn't help Ethan at the moment.

"So what the hell am I supposed to do?" He wasn't asking anyone in particular; it just seemed like the thing to say.

"I've already checked for you, sir," Mark said. "There's only one more flight left today going to Portland and it has two stops. You won't land until six thirty tomorrow morning."

Ethan turned around and looked at him in shock. "It's a forty-five-minute flight! That's ridiculous!"

Mark nodded nervously. "You could rent a car and drive back. It's not ideal, and I know it's a five-hour drive but…"

"Unbelievable," he muttered and stalked away to

get his head together. It was almost six o'clock in the evening; he hadn't eaten dinner and he was exhausted. There was no way he could safely make that long a drive without killing himself or someone else. He walked back over to the two men. "And you can guarantee me I'll be in the air by eleven tomorrow morning?"

They both nodded. Ethan turned to the pilot. "Where will you spend the night?"

Mark shrugged. "There aren't a lot of accommodations here, but there is a motel about ten miles up the road. I'll probably just crash there." Ethan made a noncommittal sound. "What about you?"

That was a good question. The first thing that popped into Ethan's mind when he heard he was going to be stranded here for the night was that he could get right back in the car and return to Summer. They'd have their night together and he'd get her out of his system and be able to go on the climb with one less thing messing with his head. Then he realized how shallow that sounded and how he had told her she deserved more, deserved better. And he was right.

With a sigh of resignation, he thanked the two men, told them he'd see them in the morning, and went to the car to find someplace to spend the night that wasn't too far out of the area—and more than the no-name, by-the-hour places that he had driven by on his way to and from where Summer was staying.

It was a far cry from what he wanted to do and where he wanted to be, but like everything else in his life lately, he might not like it, but he'd have to accept it.

The yoga was relaxing.

The soak in her private hot spring was great.

The yogurt-and-granola dinner left a bit to be desired.

It was barely eight o'clock and Summer wasn't the least bit tired. The peace and quiet was all right, she supposed, but it left her too much time to think.

About Ethan.

About the kiss.

About him leaving.

While Summer loved her family to pieces, sometimes they were a royal pain in the rear. It was times like this when she could totally relate to her brother James and his almost fifteen-year sabbatical from all things Montgomery. If she thought she could get away with it, Summer would gladly have packed up and moved away where no one could interfere with her life. Particularly her love life.

If she had one.

"Please," she said. "I could totally be having a love life right at this very moment with Ethan if it weren't for my interfering family." Unfortunately, as much as she wanted to think she could move away and be without them, Summer was too much of a family girl. She loved them.

Even when she hated them.

Like right now.

She threw her clothes back on over the bathing suit she'd been wearing from her earlier soak, and with nothing pressing to do, she decided to take Maylene on a walk around the grounds and got out her leash. It wasn't the most exciting way to spend a Friday night, but with any luck she'd exhaust them both so that going to bed early wouldn't be quite so hard.

The property was massive. Besides the tepees, there were dozens of small cabins scattered around and a large main resort building for those needing a little more in the way of creature comforts. While none of it was deluxe, Summer was sure she could head into the main building at some point tomorrow and grab a hot meal and a shower. There were bathrooms and showers out by the tepees that would be fine, but she had no desire to make regular use of them. Not when there was a perfectly enclosed private locker room in the hotel. Roughing it was one thing; roughing it with no other options was quite another.

Maylene trotted happily along the property, her rhinestone collar sparkling. They stopped occasionally, and Summer talked to some of the other guests along the way, but an hour later she found herself right back at her tepee.

"Not the most exhausting walk I've ever been on," she said dryly as she stepped back into the tepee and contemplated the door. It was a flap. There was no other way to describe it, and although there were ties, it didn't seem the safest way to make sure no one came in. Why hadn't she thought about that before?

Maylene danced around Summer's ankles as she tried to disconnect the leash. "Easy, girl," she cooed, and once the dog was free, she scampered over to her water bowl and took a drink before promptly curling up in her own little bed. She was snoring within seconds. "Oh, to be able to sleep like that."

It was still early and Summer wasn't tired. She had her e-reader with her and it was loaded with books, but that wasn't appealing. She was restless. The fresh air and the walk had been all well and good but didn't seem to take the edge off what she was feeling. The temperature was very comfortable inside the room, and with nothing else appealing to do, Summer stripped back down to her bathing suit and climbed back into the hot tub. A sigh of pure bliss escaped as she felt herself relax.

"Must be some magic water to make you moan like that."

Summer screamed and jumped up from the water. "Ethan?" She placed a hand over her rapidly beating heart. "What in the world? I thought you went back to Portland! You scared the hell out of me!"

Ethan hadn't meant to scare her; he honestly thought she would have seen him sitting on the sofa on the side of the room. Unfortunately, she had been so engrossed in her own thoughts and talking to the dog that she hadn't noticed. Not that he was complaining; watching her strip out of her yoga clothes had been quite entertaining. All that was missing was music, and he would have called it the most erotic striptease he had ever seen.

"The maintenance didn't get done. Something about a wrong part being sent and it won't be in until the morning."

"Where's Mark?" Summer was familiar with the pilot who had been flying the Montgomerys around for almost ten years now.

"At a motel."

"And there was only one room?" she asked, one brow quirked.

Shrugging, Ethan stepped closer to the tub. "I don't know. I didn't bother checking."

"And why not?" Was that her voice sounding so breathless?

Now he was standing right in front of her. The sight of the water droplets making their way down her bikini-clad body had him twitching with need. "I didn't want to go to a motel."

Summer's heart rate still hadn't calmed, only now it wasn't because of fright but because she was nervous about where this conversation was leading. Risk. She had to remember she needed to take this risk. Right now. With Ethan. "And what did you want?"

Ethan didn't answer. Instead, he held her gaze as he kicked off his shoes. He barely blinked as he pulled his shirt over his head and tossed it to the side. He almost groaned when Summer licked her lips as he unbuttoned his jeans and pulled them off. When he was down to his briefs, he stepped over the edge of the tub until he was close enough to touch her. "You," he said gruffly. "I want *you*, Summer."

No words had ever sounded sweeter to her.

Her mind raced with some kind of seductive come-back, but the words wouldn't come. Ethan's hands came to rest on her bare waist and she gasped. They moved slowly up her rib cage and settled on her breasts. Summer closed her eyes and sighed. All too soon, Ethan's hands once again moved up to cup her face.

"I'm a bastard for coming back here," Ethan said. "I meant what I said earlier; you deserve better than this, more than what I can give you, but heaven help me, I couldn't stay away."

"I didn't want you to," she admitted softly. This time, it was Ethan who initiated the kiss, and it was just as electrifying. Steam rose up around them, and Summer couldn't say if it was from the springs or from the two of them, because she certainly felt ready to combust. Slowly, they not only sank into the kiss, his lips slanting over hers again and again, but they also sank to their knees in the water.

"So good," he murmured as he sipped droplets from her lips and across her cheek, down her throat, and to her collarbone, tasting the water on her skin. "You taste and feel so good, Summer." His words were part praise, part growl. It was awkward as they settled themselves into the tub with Ethan's back against the side and Summer straddling his lap, but once they settled in, it was pure bliss.

There were so many questions rattling around in Summer's head, but she was afraid to voice any of them for fear of ruining the moment. This had been her dream, her fantasy, and it was really happening. Running her hands up his arms, his biceps, and his shoulders, she relished the feel of him. His muscles were hard and yet smooth. He had a tribal band tattoo on his left bicep and it fascinated her briefly. When had he gotten it? What did it mean? She didn't linger; her hands continued the journey up to touch his face, his strong jaw, before sinking into his hair and pulling his mouth back to hers. Beneath her, Ethan shifted and the size of his arousal pressing against her was pretty impressive. She had always thought he was impressive, both in looks and physique. But feeling it this up close, this intimately, was beyond her realm of comprehension. Summer felt as if she were somebody else because she had never felt this good, this wanted.

"Tell me you want this, Summer," he said breathlessly when he lifted his mouth from hers. His hands were anchored at her waist, securing her to him. "I need to know you're not having second thoughts."

She smiled sexily at him. "I wasn't the one who left earlier."

It was all the answer he needed.

―⌇⌇⌇―

Ethan woke up much later and felt immediately startled by his surroundings. There was loud snoring beside him, and at first he was certain he was hearing things; that noise couldn't possibly have been coming from Summer. Then he realized it was coming from the pup. He breathed a sigh of relief because that kind of sound would have been hard to deal with coming from a human, let alone someone as sexy and girlie as Summer.

Now that he was a little more awake, he settled in and felt Summer curled up beside him. He smiled into the darkness. It was so quiet and so peaceful and so unexpected that he almost wanted to pinch himself to make sure it had all really happened.

Once Summer had reminded him that he had been the one to leave, it was like waving a red flag in front of a bull. It had released his inner beast, and while he'd worried he was being too rough, too demanding, he had scratch marks on his back to prove that Summer had been right there with him for the ride.

And what a ride it was.

Damn.

In all the years he had known the Montgomerys, Summer had been outgoing and friendly but always very…feminine. She was athletic but didn't play sports with her brothers or try to fit in that way, but for all of the outlandish career choices and hobbies, Ethan still pictured her as being a bit more reserved.

Boy, was he wrong.

Why had he never noticed the wildness in her? The passion? In his own head, his own fantasies, Summer was like that, but he had never expected it to be the reality. She had completely destroyed him over the course of the night. Rather than getting her out of his system, it had only made him hungry for more. With one arm around her, Ethan pulled her closer and grew hard at the feel of her naked body moving even closer to his. With no windows in the tepee, he had no idea what time it was. They could have been asleep for hours or minutes; he had no idea. All he knew was that he needed her again. Now.

He let his hand massage its way up and down her spine until it came to rest on her bottom, where he gently squeezed. Summer let out a small moan. With his other hand, Ethan reached down and touched her leg entwined with his and ran his hand up until he reached her thigh. She squirmed a little bit and rubbed herself against his hair-roughened thigh right before letting out a little purr.

A man could get used to waking up like this.

Unsure of what his next move should be because his inner beast was ready to just roll her over and start again, Ethan was surprised when Summer seemed to come fully awake and took the decision out of his hands. With lightning speed, she straddled him. He was about to speak, but—although the tepee was pitched in darkness—it was as if she sensed it and placed a finger over his lips.

Leaning forward, Summer kissed him thoroughly before making her way down to kiss his chest. She thought she could spend hours just licking and kissing and touching Ethan. His body was a thing of beauty. She was almost tempted to turn on the small bedside lamp just to be able to see him, and yet… She smiled wickedly as she moved. Feeling him in the dark and letting her imagination run wild was quite something. Talk about sensory overload. Every hiss of his breath, every time she made his body jump empowered her.

They may only have this one night. When the sun came up and Ethan drove away, all she would have was this memory, so she'd be damned if she was going to waste time sleeping when she could be enjoying one of the sexiest men she had ever known, ever wanted. Ever had.

Sleep was highly overrated.

Ethan was getting dressed as he looked down at Summer sprawled across the bed, the blankets barely covering her. He was exhausted, but it was the best kind of exhaustion he had ever experienced. He looked at his watch and saw that it was ten o'clock. If he was going to make sure the jet took off on time, he really needed to get to the airport and oversee things. There was no way he could afford to be away any longer. Luckily he was fairly organized and all of his packing for the climb was already done; he was just going to need to put some last-minute stuff together and grab a nap.

He smiled. There had been a time when he had made fun of people who couldn't handle a night out and needed a nap the next day. Now he was proud of the fact that he was one of them.

"You're looking pretty smug right now," Summer said sleepily from the bed. At the sound of her voice, Maylene perked up and rose from her bed on the floor. With a quick shake and stretch, she jumped up beside Summer and began to bounce around her. "I wish I had her energy."

Ethan chuckled. "Don't we all." He thought it would be awkward, the whole morning-after thing, but as Summer rose gloriously naked from the bed, it seemed like the most natural thing in the world. "Let me," he said and walked over to get the dog's leash and got her hooked up. "We'll be right back." Honestly, the last thing he needed to be doing was taking her dog for a walk; he needed to leave and get to the airport. So what was he doing this for?

"Because you're trying to drag out the inevitable," he muttered to himself once outside the tepee. He knew he had to leave; he just didn't want to.

The dog skipped along the grounds, happy to be outside. Ethan wished he felt that way. The weather was a little cooler than he'd expected, and Ethan was glad for his jacket. When the dog needed to stop and sniff practically every blade of grass, Ethan grew impatient. "Let's go, dog," he said firmly, and then could have kicked himself when her big, sad eyes looked back at him. "Sorry."

He was seriously losing it. He was a man's man; he did extreme sports, for crying out loud, and here he was apologizing to a five-pound dog because he wanted to go back inside a tepee where it was warm.

Yup, seriously losing it.

Finally, the dog did what she had to do and, with

a jaunty little hop, headed back in the direction of her waiting mistress. Ethan knew exactly how she felt; he wanted to be back there too.

Summer was waiting for them in bed. She got up to fill the dog bowl, and once Maylene was off her leash and happily eating, Summer turned her attention to Ethan. "Thank you for taking her out. You didn't have to."

"I was dressed," he said, taking a step closer to her.

"Well, it was very sweet of you and I appreciate it." As she stepped closer, Summer wrapped her arms around Ethan's shoulders and smiled up into his face. "Good morning," she said softly.

"Good morning," he responded right before lowering his head to hers and kissing her the way he had been aching to do. In the back of his mind, Ethan knew it was wrong; it would have been better to make a clean break and not indulge in this again. The night was over and so was…everything. He needed to leave, to take the memory of last night and be thankful they had it. But her lips were so soft, her body so yielding…

Summer was the one who pulled back first. "If we keep this up, you'll miss your flight."

His gaze was intense as he looked down at her. "I'm the only passenger. They'll wait." Wait…what was he saying? What was he doing? For crying out loud, she was giving him the nudge he needed and he wasn't taking it. *Get it together, Reed!* he chided himself. With a growl, his hands reached up and anchored themselves in her long, blond hair and tightened their grip as he gave her one last fierce kiss. It wasn't fair. In a perfect world, this kiss would signify a temporary good-bye.

He'd see her again, be able to make love to her again as soon as he got back from Denali.

But this? This was a last kiss. One that signified an ending. They wouldn't get another chance. There would be no reunion when he got back. Pouring everything he had into it, Ethan heard Summer whimper with her own need. If she asked him not to go, if she simply asked him to stay, Ethan was certain he'd cave. The plane would leave later, and he would have another couple of hours with her to get him through a lifetime.

But she didn't ask.

When he lifted his head, their breathing was ragged. Summer's eyes were glazed with passion, and he was sorely tempted to scoop her up into his arms, walk back over to the bed, and lay her bare to him.

But he didn't.

"I have to go." The words felt wrong even as he forced them out.

Summer nodded. "I know."

"Summer…I…"

She placed a finger over his lips as she had earlier. "Don't say anything, Ethan. I know you can't make any promises, and I certainly don't want to hear you have any regrets."

He shook his head. "No. I don't regret last night. I'm only sorry that it's all we have."

While it was killing her on the inside, Summer stood tall and refused to let him see how his words were affecting her. "I know. Me too."

They stood staring at one another for long moments.

"Be safe," Summer finally said.

They weren't the last words Ethan wanted to hear,

but he knew better than to tempt fate. With a nod, he turned and strode from the room. Cramming himself into the tiny rental car, he pulled away and did his best not to look back.

It was over; they'd had their night and no one had to know.

But he knew.

And Summer knew.

Chapter 5

THE FLIGHT HOME WAS A BREEZE. ETHAN WAS BACK AT his own place a little before one in the afternoon, and after taking a quick inventory of what he still needed to do before meeting up with Zach, he crawled into bed for a short two-hour nap.

During which he dreamed of Summer.

"This is not good," he muttered when he woke up. His head needed to be clear; he needed to focus on the climb and on getting back to business as usual. Zach knew him too well and would be able to tell immediately if Ethan's head wasn't in the game. The bedside clock showed it to be almost four. He was supposed to meet Zach at the airport at seven. The nap had refreshed him, but as Ethan climbed into the shower, he conceded that another twelve hours of sleep would have been better.

The town car arrived on schedule and was loaded up. Everything was shut off and good to go in Ethan's condo. One of his neighbors was going to keep an eye on things for the three and a half weeks he'd be gone. Looking around one last time, Ethan closed and locked the door behind him and headed to the airport. What had seemed like a relatively short trip now loomed in front of him with no end in sight.

Why was he doing this? Did he even want to go? It was a little late to be having second thoughts now, but the more Ethan thought about it, the more he realized something. For far too long, he had simply gone along with things his buddies were doing rather than figuring out what *he* wanted to do. When had he become more of a follower than a leader? Resting his head back, Ethan sighed. This was so not the time for this kind of introspection.

They made great time getting to the airport, and before he knew it, Ethan was standing with Zach and listening to how excited he was about the climb. Ethan tried to respond appropriately. From what he could tell, Zach was none the wiser. It wasn't until they were actually on the plane that Zach asked about his sister.

"So did Summer give you grief about this trip?"

Ethan shrugged. "It was the same stuff she's been saying for weeks. She's just worried about you, Zach. Cut her a break."

"Look, I appreciate that she's concerned, but she's never paid any attention to the trips I've taken before or even the risks I've taken before. She's just up in arms over it because this is the first time she's been close by when I've been getting ready to go. Believe me, if Summer had lived closer to me in the last couple of years, she would have been all up in my business about my hobbies. The skydiving? The race car driving? Running with the bulls? If she had even been remotely aware that I was going on *those* trips, she would have been the exact same way. She's a worrier."

Ethan wasn't so sure. He'd known Summer for far too long. There were too many times when he and Zach had been around the Montgomerys and talked about their adventures with Summer right there, and she'd never once made a negative comment. If anything, she had been excited by the stories. This was different. He shook his head. Maybe she was onto something. Maybe this trip was more about ego than anything else. He glanced over at Zach, who was busy chatting up the flight attendant. Typical.

Zach smiled appreciatively as he watched the curvy brunette walk away before turning back to Ethan. "Like I told you yesterday, I promise to spend some time with Summer when we get back. I'll even try to be nice and not pick on her for being such a royal pain in my butt over this trip or pressure her about moving back east." They were interrupted again by the flight attendant as she served them their drinks.

"So was it awkward when you went in there all hell-bent on confronting a guy and ended up face-to-face with a puppy?" Zach barely contained his laughter at his own question.

Ethan grimaced at the memory. "It wasn't one of my finest moments," he said with a shake of his head. He told Zach how Summer had tried to play it off as another woman before finally introducing him to the dog.

"Is it wrong that I'm majorly relieved that it was a dog?" Zach asked.

"Not at all. I can't tell you how relieved I was." He took a sip of his beverage. "Cute little thing; she'll be a nice distraction for your sister."

"Remind me to buy it a hundred pounds of doggie treats if that's the case," Zach said with a laugh before holding up his glass to Ethan's. "Cheers, buddy. Here's to another great adventure!"

Ethan toasted, but he wasn't really feeling it.

—◦◦◦—

It was after midnight by the time they checked in,
and Ethan was alone in his hotel room, alone with his
thoughts. After the conversation about Summer, Zach
had talked nonstop about the climb. Realistically, Ethan
knew he was prepared; he had been training for six
months and had purchased all of the gear the guides
had recommended. If there was anything he was missing, he'd be surprised. The problem wasn't skill or
preparedness though; the problem was him. He didn't
want to go. The prospect no longer appealed, and he
couldn't really be sure if this was something that had
been building up in him for some time or just within the
last twenty-four hours.

Because of Summer.

Pacing the confines of the plush hotel room, Ethan
wracked his brain for a way out. There was no way he
could fake an illness or an injury—Zach would see right
through that. If he came right out and admitted he didn't
want to go, he had no doubt Zach would talk to him until
his ears bled and he'd have to cave and go anyway just
to shut Zach up. There was no way to fake a work emergency either, because they worked together. From every
angle, he was screwed. And not just kind of screwed, but
royally screwed. He was stuck going on a three-week
hike up a mountain he really didn't want to climb just
so someone else would be happy.

*But are you deciding not to go on the trip for the
same reason?*

He hated when his inner voice decided to chime in.
There was no easy answer to this dilemma, but if Ethan

had to choose, he'd say he felt stronger about not going on the climb than he did about going on it. That was saying something, right? Now he just had to figure out how he was going to break it to Zach.

Cursing, he flopped down on the king-size bed. When had life gotten so damn difficult? How had he let things get this far out of control? If he didn't go with Zach, Ethan knew he'd still need a little time away from work—time to try to get his head together and figure out what he was doing with his life and where he wanted to see himself in the next five years.

The immediate answer was that he wanted to see himself with Summer. Unfortunately, there were at least a half-dozen Montgomery males who were not going to be happy about it and even if he stood his ground, Ethan knew they wouldn't make it easy for him. While he felt deep down that Summer was worth the fight, would the constant fight with her family be something she could survive? Family meant everything to her; that was one thing Ethan was certain about. He wouldn't be able to live with himself if he caused discord between them.

This was clearly a no-win scenario.

"Nothing is going to get decided tonight," he muttered, rising from the bed and going through his luggage for his toiletries. "A hot shower and a full night's sleep will make things clearer in the morning." Even he didn't believe his own words.

Within minutes, he was under the hot spray, and automatically his mind wandered back to Summer. He wanted to call her, to make sure that she and Maylene were okay. He worried about her making the drive back to Portland by herself. Why hadn't she taken the company jet? It was lucky for him that she hadn't; otherwise, he would have had to make the long drive solo, but it bothered him to know that, should anything happen, she was a single woman all alone with no one to protect her except a five-pound pug.

Not a comforting thought.

When the water turned cold, he stepped out, wrapped himself in a towel, and went in search of his phone. What harm could one phone call make? They were friends, weren't they? *Friends who had incredibly hot and wild sex less than twenty-four hours ago.* "Oh, shut up," he told himself. "Don't think about the sex. Think of her as your best friend's sister. She's Summer Montgomery—a friend. Not Summer Montgomery, the sexy woman who blew your mind with her hands, her mouth, and her body." Great, now he was hard. There was no way he could call Summer while sporting a raging hard-on. Cursing himself again, Ethan walked back into the bathroom, finished drying off, and crawled back into bed, all the while willing himself to focus on the ESPN show he was watching and not imagining there was a curvy blond sprawled out beside him, reminding him he'd been a fool to leave.

"You're joking, right?"

Ethan shook his head and Zach cursed.

"This is because of Summer, isn't it?" He cursed again even as Ethan tried to speak. "You were fine with this trip until you went to see her! What the hell, man? You're here, you're packed, and we're all set! You can't just bail!"

Ethan expected the rage; he just didn't know how to make it better. "To be honest, I haven't been sure about it for a while. I didn't want to say anything because I didn't want to bum you out, and I thought I'd get more excited about it by the time we got here, but…I'm just not. My head isn't in it and I don't want to be a liability for the team."

"Bullshit," Zach spat, shoving a finger hard into Ethan's chest. "She got in your head. I freaking knew it. I should have stuck to my original plan. I should have been the one to go because I would have been stronger. You've always had a weakness for her. Maybe because you're an only child and she's like a sister to you, but believe me, whatever she said, she's wrong."

Now it was Ethan's turn to be filled with rage. "Do you think I'm not capable of making a decision on my own? Is that what you're telling me?" he snapped.

"All I'm saying—"

"Don't even!" Ethan interrupted. "You think because I spent some time talking to your sister that now, all of a sudden, I've decided not to go on the climb? What the hell do you take me for?"

"That's the thing, Ethan, I don't even know! You never once mentioned not wanting to go! We trained together, met with the guides together, and got our supplies together. What do you expect me to think? Not once did I see a hint of hesitation until all of this nonsense with Summer!"

"It isn't nonsense!" Ethan declared firmly, realizing as he spoke that it was true. "This is about me. I'm a grown man, and I don't owe you or anyone else an explanation for the decisions I make. This whole climb was your idea, and to be honest with you, I don't think you should be going either. Summer only confirmed what we all already know—you're not physically ready for something like this. Personally, I think you're crazy. You're going to be a liability to the group, but you refuse to see it or admit it. If this is something you want to do, then do it, but don't give me grief because I don't live my life exactly the way you live yours." There was both a dare in his words and a hint of finality.

Zach was silent for several moments before he stalked away about a dozen feet and came back. "Why didn't you say anything before?"

"Would it have made a difference?" Ethan didn't wait for an answer. "You're hell-bent on doing this, on proving that you can do this. I don't think it's necessary. I've got nothing to prove here."

"I don't know what to say," Zach said, his tone quieter, calmer than it had been minutes ago.

"You could say that you understand what we've all been saying and that you'll wait until next year when your leg is stronger."

He shook his head. "I...I can't. I know I can do this, Ethan. I'd prefer to be doing this with you."

"It's not gonna happen. I'm not going." His words were simple and honest.

"You're sure about this?"

Ethan nodded.

"What are you going to do? Go back to Portland?"

"No. I'm going to take the time to relax. It's been a long time since I've had an opportunity just to chill out," Ethan said.

Zach wanted to be mad; everything in him told him to

do whatever it took to make Ethan change his mind. But one real look at his friend and he knew it was pointless. Whatever his reasons, Zach knew Ethan's decision to skip the climb was weighing heavily on him. So rather than rage at him some more, he did the only thing he knew how. "Lame. Very, very lame. You going to have some spa time? Maybe get a pedicure and facial while you're at it?"

Ethan smiled. "Depends."

"On?"

"On whether or not I'm allowed one of those fruity drinks with an umbrella while I'm getting my toes polished."

Being the ever-supportive friend, Ethan showed up on the morning of the climb to wish Zach luck. He waited for the regret to kick in, or at least a sense of doubt, but it never came. That was all the proof Ethan needed to know he had made the right choice. All of his gear was at the hotel, so it wouldn't have taken long to go get it if he had been so inclined, but the truth was, his heart had never fully been in the trip. He had agreed to the climb in the first place out of habit; Zach normally came up with the idea for the adventure, and Ethan always jumped on board.

Until now.

What did that mean? What did that say about the state of his life? Was he that much of a follower all this time? Being strong-minded and independent were character traits Ethan had prided himself on; was that pride misplaced?

After Zach and the team took off, Ethan allowed himself the luxury of a couple of days at the hotel with no interaction with the outside world. He didn't call the office to let them know he wasn't going on the climb. If anyone knew he was available, he would no doubt lose the time to himself that he'd gained. The staff was efficient, but they took certain comfort in his approval.

By day three, the walls were closing in. For all his lazing around, he hadn't once thought about where he wanted to go. For years Ethan went wherever Zach planned for them. Crap. He *was* a follower. Now, with the world at his feet, he could go anywhere and have three weeks to enjoy it without interruptions.

The task was easier said than done. For all of the exotic locations he researched, few spoke to him, and the ones that did made him want to take someone with him. Like Summer. Dammit.

No, he chided himself for the hundredth time. *She's not for you. You need to move on and forget about her.* Forget about their night together and all the possibilities of a future together. It wasn't going to happen. Why? Because as much as it killed him to admit it, Ethan knew his friendship with Zach and all of the Montgomerys meant too much to him to risk on a relationship that might not work out. Could he possibly deal with all the aggravation her family was bound to put them through if they were to start dating?

The thought gave him a headache. Why her? Of all of the women he'd dated, hell, of all the women on the planet, why was Summer Montgomery the one woman he couldn't get out of his mind? Out of his system? The universe was definitely punishing him for something. There was no other explanation for this cruel twist of fate.

"Vacation," he muttered to himself. "Find yourself a place to park your ass for a couple of weeks so you can go back to Portland with a clear head." Fine words when he was all alone in his room, but how would they hold up in his real life? Could he possibly push all thoughts of Summer from his mind? "Only one way to find out."

Ethan put his tablet on the table in his room and pulled up a map of the area. In all his travels, he'd never spent any time in Alaska, and the thought of hanging out there while Zach was on the climb seemed to make sense. There was plenty to do, plenty of activities that called to him, and none of them were far away. Plus, he could be there when Zach returned and hear all about the trip as they traveled home together.

It didn't take long to realize that he was sick and tired of his own company. With a muttered curse, Ethan grabbed his room key and decided to head down to the bar for a drink. Maybe he'd talk to the bartender and see if he had any suggestions for someplace to go where he could get in a little sightseeing while feeling like he was away from civilization for a bit.

The bar was fairly crowded and Ethan found himself a seat and ordered a beer. There was a couple sitting next to him and he smiled in their direction while trying not to listen in on their conversation.

"I just couldn't believe how many we saw!" the woman was gushing. "I mean, I thought we'd see maybe one or two whales, but never in my wildest imagination did I imagine seeing six whales in one outing!"

Her husband laughed. "Can we really be sure that it

was six different whales? Maybe it was one who was just being a show-off."

"Oh, Jim," she laughed. "Don't ruin it."

He laughed too. "I'm sorry. I know how much you enjoyed it. Personally, I had a great time fishing. I don't think I've ever experienced anything quite like it. We'll have to come back again."

"Excuse me," Ethan said, turning in their direction. "I couldn't help but overhear your conversation. I'm actually looking for someplace to do some fishing. Would you mind if I asked where you went?"

"Glacier Bay," Jim said. "There's a great lodge there and a ton of outdoor activities. We went whale watching and fishing, kayaking and even took some sightseeing tours on an airplane. I'm telling you, it was the perfect getaway if you love the outdoors."

"That I do," Ethan said as his mind began to wander at all the possibilities. "Thank you. I'm going to look into that. Have a good evening." Paying his tab, Ethan took his drink and went back up to his room to do a little research.

It didn't take long to pull up a Google search and discover that this was exactly the kind of place he was looking for. Actually, if Zach weren't such an adrenaline junkie, Ethan might even consider suggesting Glacier Bay as a potential place for their next getaway. Unfortunately, he had a feeling it would be a little too tame for Zach's standards.

But not Summer's.

Damn it. Why had he gone there? Why? Because in the last month, he had learned that Summer still enjoyed outdoor activities. Back when they were younger, her brothers never included her in the things they did—the sports, the camping, the fishing—but Summer had found her own outdoor fun in the form of biking and tennis, hiking and sailing. The men of the Montgomery family considered her choice of activities to be tame, but considering them now, Ethan had to admit they certainly held a lot of appeal.

"Okay, focus," he admonished himself as he scanned the website. Glacier Bay. With a ton of activities and a lodge on-site, it would make for a great getaway that guaranteed he'd keep busy while getting to do the kind of outdoor activities he loved, without risking his life. And that was it in a nutshell—Ethan no longer felt the need to be so extreme. What was wrong with fishing? Kayaking? Or just plain hiking and enjoying nature? Why couldn't those activities be perfectly satisfying without the need to take everything to the next level of hair-raising?

With a renewed sense of self, Ethan made his reservations and began to pack. He booked a flight for early the next morning. Now all he had to do was get through the night without second-guessing himself again.

How hard could that be?

Chapter 6

"I TAKE IT THE HOT SPRINGS WEREN'T ALL THEY WERE cracked up to be?"

Summer glared at Gabriella on Monday morning as she made her way through the executive suites. "Why would you ask?"

"Because you don't look the least bit relaxed. Or rested. If anything, you look even tenser than you did when you left here on Thursday."

With a sigh, Summer dropped her briefcase on the floor and pulled up a chair opposite Gabriella. "They really went."

There was no need for clarification; Gabriella knew exactly what she meant and whom she was talking about. "They're probably getting ready to start even as we speak."

Summer shook her head. "I can't think about it. It's bad enough that my brother seems to have a death wish, but did he have to drag Ethan along with him?"

A knowing smirk crossed Gabriella's lips.

"All I'm saying is, it's hard enough worrying about one family member. Now I have to worry about two."

"Family member. Right."

Her glare deepened. "Okay, so I don't technically think of Ethan as family, but I still worry."

It was on the tip of Gabriella's tongue to say that she worried too, but she kept that to herself. "Well, if the hot springs didn't do anything for you, then there's only one thing left to do."

"What's that?"

"We need to have a serious girls' trip of our own."

Now it was Summer's turn to grin. "Hmm... I like the sound of that. What were you thinking? Massages? Manis? Pedis? Eating ice cream for dinner? Because let me tell you, I can completely get on board with that."

Gabriella shook her head sadly. "Why do you dream so small?"

"What? What's wrong with a lazy weekend eating ice cream? If you're nice, I'll even get us cookie dough."

Another sad shake. "I had something a little more... adventurous in mind."

"Oh, no," Summer said, shaking her own head. "I am leaving all of that adventurous crap to my brother. If you want to go mountain climbing or jump out of a plane, count me out."

"Stop being so dramatic," Gabriella said with a smile. "I'm talking about going someplace that's a little out-doorsy, something right up your alley."

"I'm intrigued."

Gabriella nodded. "Glacier Bay. We can leave Friday. I've got two weeks off thanks to your brother, and so do you."

"Yeah, I just found out about that this morning," Summer said with a lack of enthusiasm. "Rick gushed about what a great job I did on that project last week and then apologized that he didn't have anything more for me to do right now since this is a slow time of year." She sighed. "I was just starting to get into the swing of things, and I'm already getting booted out."

"You are totally looking at this the wrong way."

"I'd bet good money that Zach put him up to it so that I can't do anything while he's gone."

"Forget about your brother for a minute. You have just been handed vacation time without having to wait out your six months. Be happy! Be joyful! Put a smile on your face!"

Summer faked a smile. "There. Happy?"

"Honestly, there is something seriously lacking in the Montgomery genes," Gabriella said with exasperation. "It's okay to have a little fun, Summer. You're allowed to enjoy yourself. Personally, I had planned on staying close to home and just getting some spring cleaning done, but this is much more appealing. What do you think?"

Summer took a minute to think about it. "Can we do that? I mean, it's kind of short notice."

"Yep, I already checked."

Summer looked at her oddly. "You already checked? But…why?"

A blush crept up Gabriella's cheeks. "I…I had done a lot of research to help Zach with his trip. The area, you know, Alaska, it was kind of intriguing. I had looked at Glacier Bay during my search because I wanted to see what all the fuss was about."

"I don't think Glacier Bay is near Denali, is it?"

Gabriella shook her head. "It's not, but it's a relatively short plane ride." She looked away uncomfortably. "Not…not that we'd have any reason to go to Denali. I mean, the guys are already gone, and they're not going to be back until after we're already back here safe and sound."

"You're acting weird. Are you all right?"

"I'm fine." She cleared her throat. "So what do you say? We can go, see what's so appealing about the great outdoors of Alaska, and maybe have a little something to talk to the guys about when they get back."

Summer arched a brow at Gabriella. "Since when do you want to have something in common with Zach?"

Gabriella's blush deepened. "That's not what I meant," she replied quickly. "Anyway, maybe we'll meet some nice guys who aren't into death-defying activities. Although I hear whale watching can really get your blood pumping."

They both laughed.

"I'm serious, Summer. We can go and do some of the tours and hikes, and maybe you'll meet someone interesting."

"Oh, I don't know, Gabs," she began hesitantly. "I don't think I'm ready for that."

"Don't be such a wuss. If you're not into hooking up with anyone, then we'll just go with the flow and maybe, just maybe, let hot men buy us drinks. A little harmless flirting. What do you say?"

It was very tempting. There would be plenty of distractions to keep her mind off Zach's climb and Ethan's…everything. Even if they were a short plane ride away. Summer still couldn't quite come to grips with the fact that she and Ethan had finally slept together and he had just walked away. Worse, he walked away and hopped a plane to take a dangerous trip with her brother. Talk about a double slap in the face.

"I can't," she finally said solemnly. "I can't just pick up and leave. I've got Maylene to think about. She's just a puppy and…well…training isn't going as well as I had hoped."

"Then it's lucky for you that I happen to know of a fabulous dog-sitter who excels in puppy training."

"Seriously, is there anything you don't know?"

"Clearly I don't know how to make you just unclench and say yes to a damn vacation!" Gabriella said with a laugh. "Come on, Summer. Maylene will be fine. By the time you get back she'll be the perfect pet."

"My impulsive nature is what keeps getting me into trouble. I'm trying to be reasonable and levelheaded here, and you're totally not helping me."

"Being reasonable is overrated and, might I add, boring."

"You know, you tend to put off a very reasonable and levelheaded vibe around the office. This is a completely different side to you." She studied her friend for a moment. "I think I like this new you."

"So?" Gabriella asked anxiously. "What do you say? I can handle all of the arrangements; all you have to do is pack and go." She waited a moment before leaning forward in her seat. "Well?"

Summer's smile grew. "What do I say? Let's go watch some whales!"

Ethan couldn't understand what all the fuss was about. Twenty-four hours into his big Alaska adventure and he was bored. "There is seriously something wrong with me," he mumbled as he strolled over to join the line of people getting ready to board the boat that was going to take them whale watching. He had decided to take the afternoon tour so that he could sleep in a little, and while he was refreshed, he still wasn't overly impressed with what was going on. "Definitely something wrong with me."

More than one beautiful woman had shown interest in him in the last hour alone while he had been getting his ticket for the excursion, and although it should have been something that interested him, it didn't. He didn't want to be with another woman, not now. Maybe not ever. After having spent the night with Summer and making love to her, Ethan knew it would be hard to replace her with someone else. You just didn't find that kind of connection, that kind of chemistry, that often. If ever.

With a sigh, Ethan looked around at the people he was going to be spending the day with. It was amazing that in a room full of people, Ethan had never felt more alone. Everywhere he looked he thought he saw Summer. He knew that was impossible because she was back in Portland, working, taking care of her dog... having a life. Meanwhile, here he stood, nursing a cup of coffee while juggling his rain gear, binoculars, and a camera while imagining her laughter.

"Great, now I'm hearing things," he mumbled and took the last sip of his coffee. When he heard the same laugh again, he stood up a little straighter and looked around. Not more than ten feet away from him stood a woman who could easily be Summer's twin. Her back was to him, and before he could catch a glimpse of her face, a voice came over the loudspeaker announcing that they were getting ready to board the boat.

Crap.

With no other choice, Ethan moved along with the

group and couldn't help but get caught up in the excitement of those around him. This wasn't his usual activity, but that didn't mean he wasn't going to enjoy himself.

He just needed to put a little extra effort into it.

Working his way through the crowd, he found a position out on the deck. This particular boat only took about thirty passengers out at a time, so it wasn't particularly crowded, but it seemed like everyone was here with someone and he was the only person going solo.

Trying to push "One Is the Loneliest Number" from playing in his mind, Ethan focused on the water and doing his best to keep a somewhat positive attitude. He had four hours of whale watching ahead of him, so he needed to drum up some enthusiasm about it and tried not to imagine Zach pointing and laughing at him for doing something so tame.

An hour into the tour, Ethan was feeling the chill from the water and decided to go inside and grab another cup of coffee. So far there hadn't been much to see in the way of whales, but the scenery had been breathtaking. Closing the door to the deck behind him, he looked around and saw that the line for snacks and drinks was relatively short. There were only two women ahead of him and as he stepped closer, he heard that laugh again.

Summer's laugh.

He was slowly going insane. How could he possibly keep hearing her, picturing her wherever he went? Why was his mind playing tricks on him? Why was...? And then it hit him. His mind wasn't playing tricks on him. As he stepped closer, Ethan realized that the woman he heard laughing *was* Summer and that Gabriella was with her.

Unsure of what to do, he continued to stare. What the hell were the two of them doing in Alaska? Why weren't they back in Portland? He knew that Gabriella had to take her vacation time when Zach was on vacation, but why didn't Summer—or Gabriella—mention that they were coming to Glacier Bay? And to that end, why had they come all the way to Glacier Bay? This wasn't exactly the kind of vacation he would have imagined the two of them taking.

And why not? Summer was an athletic woman who enjoyed the outdoors. Ethan just had no idea Gabriella was the same way. She seemed more of the luxury spa variety. He had to wonder whose idea it was to come here. Had they gone to Denali first in hopes of trying to stop Zach again? Or him?

Only one way to find out.

No sooner had the thought entered his mind than two men approached Summer and Gabriella. He stood back and fumed silently as one of the guys said something that made Summer laugh. Hell no. There was no way he could stand by and watch her get hit on by some other guy. He was just about to make his move when the four of them took their drinks and walked back out on the deck.

"Can I help you?" the snack attendant asked, and Ethan was torn between grabbing the coffee he had come in for or chasing after Summer. "Sir?"

Quickly he ordered his drink and then went back out onto the deck. Everyone was *oohing* and *aahing* and it didn't take long for Ethan to realize that this was their first sighting of a humpback whale. It was really something to see, but Ethan only had eyes for Summer. He slowly approached where she and Gabriella were standing with their new friends. Gabriella spotted him first and he watched as she nudged Summer in his direction.

"Ethan?" Summer said, her eyes wide with surprise. "What are you doing here? Why aren't you on the climb with Zach?" She stopped speaking and quickly looked around. "Is he here too? Did you both decide not to go?"

That was it? That was all she had to say to him? His gaze bore into hers as he took in her sporty attire. She had on snug-fitting jeans, boots, a quilted vest, and some sort of colorful scarf that wrapped around her neck several times. Her hair was pulled back into a ponytail and she had just a hint of lip gloss on.

"Ethan?" she asked again as he continued to stare.

"Did the climb get canceled because of the weather?" Gabriella said to fill the awkward silence.

Ethan wished they'd all just go away. Except for Summer. She was here. He was here. Clearly it was a sign that they were allowed to have more than one night, more than one stolen night. Finally he said, "No, Zach's not here. No, the climb didn't get canceled. I decided not to go." He watched as Summer's eyes widened at his words. "I couldn't." Then he watched as she swallowed and nervously looked from him to Gabriella and back again.

"Why are you here?" she asked quietly.

"I could ask you the same thing."

"If you two will excuse us, we're going to watch the whales," Gabriella said, walking over to the rail with her two new friends.

"I don't understand, Ethan," Summer said. "Why didn't you go with Zach?"

He shrugged. "I don't think I ever really wanted to go

on the climb. It wasn't until we got there that I realized how much I didn't want to."

Disappointment swamped her. It wasn't because of her that he didn't go; it was something else. "Oh."

Reaching out, Ethan tucked a finger under her chin. "Everything you said made sense, Summer. You were right. There was no way I could go with a clear conscience. I'm sorry I couldn't talk your brother out of it, but as you know, he's pretty stubborn."

She nodded but couldn't speak. Just the simple touch of his finger and she was lost. She glanced over at Gabriella and noticed the two guys they'd been talking to had moved on. Summer sighed. As much as she wanted to stand here and talk to Ethan, spend more time with him, she had come away for a girls' trip with Gabriella. Just her rotten luck.

"Well," she began as she took a tentative step back, "I guess I better go and join Gabriella." She'd shown more enthusiasm on her way to a root canal. Her gaze lingered on Ethan for longer than it should have. "Would... would you like to join us?"

The immediate answer was yes, but Ethan looked over and saw Gabriella now waving off a couple of new guys. It made him jealous as hell to think that if they hadn't run into one another, Summer would be spending her afternoon with them. "I'd like that very much, but I don't want to be the third wheel."

"Third...?" And then she got it. Looking over her shoulder, she saw Gabriella looking out at the water with her binoculars. "Come on. It will be fun."

There were other activities Ethan would rather be participating in with Summer, and whale watching wasn't one of them. Rather than argue the point, he changed the subject. "Where are you staying?"

"Oh, we have a room at the lodge."

"You didn't mention that you were coming here when I saw you."

Summer blushed at the memory of the last time he'd seen her. "It really was a spur-of-the-moment kind of thing. Gabriella actually arranged it. After all of her research for Zach, she was curious what the big draw was for Alaska. We both had some time off coming to us, so we figured we'd check it out."

"Hopefully you won't be disappointed," he said with a smile.

Summer couldn't help but smile back. It was on the tip of her tongue to say that it would be impossible to be disappointed now that he was there and could share it all with her. Taking a step closer to Ethan, she was just about to ask if he had dinner plans when Gabriella called out to them.

"Come on! You guys are missing all of this. It's amazing! I've seen at least two whales already!"

"I guess that's our cue," Summer said softly as she turned to walk over to the side of the boat. When Ethan didn't immediately move, she reached out and took one of his hands in hers and tugged.

It might not be exactly what he had envisioned for the two of them, but for right now, Ethan would gladly take what he could get.

When the tour ended and the boat docked, Summer felt happier than she had in a long time. Between the amazing sights they'd seen and being able to spend time with Ethan, she was feeling very content.

"Did you have anything else planned this afternoon, Ethan?" Gabriella asked, and if Ethan didn't know better, he'd swear that she was onto him and his feelings for Summer. She kept nudging Summer closer to him, and if anything, she seemed pleased that he was there.

"I actually hadn't given it too much thought. I was just planning on playing it by ear. How about you? Do the two of you have plans?" The question was meant for the both of them, but he only had eyes for Summer.

"We had planned on just relaxing and then going for dinner. You'll join us, won't you?" Summer asked.

"Of course," he said. While he knew he couldn't ask Gabriella to stay behind, that didn't stop his mind from wandering to how he could possibly find a way to be alone with Summer. For now he'd bide his time.

The three of them made their way back to the lodge, all the while talking about the things they'd seen while out on the boat. Summer talked excitedly about her plans for a scrapbook and how she was looking forward to taking more pictures over the course of their stay, which led to her sharing about her brief attempt at being a photographer for a small magazine back in New York.

"You're certainly eclectic in your career choices," Gabriella said. "And you're fortunate that you have so many talents."

"Please, you've got us all beat in the talent department," Summer said as they walked into the lodge. "I'm still trying to find the one thing that I'm really good at so I can stick with it. You found your niche. You're the lucky one."

Gabriella blushed and then cleared her throat. "I'm going to grab the new *Cosmo* and a couple bottles of water from the gift shop. You want anything?"

"No thanks," Summer said, but her attention was solely on Ethan.

"So," he began, "what time were you thinking about going to dinner?"

"I'm not sure. I don't think we have reservations. What about you?"

He took a step closer. "I had kind of planned on ordering room service and just hanging out in my room. So I'm flexible."

"Oh. Okay." She was nervous and didn't quite know what to say. The thought of having dinner with Ethan in his room was beyond appealing, but she knew it wasn't going to happen. "I…um…I guess I'll talk to Gabriella and we'll call you when we have something planned."

Ethan nodded. "I guess you could. Or…"

"Or what?"

He leaned in close, close enough to watch her pupils dilate and close enough to inhale the sweet scent of her. "Or…you can come with me." He gave no other details because it was all implied right there.

She wanted desperately to say yes; it was like getting a second chance at your perfect fantasy. Could she really walk away from that? One look at Gabriella and she unfortunately had her answer. "I…I can't."

His eyebrows shot up at her response. "What? Why?"

"You and I both know why. I didn't tell anyone about last weekend, Ethan. I'm here now with Gabriella, and she's definitely going to notice if you and I leave together. And besides that, we're sharing a room. She'll definitely notice when I don't come back." Somewhere in the back of her mind, Summer knew this was for the best. She just wished it didn't hurt so much.

Ethan took a step back and nodded. He didn't want to pressure her or make her uncomfortable. He'd only recently come to grips with how he felt about her; maybe he needed to take some time to let her get to know him as a man and not as just a friend of her brother's. "I understand. I guess I'll see you at dinner." He didn't move; hell, he barely breathed. It wasn't hard to see the indecision on Summer's face, but in the end, she turned and walked over to the gift shop. He didn't move when she stepped out of his sight, and he didn't move when Gabriella turned in his direction.

"Are you out of your mind?" Gabriella hissed as soon as Summer came and stood beside her.

"What are you talking about?" Summer asked wearily as she picked up a magazine and began to flip through it.

"Care to tell me why you're standing in here with me reading *Men's Health* when you could be off somewhere with Ethan?"

Summer looked at her in shock. "Me and Ethan?" she squeaked. "Are you crazy? Where…whatever gave you that idea?"

Gabriella threw her head back and laughed, a full, throaty sound that made people turn in their direction. When she was able to catch her breath, she faced Summer. "Seriously? You are seriously asking me that question?"

"Yes."

Gabriella shifted her purse from one shoulder to the

other. "Okay, let's start with the fact that you watch him at the office all the time."

"I do not."

"All. The. Time. Secondly, he watches you just as much."

Summer's eyes widened. "He does not."

Gabriella nodded. "All. The. Time. Hell, he's standing there doing it right now. Why don't you do us all a favor and go enjoy yourself?"

"But what about—"

"I will be fine hanging out by myself. I think I'll have dinner sent to the room and enjoy eating dessert in bed." When Summer tried to interrupt, she stopped her. "My lips are sealed, Summer. No one will hear about this from me."

"But what about Zach?"

Gabriella actually frowned at the mention of her boss. "What about him?"

"You work for him. If he finds out about this, he'll freak out."

"Please. Your brother freaks out about a lot of stuff, and like I said, he won't hear about it from me. If he asks me if I know anything, I'll deny it with my last breath." She smiled. "Go. I know you said you weren't interested in hooking up with anyone, but I get the impression that statement didn't include Mr. Reed over there."

Summer was afraid to turn around. "Is he really still standing there?" she whispered.

Gabriella nodded. "And watching you like he can't wait to have you for dessert."

Summer smiled. "Then I guess I shouldn't make him wait."

"Atta girl! Go get him!"

Summer slid the magazine back onto the rack and hugged Gabriella before turning and facing Ethan. His expression was fierce, and she knew in that instant she was going to make the most of every second they had. Their night together had been too short. She was going to take her time with him and not let him leave until the very last possible second.

Taking a steadying breath, she checked her hair and fixed her scarf before she met his gaze and walked over to where he stood. When she was standing right in front of him, she stopped and looked him in the eyes. "You mentioned something about coming with you." She put a little extra emphasis on the word "coming" and watched a small smile tug at his lips.

"I did."

"Is that offer still on the table?"

His smile grew. "Sweetheart, that offer is anywhere you want it to be." Without another word, Ethan reached out and took Summer's hand in his and led her toward the bank of elevators in the lobby. Tension rolled off his body. If he wasn't mistaken, there was a slight tremble coming from Summer.

When the doors opened, he was relieved to see they were alone. Tugging her inside, he pressed the button for his floor, pulled her into his arms, and crushed his mouth to hers. Now that he knew the feel of her, the taste of her, Ethan was surprised it didn't dampen his need for her. She fit perfectly against him as her lips opened and her tongue darted out to mate with his. Turning her so her back was against the wall, he rubbed his arousal against her and nearly groaned when Summer's hand reached between them to touch him. He wasn't sure they'd even make it to his suite. If it were up to him, he'd stop the elevator and take her right here, right now, in the elevator, against the wall.

He heard the bell signal their arrival, and he nearly sagged with relief when he realized it was his floor and there weren't other guests waiting outside the elevator doors. It was torture to move away from her, but Ethan knew the sooner they got to his suite, the sooner they could resume what they'd started.

In no time at all, he had the door open and they were inside. He pinned Summer up against the back of the door and lifted her until she wrapped those glorious legs around his waist. His mouth was back on hers, and when he felt Summer's hand rake through his hair, Ethan knew they weren't going to make it any farther into the suite. It was now; it had to be now. "I can't wait," he said breathlessly as he lifted his head and looked into her eyes.

"Me either," she said and began to trail kisses along his jaw and his throat. "Now, Ethan. Right now."

It was all the encouragement he needed.

They did make it to the bedroom eventually. It was much later when Summer found herself waking up and looking for the clock. Eleven o'clock. Was that all? It seemed like so much longer. Ethan was wrapped around her in the big bed, and it felt glorious. But what felt even better was the fact that it was still early and they had almost two weeks before Summer had to leave.

Two whole weeks.

Alone.

With Ethan.

In bed.

She squirmed a little and smiled as Ethan's arm banded tighter around her waist to pull her even closer. His arousal was snug against her bottom and she purred with delight.

"You're insatiable," he murmured against her throat and then began to kiss her there.

"You seem to be holding your own quite well."

He nibbled and tasted his way up to her jaw and growled until she turned in his arms so he could kiss her properly. When he finally came up for air, he looked around the room. "What time is it?"

"A little after eleven."

"Are you hungry? Do you want me to order dinner for us?"

She smiled at his concern. "It's a little late for dinner, don't you think?"

His eyes scanned her face even as his hands roamed her body. "Did you eat dinner before we came up here?"

"No."

"Then it's not too late," he said lightly. Reluctantly, he climbed from the bed and went in search of a pair of pants. Minutes later, he came back to the bed with a menu and lay down beside Summer. "What are you in the mood for?"

She laughed. "I think I've already had what I was in the mood for."

He couldn't help but laugh with her. "Focus, woman! You wore me out, and now I need protein or something to get me through the night."

How had she gotten through the week without him? Without bantering with him and laughing with him? For that matter, how had she gotten through so many years of crushing on him without experiencing these things?

"I'm going for a big-ass steak," he announced and handed the menu to Summer.

"Typical man," she sighed, and browsed the selections. "I am going to have…"

"If you say a salad, I swear I will scream," he interrupted.

She glared at him. "I was going to say I will have a big-ass steak too. With a salad," she added before sticking her tongue out at him. One last glance through the menu and she handed it back to him. "And a slice of the chocolate truffle cake for dessert, please."

Ethan leaned in and kissed her. "Typical woman."

He went to the phone to call room service and when he came back, he found Summer standing by the window looking out at the mountains. She was wearing a big, fluffy hotel robe that covered her from chin to toes and yet he knew what was underneath. His fingers began to twitch with the need to touch her again.

He cursed himself. Why did Summer make him so weak? So needy? It didn't seem fair that for all they had in common and how much they enjoyed one another—both in and out of bed—they had to sneak away to be together. What would happen after they returned to Portland? Would they have each other out of their systems? Would they continue to have dirty weekends in secret? Ethan hated the thought. It wasn't fair. None of this was fair. Summer deserved better.

Summer turned and looked at him. "How long until dinner arrives?"

"They said about thirty minutes." He watched as Summer took a step away from the window and pulled at the sash on the robe. The robe pooled at her feet and Ethan could only stare as she walked toward him.

"Then we better make the most of it," she said with a sexy grin.

Summer tiptoed back into the room she was sharing with Gabriella before the sun came up. Leaving Ethan's bed was one of the hardest things she'd ever done, but she still felt guilty about leaving Gabriella alone on what was supposed to be their girls' trip.

Feeling like she was in stealth mode, she quietly made her way over to her bed and was just about to pull the blankets back when the lights came on and she screamed.

"What time is it?" Gabriella asked sleepily.

"Geez!" Summer hissed, her hand over her heart. "You scared the hell out of me!"

Gabriella grabbed the alarm clock and glanced at it before putting it back down. "It's four in the morning, Summer. What are you doing back here?"

"Wait…what?" She sat down on the bed. "What do you mean? This is my room."

Stacking her pillows behind her, Gabriella sat up and looked at Summer. "So you're saying that you left Ethan's bed to come and sleep here? Alone? Are you insane?"

A blush crept up Summer's cheeks. "I…I just thought that it was a little rude of me to take off like that. I mean, you and I planned this trip, and I should be here with you."

"Ugh…it's too early to have this kind of conversation." Tossing her pillows back to their original position, Gabriella flopped back down and rolled over.

"What did I say?"

Rolling back over, Gabriella sighed. Loudly. "Summer, I thought you and I were friends."

"We are!"

"Okay, then what would possibly make you believe that I would expect you to be here with me when you were already with Ethan?"

She shrugged. "I felt like a crappy friend ditching you like that."

"I'll tell you what, next time I find a hot guy to spend the night with, I get to ditch you. Deal?"

"Hmm…now that depends."

"Are you seriously still talking?"

"Uh-huh. I am," Summer said with a big smile. "So, this hot guy. Is it my brother or some other random hot guy?"

"Your brother?" Gabriella sat up and stammered. "Why…why would you even suggest that?"

"Oh, maybe because you've got a serious crush on him."

"Like the one you have on Ethan?"

"What are we? Twelve?" Summer asked with a laugh. "Anyway, back to you being in love with Zach…"

"I thought it was just a crush?" Gabriella deadpanned.

"We'll see. Anyway, if it's my brother, then yes, you are allowed to ditch me. Otherwise, I get a say in the matter."

"That's totally not fair. We're on vacation in the alpha-male capital of the world. I could totally find a hot guy here to ditch you for."

"You could, but you won't."

Gabriella narrowed her eyes at her. "And why is that?"

"For the same reason that I wasn't interested in ditching you for anyone but Ethan. Sometimes there's only one guy worth ditching your friends for."

Gabriella looked like she was going to argue but quickly closed her mouth. "Well, thanks for the insight, but I don't plan on starting my day this early. I have some quality sleep time coming to me. Don't wake me again until noon."

Summer yawned loudly. "I don't think that's going to be a problem. I'm exhausted."

"I'm sure."

"What's that supposed to mean?" Summer asked as she walked over to grab a pair of pajamas out of her drawer.

"Aw…do we need to have the birds and the bees talk? I would have thought you and Ethan would have covered all that."

"Ha, ha. Very funny."

"All I'm saying is that I'm sure you're exhausted because we'd had a very full day even before you ran into Ethan. And, on top of that, I'm sure the two of you weren't spending the night playing Scrabble."

Summer giggled. "No, we certainly were not. We—"

"Stop right there! I do not want to hear it."

"Jealous?" Summer said with a wicked grin.

"Absolutely not. It's just that I kind of work for

Ethan, and it will be really hard to face him if I have to hear about all of your sex-capades."

"They're the best kind."

"Ugh…going to sleep now," Gabriella said as she reached over and turned out the light.

Chapter 7

IT WAS A LITTLE BEFORE NOON WHEN SUMMER knocked on Ethan's door. His smile when he saw her made everything inside of her melt. "Hey."

"Hey, yourself," he said, taking her hand in his and pulling her into his room. "How are you?"

She blushed. "I'm good."

Unable to help himself, Ethan pulled her into his arms and kissed her. "Did you get some sleep?" he asked when he finally pulled back.

"I did," she said softly. "But I would have preferred staying here with you."

"You know I wanted you to. I don't think Gabriella would have minded."

"She pretty much told me the same thing when she caught me sneaking back into the room this morning."

"I won't say I told you so, but…"

"I know, I know. You told me so." She sighed and snuggled closer in his arms. "What do you have planned for today? Anything?"

"Well, the weather is being very cooperative, so I was thinking of either going for a hike or kayaking. What about you? Did you and Gabriella have anything planned?"

"There's so much to do that I was having a hard time choosing. I think I'd really like to try the kayaking."

Ethan hugged her close. "Well then, let's go grab Gabriella and see about doing that."

"Really? You wouldn't mind it being the three of us?"

"Summer, believe it or not, I really like Gabriella. I can't believe she's actually here vacationing willingly though."

"Why not?"

His eyes went wide with disbelief as he looked down at her. "Why? Have you seen Gabriella? She looks like some sort of sophisticated...model or something. The woman never has a hair out of place. The image of her hiking or kayaking is a little out of my realm of comprehension."

Summer couldn't help but laugh. "I know. I kind of thought that about her too, but she's got a bit of an outdoorsy side. Not quite like mine and certainly not like yours and Zach's, but I think she'll hold her own nicely."

"Knowing her, I wouldn't doubt it for a minute. She'll not only hold her own but probably be better at it than either of us."

Summer pulled back and grinned. "That sounds like a little bit of a challenge there, Ethan."

He grinned back at her. "Me? Issuing a challenge? Why would I do something like that?"

"Because it's exactly the kind of person you are! You rarely do anything like this for fun, there's always a challenge or a dare involved."

"Well sure, with Zach or any of your brothers. I wouldn't do something like that with you and Gabriella."

Now she pulled completely out of his arms but her grin was still in place. "Oh really? And why is that?"

"Because...you're...you're..."

"If you dare say because I'm a girl, I'll hurt you."

He pulled her back into his arms and kissed her thoroughly. "But you are a girl and not only that, you're not someone I want to compete against."

"What do you want?"

He chuckled. "Sweetheart, what I want is to lock the door and keep you in here with me and the hell with kayaking and hiking and fishing and whatever else this place boasts." He nuzzled her neck. "I'd keep you naked in the bed with me and forget that anyone else even existed."

She purred with pleasure. "Oh, that does sound really good."

"But…" he prompted.

"But…even though Gabriella is okay with us being together, I don't want to forget about her completely. Plus, I can't remember the last time I actually had this much free time to indulge in all of my favorite activities."

"So salmon fishing is high on your list?" he teased.

"Maybe not that, but there are so many other great things here to do that I'd hate to miss out."

"Fine," he said, pretending to be put out. "We'll go kayaking and admire all of the beautiful nature around us. For now. But later? You're mine."

Her grin grew into a full-blown smile that lit up her entire face. "That's what I was hoping you'd say."

"I think I'm seriously out of shape."

Ethan stroked a hand from Summer's waist to her knee and back again. "You don't feel seriously out of shape."

She laughed. "I can't believe that kayaking kicked my butt. I hurt all over."

"Well to be fair, it was a pretty long trip. I wasn't expecting it to be that long of a route."

It was well after dinner, and they were lying in bed together after Gabriella lovingly threw Summer's things at her and told her to not come back.

At least until tomorrow, when they had plans to go fishing.

Ethan was completely on board with having Summer share his room and now that she was here with him, he felt completely at peace. It was as if she was the missing puzzle piece to his life. Spending the entire day together—and now the night—had Ethan feeling like his life was pretty much near perfect. It wasn't as if he had thought his life wasn't great before, but now? He pulled Summer close to him and just relaxed against her and smiled.

Perfect.

"It was a really long route," she agreed and placed a kiss on his bare chest. "And yet Gabriella still managed to beat us both."

"I don't remember it that way," Ethan said.

Pulling back, Summer smirked at him knowingly. "Such a sore loser."

"What? Me? How can I be a sore loser when we weren't really racing?"

"Oh? We weren't racing?" She sat up and laughed out loud. "Then what was all that 'loser has to buy drinks back at the lodge' comment and then you buying drinks?" She continued to laugh before adding, "Hmm? Care to explain?"

Ethan frowned and lay back against the pillows. "Sure, try to be a gentleman and buy a couple of beautiful women some drinks and all of a sudden it's because I'm a sore loser. What is this world coming to?"

That just made Summer laugh even harder. Deciding to take pity on him, she curled back up against his side. "Okay, okay, you're a gentleman, and it was only because you were being polite that both Gabriella and I finished the route ahead of you."

"Um…you and I got there at the same time. I just let you get to the dock first because…"

"You were being a gentleman?"

"Exactly."

She leaned in and kissed him on the lips. "Thank you."

"I could have gotten there first," he mumbled when she rested her head on his shoulder.

"Oh my God! Are you going to be like this all night?" she teased.

"That depends," he said, rolling her over so that he was stretched out on top of her.

"On what?" she asked as she shimmied beneath him to have them perfectly lined up.

"On whether or not you can find something else for us to do that doesn't involve talking." His voice was deep and husky, and Summer shivered as he bent down and kissed her neck.

"I think what you're doing right now will work," she whispered.

"And yet you're still talking."

Wrapping her arms around his shoulders, Summer pulled him in close and found a way to keep them both quiet for a very long time.

—⁓—

For two more days, the three of them played outdoor enthusiasts. They went salmon fishing and took a flightseeing tour over the area. Their days were filled with sightseeing and all kinds of activities, but after dinner each night, Summer and Ethan retreated to their own little world.

"I still feel guilty," Summer said later that night as she crawled onto the bed.

"Not this again," he said lightly. "Summer, Gabriella is fine with this arrangement. Hell, she sort of arranged it herself. If I remember correctly, she had your bags packed and waiting outside the door after that first night."

A small pout crossed her face. "Maybe she was just trying to be nice."

"She had balloons, a bottle of champagne, and a box of condoms sitting with them," he said wryly.

"She hides her pain well."

Ethan laughed as he sat down on the bed beside her. "Is this your way of telling me that you don't want to be here with me?"

"What? No! Of course not. Why would you even say that?"

"Because no matter how much Gabriella's given us her blessing, you're still obsessing about it. I know none of us planned this, but I thought you were just as happy as I was that we're here together."

She reached up and cupped his cheek in her hand. "I am happy to be here with you. I never thought we'd get to have this kind of time together. But I can't help but feel a little bit guilty. I'm trying to get over it, I really am, but every time we say good-bye to her after dinner, I feel like I'm deserting her."

"Do you want to go and stay with her tonight?" he asked casually, even though he didn't really want her to go. "Have one of those girly sleepovers?"

"You know those don't really include pillow fights in our underwear, right?"

"Way to kill a guy's dream," he grumbled. "But I'm serious. If it's bothering you that much, maybe you should go hang out with her."

A small smile played across her lips. "No, I'm exactly where I want to be, Ethan," she replied. "I'll get over it and I know you're right—Gabriella's fine with me being here with you. I just overthink things like this."

"Well, stop thinking," he said as he slowly began to lie down and guided her with him. "We're fine. She's fine." Summer rested her head on his shoulder and Ethan felt her body relax.

Honestly, he wasn't sure what he'd do if she wanted to leave. He'd let her, of course, but it would be hard. He was just starting to get used to her being with him and really getting to know Summer as a woman—not the girl he had grown up with—and he was enjoying the discoveries.

When they were younger, he'd known her to be athletic, but he'd never realized so many of her interests mirrored his own. She loved a challenge and didn't shy away from trying new activities, but she did it all just for fun rather than because she was trying to prove something.

Which was what he was slowly beginning to realize he'd been doing for a long time through his activities with Zach. They had always competed with each other through school and well into their twenties and now thirties, but Ethan was finally seeing it was time to be done with that. He knew he was a good man, a good athlete, a good friend. There was no need to keep up with the challenges or try to prove that he was invincible. Holding Summer in his arms and enjoying the activities as they had for the last several days made Ethan happier than any adventure he'd ever gone on.

And it wasn't scary.

It wasn't an adrenaline rush.

And yet he was completely content.

A soft sigh beside him had him looking down and seeing that Summer had fallen asleep. As much as he loved making the most of their time together, it was moments like this that meant the most. While Ethan knew it couldn't be like this forever—they were eventually going to have to return to their normal lives and deal with whatever fallout there was going to be from the Montgomerys—that didn't mean he couldn't relish it for now.

—⁂—

"So what's on the agenda for today?" Ethan asked the next morning as he and Summer joined Gabriella for breakfast.

"Actually," Gabriella began hesitantly as they all sat down, "I think I'm just going to hang out around the lodge today. I'm going to be lazy, maybe get a massage or something, and curl up with a good book. I'm not used to all this crazy outdoor stuff."

"But you're so good at it," Summer said, reaching across the table and squeezing one of Gabriella's hands. "We're supposed to hike today, remember?"

"I know, I know. I'm seriously ready for a day just to veg. You guys go and do your thing. A day of doing nothing is way more appealing to me right now than hiking around with twenty pounds of gear on my back."

A little part of Summer totally related to that. As much as she was enjoying her time with Ethan, she wouldn't mind a day of pampering. Just the thought of a nice deep-tissue massage, a pedicure… She almost groaned with imagined delight.

"If you'd rather go with Gabriella," Ethan said, "that's totally fine. I think you'd have a great time making it a girls' day." He remembered their conversation from the previous night and thought this could be the perfect compromise.

And the thing was, Summer knew he meant it. Ethan wasn't the kind of man who would make demands on her time or belittle her for wanting a day to relax and be pampered. She was completely torn about what to do and decided to put off making her decision until after breakfast.

"Who's up for Belgian waffles?" she said cheerily.

Sensing her friend's distraction tactics, Gabriella chimed in. "While I do enjoy a waffle the size of my head, I think I'm going to be sensible and have a fruit platter."

"You can't do that," Summer said firmly, placing her menu facedown on the table.

"Why not?"

"Vacation. You are not allowed to be sensible while on vacation. This is the time when you're supposed to break all the rules and not think about diets and whatnot."

"That's ridiculous."

Summer shook her head. "It's completely true. Trust me. Look around this room. Do you see anyone having fruit for breakfast?" Before Gabriella could answer, Summer continued. "No. You don't. Why? Because no one eats fruit on vacation."

"That's the dumbest logic I've ever heard." Then she paused. "But far be it from me to commit some sort of vacation faux pas." Picking up her menu, she looked it over again. "Fine. I'm going to have the eggs Benedict with a side order of potatoes. Happy?"

"Not enough carbs in my opinion, but whatever," Summer said as she continued to scan her menu. "Belgian waffles with strawberries for me."

"Uh-uh," Gabriella said disapprovingly.

"Why? What's wrong with that?"

"If I'm not allowed to have fruit, neither are you."

"It's not fruit," Summer argued lightly. "It's a topping. Completely different."

"I don't agree. Get the chocolate chip ones or I'm getting my fruit platter. And then it will be your fault that everyone stops and stares at me like I'm a freak."

Beside them, Ethan rolled his eyes. "If the two of you keep up this kind of conversation, the only thing I'm going to be having for breakfast is a strong drink."

"Ooo...mimosas!" Summer said excitedly. "Why didn't I think of that?"

"Seriously?" Ethan asked. "That's your idea of a strong drink?"

"A strong breakfast drink," Gabriella corrected.

"Note to self, drink heavily before having breakfast with these two," Ethan murmured as he looked at the menu. "And in case anyone's wondering, I'm having the outdoorsman platter—eggs, bacon, home fries, and pancakes. I think I've hit all the necessities." He looked at Summer expectantly. "Did I miss anything?"

"Nailed it in one," she said and leaned over and kissed him on the cheek before looking at Gabriella. "See? He knows the rules of vacation eating. You don't see him eat like that at the office, do you?"

"Can't say that I have. But then again, I'm usually too busy running around for Zach to notice what Ethan's eating. Maybe I'll have to call his assistant and ask some questions." Her eyes twinkled as she looked at the two of them.

"Oh no," Ethan said with a chuckle. "Leave Donna out of this. No one knows that I didn't go on the climb, and I'm enjoying the peace and quiet."

They all grew silent for a moment. "How do you think Zach's doing?" Summer asked, suddenly serious. "Do you think he's okay?"

Ethan put his arm around her. "I'm sure he is. I know his leg wasn't as fully healed as it should have been, but I'd like to think that he's being careful and not doing anything to aggravate it."

Gabriella snorted with disbelief and then quickly coughed to try to cover it up. When both Summer and Ethan looked at her expectantly, her eyes went a little wide. "What?"

"Out with it," Summer said. "Say what's on your mind."

"Your brother knows he shouldn't have gone on this climb, and so does everyone else. He likes to think he's invincible, but he's not. This whole thing was poorly timed, and I understand that he didn't want to wait another whole year before the climbing season came around again, but he's only hurting himself. I mean, what is he trying to prove?"

It was on the tip of Ethan's tongue to defend Zach, but he didn't. Not really. "Zach's addicted to taking the risks. He's an adrenaline junkie. We both are. It's not something that everyone gets, and yeah, maybe he could have been a little wiser about this particular trip, but I think he's going to be all right."

"I never understood it," Summer said. "All my life I sat back and watched Zach do one stupid adventure after another, and I just don't see the appeal. I enjoy going out and playing sports just like the next guy, but I don't see how practically killing yourself can give you any kind of a thrill."

"It's a great feeling when you do it," Ethan said with just a hint of defense. "I can't describe it, but it's an incredible high when you jump out of a plane and soar through the sky or when you bungee jump off a bridge and barrel toward the ground and bounce away just in time. It's…it's amazing."

"It's stupid," Gabriella said before thanking the waitress who poured their coffees. "People who do that sort of thing are clearly trying to prove something. We all get it—Zach's a man's man. He doesn't need to jump out of a plane or climb a mountain with a bad leg to prove it. Why can't he just be happy doing normal things?"

"The things he does are normal to him. He's a gifted athlete who's conquered all of the usual sports. So little by little, he upped the ante," Ethan said, taking a sip of his own coffee.

"To what end?" Gabriella asked. "When is enough

going to be enough? I thought the broken leg would have slowed him down a bit, but all it did was make him angry and push him to do something completely stupid!"

"I don't think it's the smartest thing he's ever done," Ethan said evenly, "but I'm hoping he's going to see that he needs to slow down a bit. Maybe after he gets back, Zach will realize that his body can only take so much and he'll finally relax a little."

Gabriella shook her head with disbelief. "I think something major is going to have to happen for him to see that."

Summer sat back and quietly sipped her coffee and listened to the exchange. Unfortunately, she knew Gabriella was right. Her brother was so damn stubborn that it was going to take something major to wake him up and snap him out of this obsession for dangerous sports. She'd lost count of the times she had begged him—for his own safety—to wait before going on this excursion. His leg wasn't healed from jumping out of that plane back in the fall.

Zach had argued that it had been six months and he was fine, but Summer knew better. After all her training as a yoga instructor, she had learned enough about how the body works—and heals—to see the telltale signs of an injury that wasn't fully healed.

And Zach wasn't fully healed no matter how much he protested.

"Look, we could go back and forth about this all day, but in the end we have to trust that Zach knows what he's doing," Ethan said and smiled as their waitress approached to take their orders.

Time for another change of subject, Summer thought

to herself. "So…a spa day?" she asked cheerily. "I'm sure it's going to be fabulous."

"You could totally join me," Gabriella said. "I wouldn't say no to the company."

"As much as I know my body would absolutely love it, I'm kind of excited about the hike. Everything is just so beautiful out here, and we have such great weather again today that I don't want to miss out."

"Summer, you don't have to explain yourself to me. I'm the one changing plans. I knew you guys were going to go on the hike. I'm the one crying 'uncle' because I'm out of shape."

A snort escaped Summer's lips before she could stop it. "Sorry. But um…out of shape? Hardly. Please. Don't make me smack you."

"You have no idea," Gabriella countered.

"Enough!" Ethan said. "I have to stop the two of you right there because I cannot sit through another of these crazy conversations. Gabriella? Enjoy the spa day. Summer? You and I are going to get a bag lunch to take with us and we are going to go and hike like we planned. And tonight when we all meet for dinner, everyone will be happy. Okay?"

Both women looked at him as if he had spoken Greek. "Geez, lighten up," Summer mumbled.

"I know, right?" Gabriella agreed just as quietly.

With a roll of his eyes, Ethan took his coffee mug in his hands and decided the only way to win was to keep his mouth shut until they were done with breakfast. This was a whole new experience for him—witnessing this much female conversation. He knew that Summer and Gabriella had only known each other for a short time, but they acted as if they'd been best friends forever. He was glad Summer had made a friend here; it might work to his advantage if he hoped to convince her to stay in Portland, even if she didn't want to work for Montgomerys.

This was probably something he should approach Summer about. While right now everything was wonderful and they were both happy, the truth was that they hadn't been living in reality. The time in the tepee and now here in Alaska were far away from their normal lives. What was going to happen once they returned to work? To Portland? To being surrounded by nosy Montgomerys?

Their breakfast arrived and Summer looked at her giant waffle and turned to Ethan and smiled. Her entire face lit up, and it just confirmed what he already knew: He was in love with Summer Montgomery.

—◦◦◦—

"This trail is a little bit boring, don't you think?" Summer asked several hours later as they made their way down a marked path.

"I hadn't really thought of it that way. There's so much to see—different kinds of birds and plants… The weather is just fantastic—perfect for hiking." He reached out and took one of Summer's hands in his. "And the company is perfect."

"Aw, aren't you sweet," she cooed and pulled him close for a kiss and sighed. "It is a beautiful day and everything is really pretty to look at… I was just hoping to see a little something more."

"More? Like what?"

"Oh, I don't know. Deer. Bears. A moose. You know, wildlife."

Beside her, Ethan chuckled. "Summer, trust me when I say that you do not want to have an up-close encounter with any of those animals."

"I'm not saying up close. I'd just like to see one—even off in the distance." She looked around and then came to a complete stop.

"What? What's the matter?" he asked.

"You know, that guy at the trail shop said there were a lot of 'secret' paths to check out." She looked around again. "You can see a couple of rough trails through the trees over there. Let's go and check that out!" Tugging Ethan by the hand, Summer tried to move over to what she thought was a trail.

"Summer," he began and held his ground, "I don't think it's a good idea to wander off the path. We've got maps right here and we already chose the longest one to explore. Come on. You have no idea what those paths are like. Let's just stick to the ones mapped out for us."

She pulled her hand free of his and crossed her arms. "If you were Zach, would you stick to the mapped-out, boring path?"

"That's completely irrelevant."

"Is it?" she asked and crossed her arms across her chest.

Why hadn't he remembered her stubborn streak? "It doesn't matter what I would do if Zach were here. You're here. I'm here. I thought we were having a good time."

She dropped her arms to her side. "We are," she

said begrudgingly. "I was just expecting something a little more exciting. All those travel and tour brochures showed the wildlife and the only thing I've seen is a squirrel. And he wasn't even doing anything entertaining."

"What were you expecting? For it to be juggling or something?" he teased.

"No," she said with a pout. "Maybe. I don't know."

Ethan pulled Summer into his embrace and took a moment to enjoy the feel of her in his arms. "What's going on?" he asked softly.

"I don't know… I feel like you're always off doing these really cool, crazy things and that this seems a little tame for you." She shrugged. "I'm not big on dangerous stuff, but I wanted us to have our own little adventure. Just the two of us."

"Sweetheart, we've been having our own adventures for days," he said and placed a kiss on the top of her head. "I don't need an adventure. I just want to spend time with you."

Summer looked up at him and smiled. "Really?"

He nodded. "Absolutely. I'm thankful that we have this time, without any prying eyes, just to get to know one another."

"Ethan, we've known each other for years," she said with a chuckle.

He shook his head. "No. The Summer Montgomery I knew was a girl. When you showed up at the office for the first time? I thought I was going to have a heart attack."

"Really?" she purred and snuggled closer. "Do tell."

"You've blossomed into this amazingly beautiful woman," he said and kissed her temple. "I mean, you were always beautiful, but when you walked into my office that day, it was like you'd transformed. Gone was the young girl I always pictured when I thought of you and in her place was…" He pulled back and looked into her face. "You." He sighed. "I look at you sometimes and it's like I can't breathe. And even standing here right now with you in my arms I can't believe it's real."

"I feel that way too," she said quietly. "I'd had a crush on you for so long and you never noticed me and…"

"Wait, wait, wait… You had a crush on me?"

She rolled her eyes. "Oh come on, Ethan. You can't tell me you didn't know!" she said with a laugh. "Everyone knew! Hell, my brothers used to throw things at me to stop me from staring at you!"

Ethan stopped and thought about that for a moment and then started to laugh. "Seriously? That's what that was about?"

"What?"

"I remember your brothers always throwing stuff at you…popcorn, socks…I think I remember James throwing a basketball at you once and I thought it was odd."

"They told me I was being a nuisance."

Shaking his head, Ethan continued to laugh. "Not to me, because clearly I didn't even notice."

"Thanks a lot!" she cried and went to pull away, but Ethan pulled her in close.

"Don't take it like that," he said and wrapped his arms around her. "I just meant that I never knew. I always thought you were beautiful and sometimes I had to wonder if your brothers ever caught *me* staring at you."

"I don't know. Did they ever throw anything at your face for no reason?" she asked with a smirk.

"Not that I can remember. But it doesn't matter. All I know is that you're here now and I'm seeing you, Summer. Really seeing you."

Her eyes went wide at his words and the sincerity behind them. "What do you see?"

"I see a woman I want to get to know better. A woman who is sexy and intelligent and just…everything."

"Wow." She sighed and stood up on her tiptoes and kissed him gently on the lips. "Thank you."

"For what?" he asked.

"No one's ever said anything like that to me before," she replied quietly, blushing.

"Good," he said huskily. "I like knowing that I'm the only one."

They were standing in the middle of the path, gazing into each other's eyes, when a small group of hikers walked by and effectively killed the moment. Ethan looked around and knew that they could continue on the path they had been taking—the safe one—or he could give in to Summer's request and take them on a bit of an adventure. Taking her hand in his, he pulled her toward the unmarked path.

"Wait. Ethan, what are you doing?"

Looking over his shoulder at her, he winked. "I thought you wanted an adventure."

Her smile grew wide. "Really? You're seriously going to take us on this unmapped trail? For real?"

"Stop asking or I'll come to my senses," he teased and led the way through the trees until they found a slightly wider path to follow.

They hiked for several hours, admiring the scenery and talking about everything and nothing all at the same time. Summer found out all about Ethan's hobbies besides extreme sports—chess, reading mystery novels, and listening to classic rock music—and found that even if she hadn't been insanely attracted to and falling in love with him, he'd be someone she'd still want as a friend.

Ethan still wasn't one hundred percent comfortable taking Summer off the beaten trail (so to speak) but was enjoying their conversation. While he had heard all about her multiple and sometimes quirky career choices, each and every one of them meant something to her. She wasn't as flighty as Zach had made her sound; she was just trying to find the right fit for herself without letting anyone dictate it for her. He admired Summer for that.

"So which job did you like the most?" he asked as he climbed over a fallen log.

"I love doing the yoga classes. It's a win-win situation; I get to teach but I also get the benefits of the class. It's one of the only jobs I've ever had where I never felt any stress."

"That makes sense. And from what I could tell, you're pretty good at it," he said with a wink and then noticed the confused look on her face. "That day at the tepee? You were doing yoga out front. Remember?"

"Oh, right," she said. "I had forgotten that part."

"I don't know anything about yoga, but you certainly seemed to know what you were doing."

Summer stopped and looked around. "Tell you what, why don't we stop here and have our lunch and I'll show you a pose or two."

Ethan's eyes went wide. "Um…what?"

"Don't be such a baby. I'll just show you some basic poses. They'll be easy for you."

"Summer, I'm not doing yoga in the middle of the forest. Not even for you," he said lightly as he pulled his backpack off and began taking out the supplies they had for their lunch.

"Spoilsport," she mumbled and crouched down on the ground to help him. Within minutes, they were sitting quietly on a flannel blanket, enjoying the sandwiches they'd had the lodge restaurant pack up for them.

When she was done, Summer lay down and looked up at the sky through the blanket of trees. "This really has been a perfect day, don't you think?"

Ethan finished his sandwich and lay down beside her. "It certainly has."

"I bet Gabriella's enjoying herself too."

Ethan nodded. "I'm sure."

"Would it be wrong to take a nap right now?" she asked around a big yawn.

"Yes. As it is we probably shouldn't be where we are. It would be even worse to fall asleep here and get lost."

"Fine. Can we just rest for a little bit?"

Leaning over, Ethan put an arm around Summer and tucked her in close to him until her head was resting on his chest. "I think that would be okay."

It didn't take long for him to realize his error in judgment as his own eyes began to drift closed. "We can't fall asleep," he said softly and then yawned.

"We won't. I promise." Even as she spoke the words, Summer relaxed against him and her breathing slowed and evened out.

Some time later, Ethan awoke with a start. The sun

had definitely shifted, and he immediately began to panic. A quick glance at his watch showed that they had indeed fallen asleep—two hours ago. "Summer!" he said sharply. "Summer, wake up! We fell asleep!"

She didn't immediately move to get up. Instead, she stretched and yawned and blinked a couple of times to bring the world into focus. "What's the matter?" she asked innocently.

"What's the matter?" he snapped impatiently. "We fell asleep! I have no idea how long it's going to take us to find our way back to the path and get back to the lodge before it gets late!"

Standing, she stretched again. "Relax. It won't get dark until almost eleven tonight. We've got plenty of time. What time is it?"

"It's almost four," he said. "I know it doesn't get dark until late, but I don't want to be out wandering around until that time. Come on, we need to get our stuff packed up and head back."

While Summer knew Ethan had a point, it didn't make her feel any better. So they had fallen asleep. What was the big deal? She knew better than to voice that question out loud and decided to keep it to herself. Once everything was cleaned up and back in their packs, Ethan took out his compass and Summer watched in fascination as he mapped out in his head where they needed to go.

"We came in from that direction," she said, pointing back over her shoulder. "Why can't we just head back that way and follow the path?"

Ethan frowned. "I didn't think we came in that way. I thought it was from this side." He pointed directly in front of him.

Summer looked around and her shoulders sank. "Now I'm confused," she said.

"That's why we have the compass," he said with a hint of sarcasm.

"Hey," she snapped. "I'll admit it was a bad idea to fall asleep out here, but might I remind you that I wasn't the only one? So quit being snippy with me. You were just as sound asleep as I was."

He didn't bother to argue and put his attention back on the compass and then pulled out the map from the original trail.

"You know what? You use your little compass and map and all that. I know we came in from this direction so I'm heading back."

"Summer, don't go wandering off," he warned.

"I'm not wandering. I'm heading back to the trail. Which is this way!" And off she went, stomping off down the narrow trail.

"Damn it," Ethan cursed and immediately went after her. He knew she was heading off in the wrong direction; what he didn't realize was how fast she could walk. "Summer! Wait up!" He picked up to a light jog and finally caught up with her. Taking her arm, he stopped and spun her around. "This isn't the way," he said and pulled out the map and compass to show her. "We are heading farther away from the lodge right now. We need to turn around and head that way. Now come on."

"I'm not going anywhere until you apologize," she said defiantly.

"Seriously? We're going to do this now?"

"I expect this kind of attitude from my brothers, but I didn't expect it from you!"

"What attitude? You know what? We don't have time for this. It's getting late and—"

"And it won't be dark for another six hours so save it. I'm not going to take the blame for this, Ethan. We both fell asleep."

He let out a frustrated sigh and mentally counted to ten. "Okay. Fine. I'm sorry I snapped at you. I just…I just don't want anything bad to happen while we're out here where we're not supposed to be."

"Nothing bad's happened, Ethan. We lost track of time. It's not a catastrophe."

"Not yet," he mumbled.

Summer shot him a warning glare. "Fine. Let's just say, for argument's sake, that it's not a catastrophe. Which way do we need to go?" She was feeling more than a little annoyed and defeated but didn't argue when Ethan began to lead them in the opposite direction. Summer knew he was definitely more skilled in situations like this, but she knew she wasn't an idiot either. One way or another, they would make it back to the lodge safely.

Having three older brothers had taught Summer many things, but one valuable lesson was that you didn't say "I told you so" until a crisis was averted. After an hour of walking, nothing was looking familiar, but rather than speak up, she kept it to herself. Ethan was muttering to himself and was constantly looking at the map and the compass, so she knew that questioning their where-abouts would not be appreciated.

Unfortunately, by the fourth time he stopped and checked on their location, Summer couldn't hide her concern—or annoyance. "Problem?" she asked.

"I don't remember tracking for this long, and none

of these trails look like the one we walked in on." He looked around again. "I think we may need to call the lodge for help." Reaching into his pocket, he pulled out his phone and cursed.

"What's the matter?"

"It doesn't look like we can get any reception out here. Try your phone," he suggested.

"It's back at the room."

"What? Why?"

"I forgot to charge it last night and I knew you had yours, so there was no reason for me to bring it," she said defensively. "Look, we need to just calm down and keep walking. If you say the lodge is this way, then that's where we'll keep going. It's not a well-marked path, so it's no wonder it doesn't look familiar."

"I knew we should have stayed on the damn marked trail," he cursed as he started walking again.

The tension was palpable as they walked, and the longer they did, the more certain Summer became that they were going the wrong way. Not caring whether Ethan approved, she stopped and pulled a bottle of water from her pack. She watched as he continued to walk while she took a long drink.

Ethan finally realized that Summer wasn't with him and turned around and stalked back over. "What's the matter?" he asked none too gently.

"I needed to stop and take a drink, that's all." They stood silently for a moment before Ethan grudgingly pulled a bottle of water out of his pack and did the same. "Any idea how much farther until we reach the trail?"

"Should be soon," he said distractedly and then quickly turned around. "Did you hear that?"

"Hear what?"

"Like…someone is walking through the leaves. Listen." They stood silently, and Ethan continued to look around for where the sound was coming from.

"Ooo… Ethan, look! It's a moose!" she cried. "Look at it! I think it's a baby! Where's my camera?" Summer began going through her pack in search of it.

"You brought a camera and not your phone?" he asked incredulously.

"Well, like I said, the phone is charging and I had hoped to get some pictures while we were out today. Here it is," she said as she stood and aimed the camera in the direction of the moose.

"Summer," Ethan warned. "Just…don't, okay? Put the camera away. You don't want to startle it. When a moose gets startled or feels threatened, it will charge at you."

"It's just a baby, Ethan," she said and continued to try and capture her shot.

"And that means the mama moose isn't too far away." He stepped closer and carefully guided Summer's camera down. "Trust me."

She sighed with annoyance. "I'm not going to startle it. Just one quick picture and then I'll put the camera away." Moving over slightly, Summer quickly took aim and got her picture. "I can't wait to show Gabriella!"

Ethan wasn't listening; he was watching the moose and, sure enough, not ten feet behind it was the mama. "Summer, I need to you to listen to me and focus. We need to carefully back up and get behind those trees over there." He pointed over his shoulder to a large cluster of evergreens. "Don't think. Just slowly pick up your pack and back up."

"But—"

"Now!" he hissed as the mother and baby began to amble in their direction. Grasping Summer's hand in his, he began to move them slowly, eyes never leaving the animals that were heading their way.

Summer cursed as she tripped on a hidden pile of twigs and almost went down. The noise was enough to startle the female moose, which began to charge in their direction. Before she knew what was happening, Ethan was dragging her along through the uncharted terrain. They ran this way and that for several yards before Ethan dodged to the right and quickly tucked her against the back of a tree, where he pressed his body against hers until the animals went by.

His breathing was ragged and Summer was trembling. "Oh my God," she whispered.

"Are you okay?" he asked shakily, his hands skimming over her to make sure she was all right.

"I'm...I'm fine. Scared, but fine." She was clutching the front of his shirt as she looked up at him. "I'm sorry. I'm so sorry. I should have listened to you. I never should have suggested—"

"Shh... It's all right." He gathered her into his embrace and just held her. His heart beat rapidly as he tried to relax.

"I never thought moose were wild like that. I always thought they were relatively tame," she said as she moved to put a little space between them.

"Normally they are, except when they feel threatened. They probably don't see a lot of hikers in this area, and we startled them." Looking around, Ethan wasn't sure where the animals had run off to. Nor was he certain where he and Summer were. Somewhere in the attempt to get away, he had dropped the compass and the map. He cursed.

"What? What's the matter?"

"I have no idea where we are or how to get us out of here. I dropped the compass, and I don't think we should waste time looking for it. It's getting late and we're supposed to meet Gabriella for dinner and I have no idea how far we are from the damn lodge!"

"Try your phone again," she suggested.

Pulling it out, Ethan looked at it and put it back in his pocket. "Still nothing."

"Do you have a compass app on there?"

He looked at her as if she was crazy.

"Seriously, they have a compass app. How could you not have one? Everyone has one. Even I have one."

"Yeah, lots of good it's doing us back in the room," he mumbled and then immediately apologized. "I'm sorry. I…I just don't like that this day has gotten so out of control. Everything was going great and then…"

"Then I made us do something stupid," she finished.

"We just weren't prepared for something like this," he said rather than disagree with her directly.

"If you were with Zach and you got lost, what would you do?"

Ethan rolled his eyes. "Not this again. What does it matter? I'm not with Zach. I'm with you."

"Pretend!" she snapped. "For crying out loud, what makes the situation any damn different? You're lost in the forest with someone; what do you do?"

He glared at her for a solid minute. "Seriously? If it were the two of us, we wouldn't have gotten lost. And if by some small chance we did, we'd keep walking until we found a trail—any trail!"

"Then let's do that!" she snapped again. "I'm not some delicate little flower who can't handle this kind of situation, Ethan. I don't need you coddling me and worrying about how I'm doing and if I can handle it. And I find it a little insulting that you're acting like I am!"

"Believe me, I don't think you're a delicate flower, Summer. But it's my responsibility to make sure you're safe!"

"Would you be this concerned if I were Zach?"

"What the hell kind of question is that?" he demanded.

"I'm just saying that you and Zach go out on all these crazy adventures with each other. Do you ever freak out like this with him?"

"This is completely different!"

"Why? We took a risk—which you clearly like to do—and you've done nothing but complain the entire time! Why? What is so damn different all of a sudden?"

"Because it's you!" he yelled and raked a hand through his hair. "All day today—hell, all week—I've finally begun to realize that I don't need all that adventure shit! We have done some fantastic stuff together this week and I've loved every damn minute of it, and do you know why?" He didn't wait for a response. "Because I'm with you! I don't need to prove anything when we're together. There isn't a competition, there aren't any dares, and there's no threat to my health! Dammit, Summer, I don't need any of that because I'm happy with you. And the thought that I did something that could possibly get you hurt is killing me!"

All the anger she felt only moments ago quickly

faded away as tenderness for Ethan swamped her. There were no words she could say to convey all the emotions swirling inside her. Instead, she dropped her pack to the ground, went over, and wrapped her arms around him.

And they clung to each other for what seemed like forever.

Chapter 8

IT WASN'T QUITE DARK WHEN THEY FINALLY WALKED back into the lodge, but the sky was well on its way there.

"I am going to soak in the tub until room service brings dinner," Summer said as they waited for the elevator.

"I may join you," Ethan said, wrapping an arm around her and pulling her close so he could kiss her temple. "For a little while there, I didn't think we'd make it back."

"I'm not going to lie to you, for a little while there, I didn't either." The elevator arrived, and they quietly boarded and rode in silence up to their floor. When the doors opened and they stepped out, Summer let out a little squeal as Ethan scooped her up in his arms. "Ethan! What on earth are you doing?"

"What I've wanted to do all day," he said as he fumbled for the room key. Once they were inside, he let Summer slide down his body before backing her up against the wall and covering her mouth with his.

Summer wrapped her arms around him and felt Ethan's hands roam up and down her body until they landed on her bottom. He gently squeezed and then lifted her until her legs wrapped around his waist. She purred and rubbed herself against him and almost cried out when he lifted his mouth from hers.

"All day," he panted, kissing her cheek, her throat,

"even when I was angry and scared about what was going on, all I could think about was making love to you." And then his lips were back on hers, kissing her, loving her, devouring her.

"I wish you would have," she said after some time. "When we fell asleep on that blanket, I dreamed of waking up and making love with you—out in the middle of the forest. It was a very sexy dream."

"How about a very sexy reality?" he whispered, one hand coming up and cupping her breast. "We may not have the forest above us, but I can guarantee you it will be even better."

"Guarantee?" she moaned as her back arched and her head ground against the wall.

"Guarantee," he growled and carried her over to the bed. "Let me prove it."

And he spent the next hour doing just that.

———

"Food's here," Ethan called out as he took the room service tray from the hotel waiter and closed the door.

Summer stepped out of the bathroom in her robe and her hair up in a towel. "I know it's wrong to be eating a bacon cheeseburger at eleven o'clock at night, but that just adds to the appeal." She giggled. "Is that wrong?"

"Definitely not," he said and set the table for them.

Summer was walking across the room when she spotted her cell phone. "I really need to call Gabriella. She's probably worried sick about where we are." The light in the upper left corner was flashing, so she knew she'd either missed a call or a text. She scrolled the screen and frowned.

"What's the matter?" Ethan asked.

"It looks like I missed a call from my dad, and Gabriella was trying to get in touch with me. A lot." She looked up at Ethan. "I knew she'd be worried."

"Did she leave a message?"

Holding up her hand, Summer dialed her voice mail and listened. And paled. "Oh my God."

"What? What is it?" Ethan was immediately beside her as she sat down on the bed. "What happened?"

"I…I'm not sure. Something about Zach and the climb." She quickly clicked out of voice mail and called Gabriella. "I don't care how late it is, I have to know what's going on."

"Oh my God, Summer! Where are you? Are you all right?" Gabriella said as she answered the phone.

"Me? I'm fine. What's going on? What happened?"

"Where have you been? I've been calling you all afternoon and all night! We were supposed to meet for dinner!"

Summer quickly relayed the events of the day, including their close call with the moose.

"Yikes. That must have been scary!"

"Oh, it was, it was. I'm sorry that we worried you. But what's going on? Has something happened to Zach?"

Gabriella sighed. "Okay, there's kind of bad news, bad news, and really bad news. Which do you want first?"

"Just tell me!" Summer demanded.

"Okay, the tour company called your father because… there's been an accident on the mountain. We don't have all the details yet."

"Oh my God!" Summer cried. "What happened? Is Zach okay?"

"We don't know yet. Once he hung up with the company, he tried calling Zach and Ethan. He didn't know that Ethan had decided against going on the climb so I had to be the one to tell him that."

"Oh no…"

"Then he said he couldn't reach you on the phone, so I told him that I'd try, and then when I couldn't get in touch with you after a couple of hours, I got really worried and…called your dad back."

"What did you tell him?" A sense of dread swamped her.

"I told him everything. That we were here in Glacier Bay and so was Ethan and that the two of you had disappeared and I had no idea where you were!"

"You didn't!"

"What was I supposed to do? The two of you were supposed to be back hours ago! For all I knew, something terrible had happened to you!"

Summer let out a breath. "Okay, okay. I get it. What did my father say?"

"Um…"

"Gabriella?"

"Let's just say that he's on his way to Alaska. With Ryder, James, and your uncle. And he's not happy."

"When is he arriving?"

"Well, I had no idea where you and Ethan were, so there wasn't anything I could do to delay them, and they're heading directly for Denali. I asked around with the concierge and found out that we can get a flight out of Juneau tomorrow that will take us there as well. It's a tiny plane, but he said that flights go out of there regularly."

Summer's mind was spinning. Where was Zach? Was he hurt? What was she going to say to her father about her and Ethan?

"If you'd like, I can make the reservations for us for first thing in the morning. We'll probably arrive the same time as your family."

"You're not on the clock, Gabs," Summer said. "We can—"

"I've already talked to the concierge and so he has the information. I'll just tell him to go ahead and get it scheduled. I'll call you back in a little bit with the times."

"Okay, thanks."

Ethan had risen from the bed and had been pacing as Summer talked. When she finally hung up the phone, he stopped. "What happened?"

She told him what she knew. "We won't know anything more until we get to Denali." She paused. "I should probably call my father and give him one less thing to be freaking out about."

"Do you want me to call him?"

She shook her head. "No. But he'll probably want to talk to you anyway."

"No doubt," Ethan murmured and walked over to the table where their food was. Taking the lid off his plate, he grabbed his burger and took a bite. His appetite was pretty much shot, but he knew he needed to eat as a necessity, considering all they'd gone through that day and what they were going to be facing in the morning.

He couldn't imagine what could have gone wrong on the mountain and could only pray that it didn't have anything to do with Zach and the fact that his leg wasn't fully healed.

He could hear Summer talking to her father and knew he'd better prepare himself for his turn on the phone. Robert Montgomery could be a real hard-ass at times, and Ethan had a sinking feeling that a lot of questions were about to be hurled at him and none of them were going to be pleasant.

"He wants to talk to you," Summer said quietly as she held her phone out to him.

"Thanks," he said with a weak smile and took the phone. "Hey, Robert."

"You have a hell of a lot of explaining to do," Robert Montgomery snapped. "Why the hell aren't you on that climb with Zach? And what the hell are you doing with my daughter?"

Ethan took a steadying breath and stepped away from Summer. "I decided against going on the climb for a lot of reasons, Robert," he began. "I realized my heart wasn't really in it. I know I probably should have said something sooner, but…it didn't really hit me until it was time to go."

"Did you think Zach was ready for it? The climb? Because Summer thinks he wasn't."

"Honestly? I don't. I think he needed more time to get in shape. His leg wasn't fully healed no matter what he said."

"And you couldn't stop him?" Robert demanded. "You're his best friend! Why didn't you stop him?"

"Robert, I tried! Summer tried. He wouldn't listen to anyone. You know how stubborn Zach is; he thinks he's invincible."

"No, you could have stopped him, and Summer should have. I know she has some training with that…

yoga stuff she does. She should have talked to his doctor and made sure that Zach didn't get clearance to go."

"It's not her fault, sir. Summer did everything she could to stop Zach. He wouldn't listen."

Robert grew silent. "And what about you, Ethan? What are you doing in Glacier Bay with my daughter?" His words were laced with barely concealed rage.

"I had no idea Summer and Gabriella were planning on coming here. I decided to stay in Alaska while Zach was on the climb and planned on meeting up with him when he was done. It was a complete surprise to see the two of them while we were all out whale watching. But…" he began hesitantly, "we've been spending time together. We were out hiking today."

"Is that all it is? Just out hiking together, or are you messing around with my daughter?"

"I don't think that's something we need to talk about right now. What time are you arriving in Denali tomorrow?" It was a risk to blatantly change the subject, but Ethan felt it was necessary. He wasn't going to be bullied by Summer's father right now, no matter how much he loved her.

"This isn't over, Ethan," Robert said curtly. He gave Ethan their flight information and told him they'd talk more tomorrow before hanging up.

"Well, that went well," Ethan murmured and handed the phone back to Summer. He sat down at the table and finished what was left of his dinner. He slouched down in his seat and looked over to where Summer was standing and held out his hand to her. "How are you doing?"

She took his hand and sat down next to him, a tear rolling down her cheek. "You know what's funny? No one in my family takes me seriously most of the time. And now? Now all of a sudden I'm being blamed for not doing more to stop Zach because I knew his leg wasn't ready for it. They all laughed at the idea of me studying yoga, and all of a sudden they believe in my skills. It's crazy." She wiped another tear away, but they began falling in earnest.

Ethan reached out and pulled her onto his lap and held her close while she cried. "It's going to be all right," he said quietly. "Everyone's just upset right now. He just wasn't thinking."

"Yes he was," she said against his shoulder. "My father's always thinking. He thinks it's my fault that Zach's hurt."

"We don't know that he's hurt, Summer. We just know something went wrong. And even if he is hurt, it's not your fault."

Summer rested her head on his shoulder for another minute and then reached out and snagged a french fry from his plate. Ethan helped her off his lap and into her own chair. Uncovering her plate, she began to pick at her food.

"You really should eat. It's been a long day, and I'm sure we're going to have to be out of here early tomorrow to meet up with everyone in Denali."

"I know you're right." She took a couple of bites of her burger and even managed to eat a couple of fries before Gabriella called back. Ethan took the call while she sat back and listened. He hung up a minute later. "Well?"

"We've got a seven a.m. flight. A car will be here to pick us up at five thirty. We need to get everything packed up tonight and try to get some sleep."

Summer nodded and knew that no matter how hard she tried, sleep was going to be elusive tonight.

—⁓—

Summer was ready to scream by the time the plane finally came to a halt the next morning. Never had a flight seemed so long to her. There was a car waiting for them as soon as they stepped down, and within minutes, their luggage was loaded and they confirmed that the rest of the Montgomerys were scheduled to land within the hour. Robert had requested that Ethan, Summer, and Gabriella go on ahead of them to meet up with the head of the tour company.

Ethan had been particularly quiet during the flight. He had made several calls from the airport but managed to keep it quiet and didn't talk about them once he hung up. But now that they were finally close to their destination, her curiosity got the better of her and she needed to know exactly what they were getting themselves into.

"Has there been any news?" Summer asked as the car pulled away from the airport. Ethan didn't look at her, and his silence spoke louder than any words could. "Ethan?"

He turned toward her, his expression grim. "A brief message came through. Several climbers…fell. The transmission ended after that and, unfortunately, the weather is too unstable to get a helicopter up to them yet. All we can do is wait." The look of utter devastation on Summer's face was almost more than he could bear. He was just about to speak when Gabriella interrupted.

"Well, that's not good enough, dammit!" Sitting up straighter, she reached for her executive bag, pulled out her tablet, and began researching emergencies like this. "What kind of company can't keep a signal with its people? How could several climbers fall? What weather conditions prevent professionals from keeping everyone safe?"

"It was a freak storm," he said dejectedly. "No one saw it coming."

"But they are professionals," Gabriella countered as she tossed her tablet aside on the car seat. "They are supposed to be prepared for things like this. How could this have happened?" Gabriella hated the tremble in her voice, hated that they were there and had to deal with this at all. Most of all, she hated not being in control.

"We won't know until they can get up there and rescue them. Getting angry isn't going to help matters, Gabriella. You'll need to remember that when we meet up with the tour people."

She glared at him. "I'm not going to sit back and be fed a line of bull, Ethan," she snapped. "If something doesn't sound right, you can be sure I'm going to speak up. Zach deserves to have us all down here fighting to get him the hell out of there and make sure he's safe."

Summer had been sitting back and listening for as long as she could before her own temper flared. "That's enough!" she yelled and then took a moment to let everyone calm down. "We're all a little freaked out right now, but arguing amongst ourselves isn't helping anything. Let's go meet with these people and ask them what we want to ask and go from there, okay?" Ethan and Gabriella both nodded. The remainder of the drive passed in silence.

Once they arrived at the tour company's office, however, the three of them walked into a loud, chaotic scene that only got louder once they all started asking questions. Summer's head was spinning with all of the commotion, and finally Ethan let out a loud whistle to get everyone's attention.

"I'm Ethan Reed and I'm looking for Mike Rivera!" Several things happened at once: the noise level went down a bit and a tall, harried-looking man stepped forward and held his hand out to Ethan. "Mike?" Ethan ventured a guess.

"Good to meet you, Ethan. I'm sorry about the circumstances." He nodded to the opposite side of the room. "Let's go into my office where it's a little quieter." Without thinking, Ethan took Summer's hand and pulled her along with him. Gabriella followed behind them. When they were all seated in the office, Mike sat down behind his desk and addressed them all. "Is the rest of your family on the way?" he asked, and Ethan nodded. "I cannot even begin to imagine what you're feeling, but let me tell you that we are doing everything we can to get to the team."

"When will that happen?" Ethan asked.

"We're working with a team of meteorologists right now to figure out when our best chance is of getting up there and getting everyone out before the weather turns again."

"And what are they predicting?"

"The window of time we need and the window of time where there's a break in the weather aren't working to our advantage. We need two to three hours to get up to where the team is, evaluate injuries, get everyone loaded on the helicopters, and get back down. Right now, we're looking at weather conditions that are only going to allow us maybe an hour to get it all done."

"Can't you at least try to go and get the injured climbers?" Summer asked. "By waiting, you could be endangering the lives of those who are injured even more than they already are."

Mike shook his head. "Our experts are evaluating—"

"You could drop off supplies for the rest of the team," Summer interrupted. "Get them blankets, food, and working communication equipment."

"I can understand your concern, Miss…"

"Montgomery. My brother Zach is up on that mountain. All of this waiting isn't cutting it, Mr. Rivera. We need to get someone up there now. You've already lost an entire day with your waiting-for-the-weather tactic. You need to take action!"

"Summer," Ethan warned.

"No, I'm serious!" she cried. "If climbers are injured and the weather is treacherous, then you need to be doing something actively right now to get them out!"

Mike Rivera looked to Ethan for help. "Summer," Ethan began patiently. "They know what they're doing. They need to make sure no one else gets hurt; you can't just send people out into a storm."

"Why not? It seems to me like they've already done that. " She turned back to Mike. "You clearly ignored the weather warning and just went about your business. Why not just do it again? Or is it because now you'd be risking more of your own people?" She stood and braced her hands on the man's desk. "What's a couple more lives to someone like you? You've already been paid in full by the people you're leaving up on a mountain to die!"

"*Summer!*" Ethan snapped.

She spun around to face him, her eyes filled with fury. "That is my brother and your best friend up there. Why are you just sitting back and taking this nonsense?" Before anyone could respond, Summer stormed from the room.

Getting through the crowd of people wasn't difficult—especially when she didn't care whom she shoved to do it. She was trembling with anger as she plowed through a maze of hallways before finding an exit and practically kicking the door from its hinges. It wasn't until she was outside and unsure of where to go that she found Gabriella right beside her.

"Are you okay?" Gabriella asked gingerly.

"No, Gabs, I'm not. I'm abso-freakin-lutely not! They sent my brother out there knowing there was the possibility of dangerous weather, and now they're too scared to do anything about it. What if he's injured? What if he badly needs to be in a hospital right now? What if the temperature drops and he gets hypothermia? I mean, how can they possibly expect us just to sit idly by?"

Gabriella grabbed one of Summer's hands in hers and tugged her in close for a hug. "I'm just as frustrated as you, and if you hadn't spoken up, I would have. I don't know why Ethan isn't making more of a fuss in there."

"Ethan never makes a fuss," Summer grumbled. "He doesn't like to rock the boat. Ever."

"Is that why he waited until Zach was firmly out of the picture before finally acting on his feelings for you?"

Summer took a couple steps back and grimaced. "Unfortunately, yes."

"Sounds cowardly."

She wanted to disagree but couldn't. Unfortunately, now wasn't the time for talking about relationships. "I know, and if it were any other time than right now, I'd be harping on it, but I can't. I have to focus on Zach and getting him back safely."

"So what are we supposed to do?" Gabriella curbed the need to vent her own frustration.

Summer shrugged. "I'm not sure. I know these guys know what they're doing, and I haven't a clue. There's only one team that specializes in this kind of rescue, and I don't have a choice but to defer to them, but I don't have to like it. And I certainly don't have to keep my mouth shut about it either."

Gabriella couldn't help but smile at Summer's attempt at being rebellious. "Okay then. Do you want to head over to the hotel? Or do you want me to leave you alone?"

"Not really. I think I need a couple more minutes to cool off before I go back inside. Otherwise I'm bound to want to punch somebody in the face, and I can't decide if that somebody is Ethan or Mike Rivera."

A laugh escaped before Gabriella could stop it. "I'd pay good money to see that happen."

"To which one?"

"Either." They both laughed and it felt good to have some of the tension leave their bodies. "It's going to be okay, right?"

Summer nodded but she wasn't sure she believed it. "Okay, I think I'm done cooling off now," she said with a shiver.

Gabriella pulled her jacket a little closer around her. "You picked the perfect place."

Summer nodded and hugged her friend. "I'm so glad your brain works the way it does, because if it were left to me, we'd all be standing here freezing. I always manage to look at the high temperatures and never pay attention to the lows." She chuckled.

"Yeah, lucky me. It's the main thing people notice about me. My efficiency."

"That's not true. First they notice your scary good looks and killer figure, then the efficiency thing."

"And that scares them off."

Summer quirked a brow at her. "Who have you scared off with your efficiency? And for that matter, what kind of idiot would be scared off by that sort of thing?"

Gabriella shrugged. "It doesn't matter. It makes me seem like a freak sometimes when I can think so level-headedly in stressful situations and can troubleshoot at the drop of a hat."

"If you ask me, that's a blessing."

"You wouldn't think so if it were you."

"Right now? I most certainly would." She stopped and considered her friend. "How would you troubleshoot this particular disaster? I mean, if it were you up there and had all of the data we've had access to. What do you think they could or should be doing that they're not?"

Gabriella stood silently for a moment. "I think they are doing okay going on the information they have, but…"

"But?"

"But they should have sent the rescue team out already. We're losing a lot of time and have no idea how many people are injured. I understand the need to make sure the weather's stabilized, but…I think that too much time is being wasted."

With a nod, Summer took Gabriella by the hand and dragged her back into the building. "Then that's where we're going to tell them to begin."

———

As expected, the arrival of the Montgomery entourage was eventful and chaotic.

"It's a damn media circus out there!" Robert Montgomery boomed as he walked through the door to the office. He did a quick scan of the room and assessed the situation immediately. His voice was loud and commanding, and soon Mike Rivera was standing before him with an outstretched hand.

"You must be Robert Montgomery," he said nervously. He introduced himself and then gave him a quick rundown about the status of the search and rescue. "We've got a team set up at the base of the mountain and I'm getting all of the updates at the same time they are, sir. We should be getting word shortly."

Robert eyed him skeptically but then chose to focus his attention on his daughter, who was anxiously standing to the side. He strode over to her and he could immediately see she was exhausted; she was pale and she had dark shadows under her eyes, and he felt a mild tug of sympathy. "Are you okay?"

Summer nodded and waited…waited to see if he'd hug her or lecture her.

"All of this could have been avoided," he said to her and then glared at Ethan when he stepped closer. "The two of you knew that Zach was endangering himself and others, and you didn't stop him."

"Well…um…" Summer began.

Ethan stepped forward and interrupted. "Robert, we've been over this already. No one would have been able to stop Zach from going. We need to stop playing the blame game and focus on getting him down safely."

Robert eyed him skeptically as well. He didn't like that Ethan had spoken up when he had been talking to his daughter, but he supposed that he had a point. They couldn't change what had happened, and they needed to focus on finding Zach and making sure he was all right.

Unfortunately, in the midst of all this chaos, there were other things that were going to require their attention. He knew he couldn't do it all himself, and Summer didn't look like she was in any shape to do more than wait for news with the rest of them. He glared at Ethan again and knew he wasn't prepared to have a rational conversation with him just yet. That left Gabriella.

With a nod, Robert turned and began barking orders at Gabriella. "I need you to call the Portland office. Someone may have heard the news by now, and I want you to make sure no one is giving any comments to the press. Once word gets out that it's Zach Montgomery up on that mountain, we're going to have clients and employees alike who are going to start to get antsy. We want to assure them that everything is fine and the people we have left in charge are more than capable of handling things."

With a quick nod, Gabriella strode away. When she had left the room, Robert returned his attention to Mike and walked over to speak to him privately.

Summer was momentarily relieved, but she knew as soon as her father had exhausted all his options, he'd come back to letting her know how this was all her fault. She was doing her best to brace herself for it but wasn't succeeding.

"Hey, kiddo," her brother Ryder said as he walked over and hugged her. "How are you holding up?"

Summer almost wanted to cry. There was no condemnation in his tone; he was comforting her, being her big brother, and it was enough to shatter her already fragile state. She took a shaky breath and clung to him until she knew she'd be able to speak without falling apart.

When she looked up at him, he smiled.

And that was when her first tear fell.

Ryder hugged her close again and let her cry it out. When he felt her shudders subsiding, he led her over to an isolated corner and sat down. "You know how he is, Summer; he speaks first and thinks later. He hates not being in control, and this whole thing makes him feel helpless."

Composing herself, Summer tested her voice. "He basically told me it was my fault if Zach was hurt because I couldn't talk him out of going on the climb."

Shaking his head, Ryder said, "You had nothing to do with this. There are always risks like this and it sucks. We're all scared, but arguing amongst ourselves isn't going to help Zach. You're not to blame here, and I think Dad knows that. He's worried sick about Zach. He's tough on all of us, but that doesn't mean he doesn't care."

"He's got a funny way of showing it," she muttered.

"You *must* be talking about Dad," James said as he came over to join his siblings. Summer rose to hug him, and he held her just as fiercely as Ryder had. He pulled back and looked at her. "You look exhausted. Did you sleep at all last night?"

"Some," she said quietly, "but every time I close my eyes, I imagine the worst. I just feel so helpless! Maybe Dad's right. Maybe I didn't try hard enough to stop Zach."

James chuckled. "Please, we all know that Zach doesn't let anyone tell him he can't do something. It's frustrating as hell." He noticed the uncertainty on Summer's face, and he placed his hands on her shoulders reassuringly. "You're not to blame here, Summer," he said softly.

She sagged with relief. "Thank you." She turned and reached out a hand to Ryder and pulled him in close. "Both of you. You have no idea how much I've been agonizing over this whole thing. Zach and I argued for weeks before he left. I knew he wasn't strong enough for a trip like this, but no one expected it to reach this level of severity. Ethan and I—"

"Did the best you could," Ryder said curtly as he glanced across the room to where Ethan was standing. "Any idea why he didn't go with Zach? I thought that was the plan all along."

Summer blushed and looked down at the ground. "He said he just changed his mind and realized it wasn't something he wanted to do."

Ryder looked first at Summer, then to James, who shrugged, and then over to Ethan, who was now watching them with apparent discomfort. "It seems odd," Ryder said. "They do everything together. Did he and Zach argue about this before Zach left? Do you think maybe Zach was distracted?"

Summer's head snapped up. "Why are you looking to blame this on Ethan?" she demanded. "And, for that matter, who says that this whole thing happened because of Zach? For all we know he had his head exactly where it should have been and it was somebody else's screwup! Ethan wasn't even there!" She pulled away from her brothers with a huff and missed the concerned glances they shared.

"Excuse me for a minute," Ryder said carefully as he walked away.

James took Summer by the hand and motioned for her to sit down. Something was going on, but he couldn't quite put his finger on it, so he did the only thing he could think of: he distracted his sister. "Did I mention that Selena and I are going to do some work on the house?"

Confusion covered Summer's face. "Why? The house is beautiful! And you just moved in not that long ago. What could you possible find to do to it?"

He chuckled. "Well, with the baby coming soon, and knowing that family will be descending on us for quite some time, we decided to do a massive renovation in the yard."

Now she was really confused. "The yard? What does the yard have to do with extra people in the house? And you're the big-shot landscape architect guy. Something yard related should be a cinch for you, not a massive renovation."

James leaned back in his chair and relaxed. "Oh, I am, but we're doing something a little more elaborate. We decided we wanted to put in a pool."

"The yard is certainly big enough."

He nodded. "And in the far corner of the yard, we're going to build a pool house that can be used as a guest bungalow. Just a one-bedroom thing. But this way, it's a little extra space where guests can stay and still have their privacy."

"Sounds amazing," she said with a smile. "Selena must be thrilled. How is she feeling?"

The thought of his wife made James smile. "Good, real good. I know you haven't been away long, but in the last seven or eight weeks she's really started to show. It's such an amazing thing to see." A goofy grin covered his face as he pictured Selena in his mind. "We felt the first kick not too long ago and at night, I just like to lie in bed beside her with my hand over her belly and wait to feel it again."

Summer wanted to cry. She was so happy for her brother—he was happily married to the only woman he had ever loved and they were getting ready to have their first baby—but she was jealous too. Her brothers were supposed to want to be bachelors; they were supposed to enjoy their freedom. She was the one who was supposed to get married and have a baby first. As it was, all her brothers—including Zach—would be married and have a ton of kids, and she'd be the lonely spinster aunt.

She'd probably have to get rid of Maylene and get a cat. Why? Because that's what lonely spinster aunts do. Things were certainly progressing with Ethan, but she had no idea what was going to happen now that her family was here. This was going to be a huge test to their new relationship. She knew he didn't like to rock the boat and that her family could be intimidating. Most of the men she'd been involved with had backed off after one Montgomery or another had glared at him or asked him what his intentions were. Summer shuddered remembering those fiascoes. Would Ethan cave under their scrutiny? She frowned at the thought.

"What?" James asked when he turned back to her, out of his reverie of marital bliss. "What's the matter?"

Shaking her head and pushing away her negative thoughts, Summer went back to asking about the house. "So are you doing the work yourself?"

"Are you kidding me?" he asked with a laugh. "I'm going to do the landscaping myself, for sure, but the construction?" He shook his head. "That is totally not my thing."

"So have you hired someone already?"

He nodded. "I lucked out. I was asking around town if anyone could recommend a contractor and the name that kept coming up was Aidan Shaughnessy."

Summer's brow furrowed for a minute. "Why do I know that name?" She wracked her brain, trying to remember why it sounded so familiar.

"We used to hang out with them when we would spend the summers on the coast, remember? Big family...a lot like us: five brothers and one sister. You were a couple of years older than the sister but we used to go to the beach with them every once in a while."

"Oh, yeah! So Aidan's a contractor now? That's awesome. Have you talked to him already?"

James nodded again and smiled. "I'm telling you, it was good to see him. I'm starting to get back into the swing of things and reconnecting with people from home, so working with a friend has been good. He's an amazing contractor and his business is huge in the area.

I think he's kind of doing me a favor by squeezing this job in. It seems to me he's got signs up all over town on projects his company is doing."

"Well, good for him!" Summer said, and she genuinely meant it. "I think it's going to be an exciting time for all of you. You'll get to reconnect with an old friend, Selena's getting a beautiful yard makeover and some extra space… I mean, you guys are totally living the dream."

Everything she said sounded sincere, and yet James noticed a hint of sadness in his sister's eyes. It could stem from stress over Zach, or have something to do with the reason she left New York, but all of James's years of being a cop told him it was something else. He looked around the room and wondered what to do. James spotted his uncle and discreetly motioned for him to come over.

"Well, there's my favorite princess," William Montgomery said with a grin as he approached. "How's my girl doing?"

Summer stood and wrapped her arms around Uncle William. James quietly walked away to give them some time alone.

William sat with Summer, looked down at his niece's face, and was instantly concerned, even though his own expression gave nothing away.

"I'm worried about Zach, of course," she said and rested her head on his shoulder just as she had when she was a little girl.

In return, William rested his head on top of hers. "We all are. But I have great confidence that today the rescue team is going to be successful."

"From your lips to God's ears," she said wistfully.

William smiled. "I want you to know I'm proud of you, Summer." She lifted her head and looked at her uncle as if he were insane. "It's true. You came up here and represented the family, and you're making sure things are happening as fast as they should."

"But—"

"While you were over here with your brothers, I was with your father talking to Mike, and he told us how much input you've given and how wonderful you've been. I know this hasn't been easy, but you stepped up and you took care of it."

She averted her gaze. "It really wasn't all me; if anything, Ethan and Gabriella have done most of it. I feel like I've been more of a burden. Ethan has dealt mostly with Mike, and Gabriella handled all the arrangements to get us here. I'm just sort of along for the ride."

Interesting, William thought. He cleared his throat. "Still, it was convenient the three of you were able to get together so quickly and get here. We were all a little shocked to find out Ethan wasn't on the climb with Zach. We thought they were doing this together, just like all of their previous trips."

Summer shook her head. "Ethan really didn't want to do it this time. He said his heart wasn't in it." The image of the two of them in the tepee by the springs sprang to her mind. She couldn't stop the blush from creeping up her cheeks. "Anyway, I'm thankful he's not up there with Zach; I don't think I could have handled it if it was both of them."

"I would have thought Ethan would take some time for himself after backing out of the trip. After all, he had already cleared his schedule," William said. "Still, it must have been a shock for you to have him back at the office so soon after he'd left."

"Oh, he wasn't back at the office," Summer responded without really thinking. "We ran into him at Glacier Bay, where Gabriella and I were having a bit of a girls' trip." As soon as she finished the statement, she realized her mistake. "I mean…it wasn't planned or anything. Seeing Ethan. Obviously Gabriella and I had planned our time there and it was just a…coincidence that we ran into him." Heat rushed up her cheeks and she felt herself beginning to sweat. Was her uncle going to figure out that she had spent an entire weekend alone with Ethan?

He looked down at her flushed face, and William smiled. *Bingo!* "So that certainly worked out well, didn't it?" he asked cheerily. When Summer looked at him in confusion, he said, "It was almost as if it were meant to be—all of you being together so you could get here to help Zach." He leaned back and smiled even wider. "Sometimes it's amazing how well things work out."

Okay, that was odd, Summer thought to herself. If this conversation had been with her father, first he would have demanded to know what she was doing in Alaska, and then he would have given her the third degree on why Ethan was there. Her father didn't believe in coincidences, and she had no doubt that no matter what she said or how hard she protested, he would have freaked out over the whole thing.

"The weather here is certainly not as cold as I thought it would be," William said, interrupting her thoughts.

She nodded. "It was a pleasant surprise. Although it's a bit colder up here than it was down in Glacier Bay. Not by much but…still."

William nodded thoughtfully. "Let's just hope that the weather cooperates now and we can get that rescue team in action and get your brother down safely." He relaxed and looked across the room and noticed Ethan watching them while trying hard not to look like he was watching. William wanted to laugh out loud again. It was almost getting too easy. Summer's nervous chatter and the way Ethan had been watching her since the rest of the Montgomerys arrived told William all he needed to know. It was just a matter of figuring out how to help these two during this whole mess with Zach.

Placing his hand on Summer's knee, he said, "No matter how you and Ethan happened to get together, I'm glad for it."

Summer looked up with wide eyes. "Together?" she squeaked. "We're not together. Not me and Ethan. I mean, we're friends…and we work together but that's it. He's Zach's best friend and…and…like I said, it was just a weird coincidence that we were together while whale watching. I mean…not together-together, but there at the same time. And…and…"

"He's a good friend," he said with happy conviction. "I always thought the world of Ethan. He's a good man, a good employee, and we're all proud of the things he's accomplished with his life. No, sir, no one can find fault with Ethan Reed." William looked directly at Ethan and saw him swallow hard. "I'm glad he was here with you to help you out, Summer." He leaned over and kissed her on the cheek. "Now, if you'll excuse me, I believe I'll go and have a word with him, to thank him."

Summer watched her uncle walk over to Ethan and sagged in her seat. They had been so careful—except around Gabriella—and the thought of anyone finding out about them, especially now, was not something she wanted to entertain. Thankful for the reprieve, however, she sat back in her seat and silently prayed that her father would keep his distance for a little while longer.

For a moment—a brief one—William Montgomery pitied poor Ethan Reed. As he made his way across the room, he noticed Ethan looking for a possible diversion, distraction, or an out-and-out escape. William chuckled to himself. Didn't the boy realize that out of the two elder Montgomerys here, *he* was the one Ethan should be looking forward to talking to?

"Ethan!" he said as he reached him and held out his hand. "It's good to see you. Although I wish it were under different circumstances."

"You too, sir," Ethan said carefully.

Placing his hands in his pockets, William took just a minute to smile. "I know this has been a rough couple of days for you." Ethan nodded. "And I'm sure part of you feels guilty about not being up there with Zach." When Ethan made to defend himself, William cut him off gently. "No one's blaming you, son. A series of rather unfortunate events took place, and they would have happened whether you were there or not."

"We can't be sure—"

"Trust me," William said, "if nothing else, your

presence up there could have meant one more injured. As it is they're having a tough time with this whole thing." Ethan didn't look convinced. "We're all thankful you're here and you're safe."

Ethan gave a mirthless laugh. "Are you sure about that?"

"You mean my brother?"

Ethan nodded.

"Pay no attention to him. He was always the hot-head of the family. He knows that you're not to blame for this."

"Well, neither is Summer," Ethan said defensively. "She cried for a long time after he called her the other night. He told her she was the reason if Zach is hurt, and let me tell you, it just about destroyed her. I had no idea Robert could be so cruel. I always knew he was strict with Zach, Ryder, and James, but I never thought he'd do something like this to his own daughter." It was impossible to hide his disgust. "There wasn't a thing I could do or say that could make her feel better. And you know what the worst of it is?" He didn't wait for William to respond. "She took the brunt of her father's anger without even defending herself. Why? Because she already feels responsible when she shouldn't." He raked a hand through his hair in frustration and looked over to where Summer was sitting. His expression softened at the sight of her. She was the most amazing woman he had ever known, and it pained him to think that her own family didn't see how special she was.

William discreetly cleared his throat. "I agree with you where my brother is concerned, Ethan, and I'm not going to lie to you: it bothered all of us. Of course, no one knew she was already feeling responsible, but either way, it doesn't excuse the things he said to her."

Ethan didn't want to look away from Summer, but he returned his attention to her uncle. "I just hope Robert doesn't feel the need to attack her verbally again now that he's here." There was a fierceness in his tone that Ethan almost didn't recognize in himself. He'd never felt so protective of anyone, and he most certainly would never have considered talking this way to any of the elder Montgomerys before. He was seriously losing it, and if he wasn't careful, William was bound to notice.

"I think my brother found someone else to vent at." He motioned over his shoulder to where Robert was standing with Mike Rivera. "That poor man. As if he didn't have enough to deal with, now he has Robert."

William didn't have much sympathy for Mike Rivera either. He believed Mike's company was at fault, and if William had anything to say about it, he'd be talking to a team of lawyers and laying blame where blame was due. How his brother could have thought even for one second to put any of the blame on Summer was still beyond him, and once this whole nightmare was over, he'd be sure to point that out.

"Anyway, I guess I should go over there and make sure things don't get out of hand." William placed a hand on Ethan's shoulder. "You're a good man, Ethan. We all know that. Thank you for being here for Zach and looking out for Summer. They're both lucky to have you."

Ethan thanked William, watched him walk over to Mike and Robert, and let out a breath of relief. That had gone better than he had expected. He was certain everyone was going to come in here like gangbusters and make all kinds of noise. So far, other than Robert, the rest of the Montgomerys had been pretty well behaved.

Ethan spotted James and Ryder speaking with one of Mike's employees, and Gabriella was on the phone in a small side office. With Robert and William still engaged in conversation with Mike, he slowly made his way over to where Summer was sitting with her head back and eyes closed. Ethan gave one last nervous look over his shoulder before sitting down beside her. "How are you doing?" he asked quietly.

She looked up and blinked with surprise at finding Ethan so close. "Tired," she said. "The waiting is killing me. It feels like we're so close and yet time is dragging."

He nodded. "I know. It actually hasn't been that long, but I know how you feel."

"I just won't be able to relax until we know Zach is all right." She reached for his hand as her eyes met his. "I don't know what I'll do if something's happened to him, Ethan. The last time we talked, he was so mad at me. I can't bear to think of that being our last..." Tears began to fall, and Ethan wrapped her in his embrace. He missed having her in his arms, and for a moment he just savored the feeling.

"Shh," he whispered against her soft hair. He loved the feel of it, he loved the smell of it, and the thought of possibly never being able to hold her like this again was almost more than he could handle—especially on top of everything else going on around him. "They're going to find Zach, and he's going to be okay, and the two of you are going to look back on everything that happened since you came to Portland

and laugh about it." He pulled back and tucked a finger under her chin. "He promised me before he left that he was going to try to make things right between the two of you, and you know your brother is a man of his word."

"He did?" she asked, her voice barely audible.

Ethan nodded and reached up to wipe away her tears. He wanted to kiss her, to hold her, to promise her everything was going to be all right. He was just about to speak when James was standing over them.

"What's going on?" James demanded of Ethan. "Why is she crying?"

For a minute, Ethan was at a loss for words.

"All of the waiting around is taking its toll," Ethan finally said as he disengaged from Summer and stood up. "She's worried because the last time she and Zach spoke, they argued. Now she's afraid—"

James held up a hand to stop him. "Say no more." Stepping around Ethan, he sat down beside his sister. "Hey," James said carefully, and put his arm around her. "I know this has been rough for you, but you know Zach; he argues with everyone lately. When he gets back, I guarantee you he's still going to be ready to argue with someone."

"But what if...?"

He placed a finger over her lips and shook his head. "Good thoughts; I only want you to be thinking good thoughts, okay?" He waited until she nodded, although he could tell that she was merely placating him. "We need to be prepared to accept that he'll have some injuries, but we need to stay positive here, kiddo. You need to be strong."

"I'm just so worried," she said wearily.

He hugged her close. "I know you are. Hopefully we'll have an update soon and then we'll all be able to relax and get a good night's sleep."

"I hope you're right because I feel like the walking dead right now." She attempted to smile and was just about to make a joke referencing the television series when her father walked over.

"It's good to see that you can laugh while your brother's life is hanging in the balance," Robert said when he came to a stop in front of her.

"Now wait a minute," Ethan began but was cut off when James rose at the same time.

"Seriously, Dad, have you learned nothing in all these years?" James asked incredulously.

"What the hell are you talking about?"

"We discussed this on the plane. I don't know why you're directing all of this hostility toward Summer. She's not to blame here. If you'd open your eyes and shut your mouth for a minute, you'd see that your daughter has been crying. She's exhausted and she's worried just like the rest of us!"

"Well, if she would have put her foot down and stopped Zach from going, we all wouldn't have something to be worried about!"

Father and son argued for another minute before Ethan cut them both off with a loud whistle. When he had their attention—as well as everyone else's in the room—he spoke. "Your son is a selfish asshole who doesn't listen to anyone!" He noticed the look of shock on Robert's face, the wary one on James's and Ryder's, the worry on Summer's, and the smile on William's. "We all tried to talk Zach out of this, Robert. Hell, even his doctor tried, but in the end he gave Zach the clearance." Ethan raked a hand through his hair in frustration. "Now I get that you're upset and worried and pissed off because this entire situation is beyond your control, but you have got to put the blame firmly where it lies—and that's on Zach."

"No," Robert said with a sneer. "She didn't try hard enough!"

"I'm sitting right here!" Summer snapped and jumped up at Ethan's side to join the fray. "I did everything I could to talk Zach out of taking this trip. You can't even begin to imagine the arguments we had over it. But Ethan's right. Zach is a very selfish person, and as upset as I am about that and as sick as I am with worry for him, I've still managed to control myself and my emotions. I'm ashamed of the way you've carried on here, throwing your weight around and acting as if you're the only one who has a say in how things are done!" It was the first time in her life she had ever talked back to her father, and it felt good!

"These people have been working around the clock since this happened and they have done everything they could to ensure no one else gets hurt. How dare you come in here and try to tell them how to do their jobs! How would you like it if someone walked into Montgomerys and did that to you?"

"I'd like to see someone try!" Robert yelled.

"That's my point exactly!" she yelled right back. "As a business owner, shouldn't you be showing Mike the same courtesy? Has your yelling and lecturing done anything to help? I mean, you just don't get it, do you?" She turned and pointed to James. "James ran away at sixteen because you wanted to dictate how he should live his life. Ryder and Zach moved almost three thousand miles away to get away from you, and I did my best to stay away for as long as possible! When are you going to learn that your way isn't the only way?"

She was breathless from her little speech, and leaned into Ethan and felt his arm come around her waist and pull her close. After her show of bravado, she wasn't sure what emotion to register first—pride in herself or excitement in having Ethan show his support of her in front of her family.

Robert was seeing red. The possessive look on Ethan's face was the straw that broke the camel's back. How dare he touch Summer as if he had every right to! And on top of that, in all his life, no one—not one of his children—had ever spoken to him the way his youngest just had. He wanted to yell, he wanted to scream, he wanted…

"Excuse me, folks!" Mike Rivera yelled as he jogged across the room. "I hate to interrupt but we have some news." All eyes turned to face him. "We got them!"

Chapter 9

THOSE THREE LITTLE WORDS EFFECTIVELY BROUGHT all arguing to a halt. In the blink of an eye, everyone was huddled around Mike's desk as they listened to the communications coming from the command center—all of the climbers were found. A million questions were waiting to be asked, but for the time being, everyone stood silently—waiting and listening for any specific information on Zach.

If the wait seemed difficult before, now it hit a painful level. They were so close, so close to finally hearing what they'd been waiting for, and having to sit through anything else was bringing everyone back to the edge.

"I'm going to need names of who is going where," Mike said into the receiver. The phone was on speaker so that everyone could hear. "How long until we have that information?"

"The first chopper just left with the first three…all were in pretty bad shape…broken bones and signs of hypothermia," a voice said over the staticky line.

Mike looked from the radio to the people around him. "Was Zach Montgomery on that chopper?"

There was a moment of silence as everyone sat still and held their breath. "Negative," the voice said and then named the three people who were on it. "This is going to take some time, Mike. There are a lot of people up there, and we can't send too many choppers up at once.

We've got a medical team up there right now to assist the injured and assess who needs immediate attention."

"I understand," Mike said. "I am going to want an update on every person as they're taken down from the mountain—I need to know which hospitals they are being sent to as soon as you have it. Do you understand?"

"Yes, sir. I should have another update for you in about twenty minutes." The line went silent, and Mike looked at the anxious faces around him. Their pain and disappointment was obvious. "I don't want you to get discouraged," he said finally. "Just because he wasn't on that first flight doesn't tell us anything about his injuries. For all you know, Zach opted to let the others go first because he's helping out." It seemed to be the perfect thing to say because there was a collective sigh around the room.

"That would be something Zach would do," Ryder said as he stepped away from the desk. Others joined in with their agreement, but Summer, Ethan, and Gabriella exchanged doubtful glances.

Gabriella left the room first and Summer followed. They walked out of the offices and down the long hallway until they found their way out the back door. Gabriella closed the door, sank onto the top step, and looked up at Summer. "I don't know how much more of this I can take," she said sadly.

Summer slouched down beside her. "Me either. I don't know what I was expecting."

Gabriella nodded. "I know I should agree with everything Mike said and we should be thinking positively, but I'm afraid too."

As much as it pained her to admit it, Summer agreed.

"I know," she said quietly. "From the moment he announced this trip, I didn't feel good about it. I thought that with my knowledge about injuries and how Zach was still struggling with his leg that he'd listen to me. But he just blew me off." She gave a mirthless laugh. "Who am I kidding? No one takes me seriously anyway."

Reaching out, Gabriella took one of Summer's hands in hers and squeezed. "I take you seriously," she said and rested her head on Summer's shoulder. "I think you're one of the sweetest and bravest women I've ever known. The way you stood up to your family out there before the call came in was amazing."

"You heard?"

Gabriella nodded.

"I thought you were making calls."

"Please, I was done about twenty minutes before the whole scene started. It was just safer to stay in the office and out of everyone's way."

"Maybe I should have volunteered to make the calls," Summer said miserably.

"No way. You needed to be out there and have your moment. I think you just about shocked the hell out of the bunch of them. I can't remember ever seeing so many Montgomery men standing with their jaws on the floor before."

Summer chuckled. "It did kind of feel good."

"I'm sure it did. You should do it more often. Show them what you're made of. Proves they can't just push you around."

Summer let that thought sink in as she closed her eyes. "I'm not sure it did me any good. I was saved by the proverbial bell."

"Mmm," was all Gabriella could say. She was mentally and physically exhausted. She was used to keeping up a fairly active pace, having worked for Zach for so many years, but this particular situation was taking an emotional toll as well. Over the last couple of weeks, even before the climb, she'd found herself really forming a bond with Summer. She respected her as a coworker and was coming to consider her a good friend. She didn't have too many of them—partly because she was a workaholic and partly because she seemed to intimidate people. She sighed. Now was not the time to dwell on that. As Summer's friend, she needed to be strong and supportive.

And then find a way to survive it herself.

"As much as I don't want to, I suppose we should get back in there and wait with the rest of them. They're probably wondering where we are."

"They probably haven't even noticed we left," Summer said and yawned widely.

"I'm sure Ethan noticed," Gabriella said with a hint of a grin. Summer turned to her with a look of anxiety. "Look, I hate the timing of all this for the two of you, I really do. But you're going to have to deal with it. I knew before the two of you even hooked up there was something there."

Summer shook her head. "I didn't believe it was even possible." Then she sighed. "I'm just not sure what's going to happen once my family finds out. Ethan may decide it's not worth all the aggravation."

"That's a load of crap and you know it." Standing up and stretching, Gabriella held out a hand to help Summer up off the floor. "I'm not going to stand here and say everyone is going to be thrilled and happy and supportive. Everyone is going to have something to say, and it might not be good. But here's the thing: Is Ethan worth it?"

"What do you mean?"

Gabriella rolled her eyes. "Being with Ethan, having a relationship with him, isn't it worth putting up with a little BS from your family? You know they'll get over it eventually. They've known Ethan for a really long time. They may not be thrilled right now, but I think the dust will clear sooner rather than later."

"I don't know," Summer said sadly. "We haven't talked about it, but it's been an issue most of my life. My family has a tendency to intimidate the guys I get involved with. Being that it's Ethan and he's Zach's best friend introduces another level of awkwardness to the situation. I wouldn't blame him if he ran screaming in the opposite direction."

"So he may be a little nervous. He should be. Your family has a way of making it seem like there are a lot more of them than there actually are. I mean, there are four of them out there—just four Montgomerys—and it feels like they consume all the space, all the air in the office!" She let out a laugh. "And it's like this all the time. They just have that big of a presence."

"But Ethan should be used to it by now! He's known us for like…forever. None of this is news to him. If you can see everyone will get used to it in time, why can't he?"

"You're jumping to conclusions here. You just said that you haven't talked to him about this yet. Why are you looking for trouble?"

Summer shook her head. "There has been so much going on with Zach and the rescue, it seemed selfish to try to talk about us and where all of this is leading. I get the feeling Ethan would rather have this whole thing go away…"

"Wouldn't we all?"

"No, not the accident and Zach, but the two of us. I don't think he had any intention of ever making a move on me. That's why I had to make the first move when I was camping in the tepee."

Gabriella's eyes went wide. "Wait…what? The tepee? How? I mean, I knew he was going to try to find you and talk to you about Zach but…"

"We were talking, and then we were arguing, and then he was saying how people need to take risks, and I agreed. And took one."

A knowing smile crossed Gabriella's face. "Good for you!"

"I thought so at first, but then he left. We agreed no one had to know. It would be our secret."

"And then Glacier Bay."

She nodded again. "And then Glacier Bay. I was so stunned when I saw him there, and when he told me he decided not to go on the climb…I actually had hope. I really thought I had gotten through to him! But he said he hadn't been into it for a while and it was no big deal."

"Oh, please," Gabriella snorted. "You got to him. He's just not ready to admit it. And the way he was looking at you when you walked away from him on the boat? Sweetheart, that was not the look of a man with only mild interest and time to kill. That was a man who looked at you and thought…*mine*. It was sexy as hell."

Summer blushed. "It was pretty hot. By the time we got back to the lodge and to the elevator, I wasn't even sure we'd make it to the room."

Gabriella pretended to fan herself. "You little vixen!"

Her blush deepened. "I never knew I had that kind of passion in me. The first time we kissed, I knew it was going to be different. It was so intense and so consuming, and every time he touches me, it just makes me want him more."

"Then you have to talk to him about this. You have to make him see that while it certainly won't be easy, it will be worth it."

"Ethan's pretty stubborn."

"Tell me about it," Gabriella said as she reached into her purse to pull out a compact and check her appearance and then cringed. She couldn't remember the last time she had gone for so long in casual clothing and without a full face of makeup. "Working with him and Zach has been a challenge because they are both so damn stubborn. I can't tell you how many times I've had to play referee and send one of them to another office!"

The image made Summer laugh. "Oh, you don't have to tell me. I grew up watching the two of them." And in all those years of watching and yearning, she knew there was still so much more to Ethan Reed and she really wanted to know all of it. How was she going to convince him it was okay?

Taking in Summer's suddenly somber expression, Gabriella placed a hand on her arm. "Hey, it's going to work out. I know it will."

"I wish I had your confidence."

"And I wish I had your curves," Gabriella said with a

sassy grin. "Now, I think we've hidden out in here long enough. Let's head back in there and see what's going on in the office. Maybe by now they've gotten word on your brother."

Together they walked back into the office and were surprised to see everyone sitting around quietly — drinking coffee and talking amongst themselves.

"I don't know what to do with this," Summer whispered. "I know how to handle them when they're loud and rowdy, but this? This quiet and meek behavior? It's unfamiliar."

Gabriella could only nod. "It's definitely not natural." She glanced around the room and felt oddly out of place. "Maybe we should back out slowly and head to the ladies room or something."

The idea was tempting, but just then Summer's father looked up at her. He didn't frown, but then again he didn't smile either. He simply looked at her warily. In her entire life, Summer couldn't remember a time when she couldn't clearly define her father's mood just by looking at him. It was definitely weird.

"Maybe he wants to talk to you," Gabriella whispered out of the side of her mouth.

"If you think I'm going to go over there willingly, you're crazy." She didn't have to.

Robert Montgomery stood and slowly made his way over to her. Once he was at her side, Gabriella excused herself to get another cup of coffee.

"We were beginning to worry about you," he said by way of an icebreaker.

It almost made Summer smile: her big, strong father finally at a loss for something to say. And she had done that. Oddly enough, she was proud of herself. "The walls in here were starting to close in on me. It was nice to step out with Gabriella and just have a quiet moment."

He nodded, hands in his pockets, and looked at the ground before looking at his daughter. "I guess it hasn't been particularly quiet since we arrived."

This time she did smile. "It was pretty loud in here before; you just picked up the slack when the crowd thinned out."

"Summer, I…I want you to know that…I'm aware." He stopped and cleared his throat. "I know I was a bit harsh with you on the phone last night. I was in shock over the news. You aren't the reason for whatever your brother is going through. That wasn't fair of me to say."

Summer realized it was as close to an apology as any of them had ever gotten. "I'm worried about him too, Dad." She gave a mirthless laugh. "I've been worried about him for weeks. When Gabriella broke the news to me last night, I thought I was going to pass out."

"I thought your mother was too when I broke the news to her. Luckily, Aunt Monica is with her as well as Casey and Selena." He frowned. "I wish you were there with them too. I never should have pushed you to go to Portland. You should be home with your mother—safe. I don't like that you're so far away, and now you're all caught up in this mess."

She reached out and placed a reassuring hand on his arm. "Dad, even if I were back home with Mom and everyone, I was still going to be caught up in this. Zach is my brother; I love him. I hate that he's going through this, and I hate that he and I fought so much before he left, but I want to be here for him. If I had been back home when you got the call, I would have fought like hell to fly here with you and James and Ryder and Uncle William."

"I wouldn't have allowed it," he said firmly.

"And I would have ignored you and gotten my own flight," she said evenly. "I'm not a child anymore. I'm a grown woman and I am free to make my own decisions. You don't have to like them. Hell, you don't even have to agree with them. You do, however, have to respect me enough to let me make them."

She thought maybe she had pushed just a little too far because she watched her father's expression tighten—the familiar, telltale tic in his jaw almost made her apologize. Then she remembered her own words just now and stood her ground.

"You're awful vocal today," he said finally after taking a couple of deep breaths. "You never used to be this vocal."

"You never gave me a chance. You never listened."

Robert wanted to argue but he knew it was pointless. She was right. Lately it seemed as though all his children were reminding him of his behavior and how much they resented him for it. Maybe it was time for a change. Maybe...

"We've got another group ready to come down!" Mike yelled from his office.

———

Twenty minutes later, they were all heading down to their cars. The only information they had was the name of the hospital Zach was on his way to. No one could or would tell them his condition.

"We have two town cars and drivers," William said as they exited the front door. "If it's all right with everyone, Robert and I will go in the first car with Ryder and Gabriella. We've got some business matters I'd like her to help us with." Everyone nodded. "Ryder, you'll need to get in touch with our other West Coast office and see what they can do to lend a hand in Portland until we're all back." Ryder nodded and climbed into the car. "Ethan and James?" He waited until they faced him. "Make sure Summer's okay." With that he climbed into the vehicle.

For the first few minutes, no one spoke in Summer's car. They were all lost in their own thoughts, so Summer was surprised when Ethan took one of her hands in his.

"How are you holding up?" he asked quietly, just as he had earlier.

"I thought I'd feel better once we knew they had rescued him. I didn't count on them not giving us any information."

He squeezed her hand. "We'll be there soon and no matter what the news is, we'll deal with it, right?" His voice was soft as he inclined his head toward hers, and when she looked up at him with her wide, dark eyes, he wanted to lose himself in them. If James weren't in the car, Ethan would have wrapped Summer in his arms and promised he'd be there for her no matter what. But he knew he had to control himself a little more.

On the opposite side of Summer, James watched the scene in front of him. Since when had Summer and Ethan gotten to be so chummy? He leaned back and did his best to observe without looking like he was watching them—a trick he had learned during his years on the force—and what he was seeing wasn't an interaction between two friends, but something a lot more…intimate.

His first reaction was to reach across the car and grab Ethan by the throat. How dare he lay a hand on his sister! Is that how he spent his time comforting her? By seducing her? *Shit*. What the hell was he supposed to do? Now was totally not the time to start a fight and yet at the same time, he wasn't sure he'd be able to keep from saying something—or just flat out threatening Ethan.

The thought of hitting Ethan was completely appealing. James's nerves were already on edge—thanks to this trip and being away from Selena—and the opportunity to hit someone would certainly help take the edge off.

But seeing how relaxed his sister looked took the fight right out of him. Ever since he'd walked into the office earlier and had seen how utterly exhausted and sad she was, he'd been wishing for a way to make her feel better. Then hearing her tell off their father had him wondering who this woman was and where had his little sister gone! But now? Sitting here and watching her interact with Ethan? James cursed under his breath and knew he'd have to find the right moment to talk to her. Or Ethan. Or both of them. A weary sigh escaped as he turned to watch the scenery go by.

Worst. Trip. Ever.

In the lead Montgomery car, Robert was giving Gabriella a list of people she needed to call and dictating a news release he wanted her to get out as soon as possible.

She tapped away on her tablet while he spoke. In the front seat, Ryder was on his cell phone, speaking to his cousin Christian, who was heading up to Portland from the Montgomerys' San Diego office.

And in the corner of the backseat, seemingly relaxing, sat William.

He waited patiently while his brother prattled on about calls and letters and whatever other nonsense he could come up with to keep poor Gabriella on her toes. Didn't he realize she wasn't here as an employee? Couldn't he tell she was just as worried as every family member was? *Sometimes Robert can be completely obtuse*, he thought to himself. When all of this was over and Zach was home and on the mend, William made a mental note to spend some time alone with his brother and do his best to help him get his head out of his rear!

When things were finally quiet, William did his best to come up with a clever question that would ensure a response from Gabriella—and no one else. "So tell me, Gabriella, have you ever been to Alaska before?"

She placed her tablet back in her bag and looked at William, her expression confused. "Excuse me?"

"I mean before this week. Had you ever traveled here before?"

She shook her head. "I don't travel much. I'm more of a homebody."

William nodded. "Well, I must say you come off like a seasoned pro."

Her brow furrowed. "What do you mean?"

"You certainly have a firm grasp on what everyone was going to need up here. You arranged flights and hotels and gave us clear information on the weather so we'd know how to pack. I just figured you must have had prior experience with the region."

Gabriella leaned back in her seat and tilted her head toward William. "Actually, I did the research for Zach. He knew he wanted to climb, and so he did all the research on things he would need for that, but he never bothered to think about what he would need prior to and after the climb." She chuckled. "I did a lot of online shopping for him."

"I'm sure he knew you'd be very efficient in getting it done for him."

"Oh, he didn't ask me to do it. I overheard him and Ethan talking about the things they were going to pack and realized they weren't going to be prepared. I made sure I didn't make it sound like I was eavesdropping; I mentioned I'd help him organize his packing list. Then I threw in my suggestions and let him think it was his idea to purchase the extra items."

William laughed. "That was very clever of you. It seems like you know exactly how to handle my nephew."

"I've worked for him for a long time," Gabriella said and realized it was true. There were times when she couldn't even remember what her life was like before coming to work with Zach Montgomery. He was like a force of nature who challenged her like none of her other bosses ever had. He was as much of a workaholic as she was, and they made an excellent team.

"You certainly have," William agreed. "How has it been with Summer around? How did Zach feel about her coming to work with him?"

Gabriella snorted out a laugh and then quickly placed

a hand over her mouth in embarrassment. "Sorry," she said as she composed herself. "He was furious. When Robert called and told Zach what was going to happen, he was fit to be tied."

"Why? She's his sister, for crying out loud! Why would he be upset?" William already knew the answer, but he was interested in Gabriella's take on the whole thing.

"Zach has mastered the fine art of running the Portland office. Everything runs like clockwork— according to Zach's clock, that is. He felt Summer's arrival was going to cause chaos and throw his carefully crafted world out of whack." She smiled. "And it kind of did."

"How so? I've heard nothing but good things from the people I've spoken to in the office," he asked conversationally. He was really enjoying himself.

Gabriella talked about Summer going from department to department and really getting involved in everyone's lives—in a good way. "Basically, everyone loves her."

"But…" William prompted.

"But…now she knows more about our employees than Zach does. It's amazing; she takes a personal interest in everyone and she has a knack for remembering things. I've been with the company for years, and I didn't know half the things Summer's learned about the people I work with. It's a gift."

William nodded. "It certainly is. So how did that throw things out of sync for Zach? It seems to me the things Summer was doing could only boost company morale."

"Yes, it did, but it also served to show what kind of tyrant Zach had turned into over the years. More than one person made a comment about how Summer must have gotten the personality gene or the heart of the family. Zach overheard some of it and it really ticked him off."

"Those people are being paid to work," Robert interrupted. "Summer needs to remember Montgomerys is a place of business, not a playground."

Gabriella frowned. "She knows it's a place of business, sir," she said a little coolly. "She simply has a knack for working with people and encouraging them in a way that makes them want to work harder and do more with a better attitude. If you ask me, that is what you need to make a successful company. If all of your employees came to work happy, they'd be more productive."

Robert was going to say more, but Gabriella's words stopped him.

"So why do you think Zach isn't more like that? Or can't *be* more like that?" William asked.

She sighed. "I don't know," she said wearily. "He didn't used to be like this. There was a time when he was much more relaxed and in touch with everyone. I don't know what caused the change; it happened about two years ago, I'd have to say. I can't think of anything particular that would have caused such a dramatic change in him, but it was almost as if someone had flipped a switch in him and the easygoing man disappeared and in his place was this…taskmaster." She made a face at the thought.

"And you're not happy with the change?"

"No. There are days I want to throw something heavy

at him just to snap him out of it." She realized her words and immediately scrambled to take them back. "What I mean is…um…I just get frustrated and…"

William took her hand. "Shh…it's all right. I know exactly what you mean. You don't have to apologize for being honest. It's one of the things I admire most about you."

"You do?" Surprise laced her words.

He nodded. "You are quite an asset to the company, Gabriella. Your coworkers admire you and just watching the way you've handled yourself in this crisis, well… needless to say, I am beyond impressed."

"Thank you, sir."

"So it gets me wondering…you seem to be, shall we say, overqualified for your position with Zach."

Her brows arched at his statement. "Excuse me?"

"It's true. I look at you and I see executive material, not executive assistant material—not that there's anything wrong with that—but I think you are capable of much more. We have more than enough offices for you to choose from and a number of open positions I think you'd be more than qualified for. I think you've done all you can do with Zach. And it sounds to me like you might be ready for a change."

"I never said—"

"Nonsense," William interrupted. "You deserve to be doing more than personal shopping for your boss. He's taking advantage of you and holding you back. We'll find him another assistant and let him worry about it. We'll wait until he's back at work, of course, but we can start planning your transition now."

"Now just a minute," Gabriella snapped, and everyone

turned to look at her. "I cannot believe you are sitting here—as we drive to the hospital no less—offering me a job and telling me to leave Zach! That is…it's…horrible!" Her anger was palpable and she wanted to wipe the smile right off William Montgomery's face. "How could you even think this was an appropriate time for this conversation? We have no idea what kind of condition Zach is in! I've been with him for years, and if you think I'm just going to up and leave him, then you're crazy." She crossed her arms over her chest and shook her head. "He's going to need me now more than ever, and I think it was in very poor taste for you even to suggest that I leave him."

The car came to a halt in front of the hospital. Robert climbed out of the car and held out a hand to help Gabriella. She stormed up to the entrance and Robert stood where he was until his brother and son came to stand beside him. When the automatic doors to the hospital closed behind Gabriella, Robert turned to William. "What the hell was that all about? We never discussed promoting her! Why would you do such a thing?"

William took the door out of Robert's hand and closed it. A mischievous grin crossed his face. "It was an experiment."

"Oh no…" Ryder groaned before rolling his eyes and making his way to the hospital doors.

"What?" Robert asked, confused. "Why did Ryder just say 'Oh no'?"

William chuckled and put an arm around his brother's shoulder and led him up the walkway to the doors. "Don't give it another thought. We've got to go inside and find the right person to talk to. We need updates and answers here."

Robert knew he was right, but he was also curious as hell about what he had witnessed in the car. "First tell me why you told Gabriella we'd make her an executive."

Stopping in his tracks, William sighed with irritation. "Your son quite possibly has some recovery time coming to him. You and I both know he's not going to like it. Zach has never liked to be held back and told he can't do something. I wanted to make sure the person who works closest with him is there for the long haul." He looked toward the hospital entrance and then back to his brother. "If she thought he was difficult before, he's going to be out-and-out impossible now."

"And are you satisfied with the results of your little exchange?"

William's grin broadened. "More than you know."

Unfortunately, no one on the hospital staff was familiar with—or impressed by—the Montgomery name. No matter how loud Robert yelled or how hard William tried to charm the nurses, no one was in any rush to speak to them.

An hour after their arrival, the group of them sat and listened to what the pair of doctors had to say. "What we're looking at right now," Dr. Eric Morgan said, "is a torn rotator cuff, four broken ribs, his leg was broken in four places along with his hip, and there was trauma to his spinal cord, causing swelling. And this is just a preliminary overview. We've done scans and X-rays, but that's not to say that we're not going to find more injuries."

"Basically," Dr. Richard Peters began, "we have a

lot of work ahead of us, and I need you to understand we won't be able to update you every five minutes." His voice was firm. Dr. Peters looked to be in his late fifties, and it would appear he had dealt with more than his fair share of anxious families. They had been assured he was the top trauma specialist in the region. "We still have multiple tests to run to fully understand the extent of Zach's injuries."

"Can we at least see him?" Ryder asked.

Dr. Peters shook his head. "Right now, we need to tend to Zach. We have to set the bones and put pins in place, so we can see more clearly what we're dealing with. Then we can give you a more specific prognosis." When Robert made to speak, the doctor held up a hand to stop him. "Your son has already lost a lot of time trapped up on the mountain; the more time I spend in here with you means more waiting for him."

"Is he awake? Is he in pain?" Robert asked as the doctor made his way across the room.

"From what the medics conveyed to us, he's been in and out of consciousness since the fall. He was unconscious when I got to him, and they're prepping him for surgery now, so he'll be asleep for some time. Depending on the extent of the swelling on his spine, we may have to keep him in a medically induced coma for his own comfort." Dr. Peters looked around the room. "I'm sorry. I do wish I had more to tell you, but until I get back upstairs and look at the results of what we've done so far, there isn't much more I can say. I'll send a nurse out to update you when I can."

And with that, he was gone.

It seemed like everyone was afraid to move, afraid

to speak. Ryder got up and went to look out a window briefly before taking out his cell phone and leaving the room. James excused himself to call and check on Selena. Robert agreed it was a good idea to call his wife, and William soon followed suit. When it was down to only Summer, Ethan, and Gabriella, Summer let out a breath. These were the people she preferred to be with right now—the people who had comforted her the best since this entire ordeal had begun.

Gabriella sat in a corner, lost in her own reflections. Ethan moved to sit next to Summer and touched her cheek. "I know I keep asking you the same thing, but I want to make sure you're doing all right."

"None of what Dr. Peters said sounds good," she sighed. "All this time, I knew that there was a good possibility of Zach being injured, but I didn't want to believe it was going to be this bad."

Wrapping her in his embrace, Ethan pulled her close and did his best to calm her. "None of us did, Summer," he said softly. "But your brother is strong, he's a fighter, and we have some of the best doctors here. If there are issues, I'm sure your father will move heaven and earth to get better ones. Zach is going to get the best care possible. You can count on it."

Her hands were fisted in his shirt as she buried her face against the warmth of his chest. The feel of him, hearing his heartbeat, did wonders for soothing her, but her mind continued to race. "All that time lost," she said. "All that time he was up there in the cold and wind. What if that time cost him?" she asked as she raised her head. "What if because of the delay, Zach doesn't make a full recovery?"

Ethan cupped her face in his hands. "We can't think like that," he said fiercely. "Right now, we need to stay positive. When we're finally allowed to see him, we need to show him we're not terrified. Your face gives you away all the time. Zach will take one look at you and know you're freaking out. You need to be strong, Summer. For Zach."

Shaking her head, Summer tried to pull away but Ethan wouldn't let her. "I don't think I can, Ethan. I'm too worried. I'm scared it really is my fault that this happened."

He released her and pulled back, staring at her as if she'd lost her mind. "What? Why are you still even thinking that? We've been over this already, sweetheart. You're not to blame!"

"I distracted him. You said so yourself when you came to find me at the springs. I had been so intent on telling Zach about how I felt about the risk he was taking with this stupid trip, and even if you managed to convince him I was fine with it or whatever you said to him, I distracted him for all those weeks. If anything, I pushed him into going because I kept saying he couldn't. I'll never be able to forgive myself if he doesn't recover. He'll never be able to forgive me either."

Ethan didn't know what to say; he thought the topic was closed after she confronted her father. He hated that she still felt guilty about this. "Summer, once everyone is down from the mountain safely, we'll find out what caused the accident. I think it's pretty safe to say for something of this magnitude, Mother Nature is to blame. Not Zach and certainly not you. Your brother isn't the type of guy who lets himself get distracted. Trust me; I've gone on more adventures and dangerous trips with him than I can count. Nothing gets in his head. Nothing and no one."

"Tell me about it," Gabriella mumbled in the corner. With a shake of her head, Gabriella stood. "Ethan is right, Summer. Your brother doesn't let anyone affect him; it's just not who he is. You could have talked until you were blue in the face, but once he started that climb, I can guarantee your concerns were all but forgotten." At the stricken look on Summer's face, she tried to make things sound a little less cold. "I don't mean he forgot about *you*. You're his sister and you know he loves you, but when Zach sets his mind to a task, he is extremely focused. You have to know this accident had nothing to do with you."

"But we don't know that," Summer retorted. Why couldn't everyone see? Why couldn't they simply understand?

"Whatever you're thinking," Ethan said, "stop. We're going to get up, go grab something to eat, and maybe play a game of cards…or chess. I'm sure the gift shop has some games we can buy to keep us busy. And there will be no more talk of you being to blame. Is that understood?" He stood and held out a hand to her.

She looked up at him warily. Now wasn't the time to argue. She'd keep her thoughts and feelings to herself. After all, how could he possibly understand what she was going through? He barely knew her. Even after how intimate they had been, he really didn't know who she was and what made her tick. Right now, she just needed a little time, a little space.

Ethan's hand was still steady in front of her. Summer looked at it and then turned to look at Gabriella standing by the window. If she was going to focus on Zach, that meant she had to put her feelings for Ethan to the side. Ignoring his hand, Summer stood and walked over to Gabriella.

"C'mon, let's go and grab a little fresh air before heading back to sit with everyone."

Gabriella looked curiously between Summer and Ethan and saw Ethan's jaw hanging open. Moving away from the window, Gabriella hooked her arm through Summer's and together they headed toward the door. "We'll meet you upstairs in a little while," Gabriella said right before they walked out the door, Summer silently walking beside her.

With fresh cups of hot chocolate in their hands, Summer and Gabriella sat side by side on a bench outside the hospital entrance. It was cold enough to see their breath in front of their faces and the steam off their cups.

"Care to tell me what happened back there?" Gabriella finally asked.

"When?"

"When you pretty much blew Ethan off after he tried to cheer you up." Gabriella took a sip of her drink and hummed with delight.

Summer shrugged. "I can't keep leaning on him. It's clear he's not comfortable letting anyone know anything's happened between us, and now that everyone's here, I need there to be some distance between us."

"I know it sucks and all, but has it occurred to you that maybe it's not that he doesn't want everyone to know but he's trying not to add to everyone's stress level?"

"What about my stress level, dammit? What about my feelings? Why is it so important not to upset James, Ryder, my uncle, or my father, but it's okay to upset me? Huh? Tell me! Why?"

"Okay, okay… Clearly this is a sore subject and I completely understand what you're feeling."

"No, you don't," Summer snapped. "Unless you've had to deal with a houseful of overbearing men all your life, you don't." Then she stopped and realized she actually knew nothing about Gabriella's life or her family. She turned to her with an apology on her lips. "Wait… do you have any siblings?"

"I do," she replied quietly. "I have a sister."

"Older or younger?"

"Older."

Summer nodded. "Must be nice. I always wished I had a sister. I have one female cousin on my dad's side. We were kind of close, but it's not the same."

Gabriella snorted. "Trust me, having a sister is not all it's cracked up to be."

"What do you mean?"

"Let's just say I moved to Portland to be as far away from her as possible."

"Well, that doesn't sound good." She hesitated and was almost thankful for a distraction. "Want to talk about it?"

"I'll give you the *Reader's Digest* version—she's older than me and didn't like having to give up her only-child status. My entire life, she did her best to torment me. She was never kind. We didn't do things together like normal sisters do; everything was a competition. The only problem was, no one explained the rules to me.

I just wanted to have a relationship with her. She wanted to make sure everyone liked her best."

"Wow. I don't even know what to say."

"There's nothing you can say. She destroyed friendships I had, caused strife between me and our parents… Every insecurity I have is because of her."

Summer looked stunned. "You are quite possibly the most confident woman I have ever met. What could you possibly have to be insecure about?"

She laughed. "This Gabriella? The one sitting here with you is not the same one my family sees. You see a confident businesswoman; they see someone who is hiding from life. You look at me and may see a well-dressed individual; they see me as someone shallow who likes to lord her money over them by buying expensive clothes. It's exhausting and endless."

"Gosh, I am so sorry. I had no idea. I naturally assumed life would be so much better with a sister rather than a houseful of brothers."

"You may be right. I'm just the wrong person to talk to about it. I've heard of a lot of women who rave about the relationships they have with their sisters, and I can't even relate. If even once she had shown me an ounce of kindness, I would have been so grateful. But throughout my life—particularly before I came to work for Montgomerys—she made sure I knew she was better than me. More successful. Wealthier. She had the whole world at her fingertips because she married well and I was just a lonely, struggling single person nobody wanted."

Summer's jaw almost hit the ground. "How can you even say that? You're stunning! How could she even imply nobody wants you?"

"I don't date much."

"By choice, I'm assuming."

A sad one, Gabriella thought miserably. "I have some issues with trust," she said quietly. "Thanks to my sister." She sat quietly for a moment. "Don't get me wrong, not every problem with my life is her fault, but she's done a lot of damage."

Summer could relate. Her brothers and her father had been so overprotective because of her family name—it was sometimes hard to know if someone was with her for herself or for her name. She knew Ethan was different, but even though there was trust, there was a boatload of other hurdles for them to get over.

Suddenly Gabriella stood. "Okay, enough of a sidebar for now. Let's go back upstairs and see if there are any updates."

"Okay, but I'm stopping at the vending machine for my chocolate fix."

"Didn't we just finish drinking our chocolate fix?" Gabriella asked with a smirk.

"Please…to deal with this group and this level of stress, there isn't enough chocolate to be found."

For all the years Ethan had known the Montgomery family, he had never felt like an outsider until now. Maybe it was his own imagination or guilty conscience, but as he sat with James, Ryder, William, and Robert, he pretty much felt completely alone.

When Summer had ignored him earlier and walked away with Gabriella, he felt as if a part of him were walking away. He was completely torn. What was the right thing to do here? Did he go on as he and Summer had and just say the hell with the consequences? Keeping quiet and not disrupting things—especially now—had seemed the smart thing to do, but now he wasn't certain. James had been giving him the stink eye since they arrived at the hospital, and Ethan wasn't sure what that was about. Then Summer had blown him off.

Deciding that another lap around the room wouldn't hurt, Ethan stood and went to the window and looked out at the parking lot below. There wasn't much else to see. It was a gray day out, but watching the people coming and going was something to do besides sitting.

He caught movement out of the corner of his eye and found Robert Montgomery standing beside him. Out of respect, he chose to check on his well-being. "How are you doing, sir?"

Robert gave a mirthless chuckle. "I hate this," he responded honestly, in a low voice. "I've never had to deal with anything like this before. None of my kids have ever been hurt, not like this. I know I have to defer to the doctors, but this waiting is making me crazy."

Ethan could totally relate. If they didn't get some definitive news soon, he was certain he'd go insane. "Sometimes it's hard to sit back and trust in the professionals. I think I would have felt better if they had let us see him. Even for a minute."

Robert was staring straight ahead out the window. "I don't know where he got the drive to want to do all of these dangerous hobbies. That was never my thing. His mother's either. Sometimes it seems like he's got a death wish."

"It's not that," Ethan said. "Zach loves what he

does—he thrives on the challenges in the business world—but he also feels a little boxed in by them. He likes the outdoors and challenging himself to see if he can conquer the extremes there as well."

"Just seems pointless to me. For all the thrill he got out of this trip, was it worth it? What if he's broken his back? What if he never walks again? Was it worth it?" He hung his head and did his best to collect himself. "Summer knew he wasn't ready for it, and we all ignored her pleas just as much as Zach did. Maybe we should have joined her. Maybe we all should have shown a lot more concern a long time ago. If we had, Zach wouldn't be here right now."

"I have to disagree with you there," Ethan said, feeling somewhat annoyed at Robert's take on the whole thing. How could crushing Zach's personality be for the better? "He could just as easily get hurt driving to and from work; does that mean he should stay closeted in his home and never go out?"

"That's not what I'm saying at all," Robert said defensively. "I think it's great that Zach's adventurous and loves being outdoors. But sometimes a person can take it a little too far. Like this."

"Robert, there's risk involved in everything we do, whether it's an extreme sport or driving in the car. For all we know, this was a freak accident. Summer thought Zach's leg wasn't ready for this, but we don't know for sure that it was the cause of the accident. She couldn't know with any great certainty either. I was all set to go on this climb too."

"And yet you didn't. You backed out. Tell me why."

Ethan shrugged. "To be honest, I'd just gotten into

the habit of going along with the things Zach suggests. We both work too much sometimes, and if it weren't for Zach, I probably wouldn't take any time off for myself. So when he suggests something, I say yes so I don't have to go through the hassle of thinking about it for myself." He grimaced at his own words. How lazy did that make him?

"But why now? Why this trip? Why did you suddenly decide this was the time you didn't want to go?" Robert pushed.

"I don't know," Ethan said. How the hell was he supposed to explain he was growing restless with his life? That after spending one night with Summer, he realized he knew what he wanted but couldn't have it? That she had gotten into his head and into his heart?

Robert eyed him suspiciously. "I know you better than that, Ethan. I know Summer was wearing down Zach; I think she wore you down too."

More than you know, Ethan wanted to say. He shrugged. "Summer and I didn't really talk that much about it. I was simply playing peacemaker between the two of them. I listened to what she had to say and relayed it to Zach. I didn't take her concerns that seriously. It just finally occurred to me that all these extreme sports weren't doing it for me anymore. That's all."

Making a noncommittal sound, Robert turned around and found his daughter standing not two feet away from them. "I was wondering where you'd gone off to," he said with a small smile. "Everything okay?"

Summer wasn't looking at her father; she was looking at Ethan with total devastation. She knew he wasn't ready to talk to her family about them, but she hadn't

expected him to sound so callous either. She was beginning to wonder who the real Ethan was. Was their time
together merely about sex? Was she reading the whole
thing wrong? She had practically thrown herself at him
back at the springs. Maybe when they met up in Glacier
Bay, he was just looking for more of the same.

And she had given that to him.

Repeatedly.

She needed to leave. To have some time away from
everything. Between the lack of sleep and the constant
worrying over her brother, Summer wasn't sure what
was real and what wasn't anymore. Forcing her gaze
away from Ethan's, she faced her father. "If it's all right
with you, I'd really like to head back to the hotel. I'm
not feeling so well."

Robert stepped forward, concern etching his face.
"Are you okay? Do you need anything?"

She gave a small smile. It wasn't often her father
showed explicit concern for anyone's feelings; it was
nice to experience it right now. "I think I just need a
couple hours of sleep. Will you call me when you hear
from the doctors?"

He nodded. "Of course, of course." In a rare show of
emotion, he pulled his daughter into his embrace.

Summer couldn't remember the last time her father
had hugged her. With her emotions so close to the edge,
she pulled him in tight and held on.

"Hey, now," he whispered and pulled back to look
down into her face. "Are you sure you're going to be
all right?"

Her voice wouldn't work; she couldn't have uttered a
word even if she wanted to, so she simply nodded.

Looking over Summer's shoulder, he said to Gabriella, "Will you go with her? Make sure she's okay?"

"Of course," Gabriella said and carefully wrapped her arm around Summer. With one last look at Robert, she said, "You'll call us? As soon as you hear anything?"

"Yes. Hopefully it won't be too long before someone gives us an update."

"It doesn't matter how small the news is," she said, her voice almost pleading. "We want to know."

"You have my word."

Chapter 10

NEITHER SPOKE ON THE CAB RIDE BACK TO THE HOTEL.

It wasn't until they were in the elevator that Summer broke the silence. "I need sleep. I mean several solid hours of sleep. I barely know my own name anymore."

Gabriella yawned next to her. "Something about a season…"

Summer's head lolled slightly to the side. "What is?" she asked around a yawn.

"Your name."

"Very funny."

They walked slowly to their room and once inside, they each went about getting changed and crawled into their own beds.

She couldn't speak for Gabriella, but Summer was asleep as soon as her head hit the pillow. If it weren't for the phone ringing four hours later, she would not be awake now. Forcing herself to sit up, she reached for her cell phone and became instantly alert when she saw her father's number on the screen.

"Hello?"

"How are you doing?" Robert asked, wanting to ensure that his daughter was all right before bombarding her with news. "Sorry to wake you so soon."

"I'm good… I'm good," she said and then yawned. "What's going on? Is Zach out of surgery? Have you talked to the doctors?"

He huffed. "He's still in surgery. He had some internal injuries. They've set the bones in his legs and got the pins in and that alone's going to make him pretty much immobile for quite some time. The nurse who came out said it should probably be another hour or so and *then* we'll meet with the surgeons."

"Wow. So we still don't know everything."

"I'm afraid not."

It was her turn to sigh. "What about you, Dad? How are you doing?"

"No…no…I'm fine. Frustrated. But fine. You know I'm not big on patience and I hate standing around."

She smiled. "I know. Do you want me to come back? To be there when you meet with the surgeons?"

"No, I want you to eat something that doesn't come out of a Styrofoam container. At the rate this is going, we probably won't be able to do more than get a glance at Zach tonight. It's already late. There's no point in hanging around now we know he's here and he's safe."

Summer knew he was right, but she still felt guilty about not being there. "Are you sure? I could be there within the hour."

"I know you're worried just like the rest of us, Summer. But it would be pointless for you to drive all the way over here at this late hour only to turn around an hour or so later and go back. Wait until tomorrow. Hopefully by then, we'll be able to see him."

"Will you call me after you talk to the surgeons?"

"I promise."

"Thanks, Dad."

"Try to get some more rest. Tomorrow will be here before you know it, and while it won't be as stressful as the last couple of days, I'm sure it's going to present its own share of challenges."

They hung up and Summer reclined against the pillows and closed her eyes. The urge to call a cab was almost overwhelming. She looked at her phone and then around the room and was doing the math when Gabriella rolled over on the other bed and said, "Don't even think about it."

"About what?"

"Going back to the hospital. Your father has been true to his word about calling as soon as he gets news, and your being there isn't going to change anything. Until Zach gets out of surgery and they get him into recovery and settled into the ICU, no one is going to get in to see him."

"Get out of my brain, witchy woman," Summer said and slouched down farther onto her bed.

"I know how your mind works because mine works the same way. When I heard the phone ring, I instantly started thinking about what we would have to do to get ready and get back there."

"I know in my head that it makes sense to stay here, but my heart is telling me to get up and go."

Doing her best to sit up, Gabriella stacked her pillows and reclined against them. "If it were still just the three of us—you, me, and Ethan—then I'd say we should go. But there are five of them there, Summer. Five big, loud, opinionated men. They aren't going to leave without all the information on Zach and whether more specialists are going to have to be called in. If we were to show up there, you would be seated in a corner without being heard and I would end up making all of the calls."

"Or you'd be *told* to make all of the calls."

"Or that." Honestly, Gabriella didn't mind making the calls; it made her feel useful. But this was Zach they were dealing with, and she had a feeling she'd be hard-pressed to stay neutral and professional.

"He told me I should get more rest. Like I'm going to be able to go back to sleep now."

Gabriella looked at the clock. "We should order dinner. Why don't you go and grab a shower—one that lasts longer than five minutes—and I'll call downstairs and place the order."

"Because you don't always have to be the one to make the calls," Summer reminded her. "Why don't you take the first shower and I'll make the call?"

"But…"

Summer held up a hand to silence her. "This is not up for debate. You go and use up all of the hot water and I'll work on getting dinner sent up and then, once we've eaten way too much, I'll take my turn using it all up. Deal?"

"Deal."

⁓

"Maybe I should call him," Summer said two hours later, as she flopped back on her bed and stared up at the ceiling.

On the opposite bed, Gabriella was in the same position. "Not a good idea."

"Why?"

"They could be in with the doctors right now. You don't want to disturb them."

"What if he forgot?"

Gabriella shot a bland look in her direction. "When has your father ever forgotten anything?"

"You're right, you're right. I know you're right," she said with a dramatic sigh. "I just thought they'd be done by now."

"Maybe the surgery is, but like I said earlier, the five of them probably had a list of questions a mile long for the doctors."

"Maybe."

"You know your father is going to want to have Zach moved closer to home as soon as possible. There's no way he's going to want to stay here in Alaska."

"I know I'm no medical expert, but I have a feeling it's going to be a while before they'll be okay with letting him fly."

"He's going to have a fit."

"Who? My father?"

Gabriella shook her head. "No. Zach. He's going to want to be out of here within a matter of days."

"That's probably why they suggested the medically induced coma. To keep him from getting too worked up."

"They can't keep him that way forever. Eventually, he's going to get up and start demanding his own way. It's a male thing."

"It's a Montgomery thing," Summer said dryly. "He can pitch as big a fit as he wants, but with his injuries, he's going to have to wait until it is one hundred percent safe for him to be moved. And where would he get moved to? Portland? Back home by my folks in North Carolina? I mean, who's to say?"

"Your folks are going to want him home with them,

but I can guarantee you that he'll want to go back to Portland. He'll need someone to stay with him, though. Since Ryder has a wife and new baby at home, and James and Selena are expecting, neither of them are going to volunteer."

"I'm here," Summer reminded.

"I know. But do you think your six-foot-plus brother is going to be easy to handle? Especially if he's still casted up? He's going to need another guy to help him out, and perhaps a live-in nurse type of person."

"Ethan can stay with him," Summer suggested.

Gabriella made a dismissing sound. "Not gonna happen."

"What? Why?"

Rolling onto her side and leaning on her elbow, she faced Summer. "Okay, I've worked for your brother for a long time, Summer, and I think I've gotten to know him, Ethan, and your family pretty well during that time. This is how it's all going to play out. Until Zach is cleared for travel, there will be a turnstile at the door because one or more Montgomerys will take turns coming and going here in Alaska. In the meantime, Ethan will go back to Portland and run the company. Your father will go and check in, stick his nose where it doesn't belong, eventually tick Ethan off, and then leave. Then your uncle will show up and be a lot kinder, a lot less intrusive, but in the end he'll also annoy Ethan and then leave."

"You've really given this some thought."

A hand went up to halt any further comments. "By that time, Zach will come back home to Portland, but he won't be able to come to the office. Then he'll essentially tell everyone to get the hell out of his life—and he will use a far more colorful vocabulary—and everyone will temporarily obey his wishes. Some poor home-health worker will show up and quit. And then another. And then another."

"Oh, Lord…"

"Ethan will try to reason with him but will also fall victim to your brother's foul mood and just return to the office and continue to run things—with limited interference from your father—until Zach can return to work."

Summer let the whole scenario sink in for a moment. "That's all very interesting."

"And accurate. Mark my words."

"There's only one small flaw in the plan."

One perfectly sculpted brow arched in response. "Oh really? And what is that?"

"Where are you during all of this?"

Rather than answering it, Gabriella turned the tables on Summer. "Or maybe you should be asking where you'll be in all of this. After all, with Zach out of commission, you'll be free to find your place in the company without him scowling at you and thwarting your every attempt to find your niche. Have you found a department that you think you want to stay in?"

"Not yet but I haven't had a chance to try them all," she said and then sighed. "I'd really like to say I'd stay here…or rather, Portland, but it's going to depend on what happens with Ethan."

"What do you mean?"

"Well, if he's not willing to do more than sneak away with me, then there's no way I can stay. I have too much self-respect for that."

"Good for you!"

"It will kill me," she said seriously, turning her head to look at Gabriella. "I don't know how I'll ever be able to see him again if he says this is all we're ever going to have."

Gabriella sat up and flung her legs over the side of the bed until her feet touched the floor. "I can't see him saying that, Summer. I think the timing just really sucks. You have to give him a little time."

"I know, I know…but did you hear him today in the waiting room? When he was talking to my father? He made it all sound so believable. So convincing. Like I really don't matter to him."

"He had to," Gabriella reminded her. "It's just temporary."

Summer shook her head. "Is it? Or is it the way he really feels?"

"Ethan's not like that."

"All men are like that," Summer said miserably. "I was involved with someone back in New York. I thought we had something amazing, and it was leading to a future together, but he was already married with kids! I never suspected a thing. He never said anything to even hint that he was married." She felt shame at admitting it out loud. "I feel so horrible for doing something so dirty."

Gabriella stood and walked over to Summer's bed and sat down beside her. "He did that. Not you. You had no idea."

"But that's what I'm saying!" she cried. "For all I know, Ethan is just having a good time right now with no intention of this going anywhere." Gabriella was about to comment but Summer cut her off. "Think about it—I basically seduced him. And there I was, a sure thing, and in a situation where we didn't have to tell anyone about it. He always had an out, Gabs. He'll always have an out. We can sleep together for the rest of our lives and not tell anyone, but as soon as I push for more, he'll use my family as an excuse."

"You don't know that for sure, but I really don't think he would, Summer. And you should know. You've known him since you were kids for crying out loud! How could you think he'd reject you?"

Because he had walked away before. At the tepee. Twice.

"I think I need to see some sort of effort on his part, something to prove to me I'm more than that to him. To prove I mean more to him than just sex."

"I'm beginning to feel like a broken record here, but I'll say it again—you have to talk to him!"

"When?" Summer asked incredulously. "The sheets hadn't even cooled at the lodge when we got the call about Zach and once we got here, there wasn't an appropriate time to bring it up." She leaned forward and rested her head on her hands. "What am I going to do, Gabs? What in the world am I supposed to do?"

The ringing of the phone brought an abrupt halt to their conversation. "Saved by the bell," Summer mumbled as she reached for the phone and answered it without even looking to see who it was. She put it on speaker so Gabriella would be able to hear everything along with her. "Hello?"

"Hey, Summer, it's James." His tone was solemn, and she had a feeling they hadn't received good news from the doctor. "We just met with the surgeons and they're letting Dad go up to recovery and see Zach. It's only through an observation window, but at least he'll get to see him."

"What did they say?" For a full five minutes, James told her about the surgery and the full extent of the injuries Zach had suffered. Some she knew about, others were new to her. James carefully explained everything in the same layman's terms the doctor had used with all of them.

"One of the doctors stayed behind while I called you just in case you had any questions I couldn't explain. Would you like to talk to him?"

Summer anxiously looked at Gabriella, who, in turn, shook her head. "No," Summer said. "It was a lot of information but I think I get the general idea." She felt sick to her stomach. "How long will they keep him in the coma?"

"A couple of days. The swelling on the spine is the biggest concern right now. Until it goes down, they won't know if it could cause paralysis." Gabriella gasped and stood and fled to the bathroom. "Summer? Are you all right?" James asked, panic lacing his tone.

"I…I'm fine," she said, her voice trembling. "That was Gabriella."

"Oh…well, is she all right?"

Summer looked toward the closed bathroom door and listened for a moment. "I'm not sure." She paused and let the news sink in. "James, no one mentioned the possibility of paralysis before. How…how soon until we know?"

"They're not sure," he said. "Right now, everything is uncertain. I think we're all in a bit of shock. I mean, I

know I was expecting broken bones and hypothermia…
that sort of thing. But paralysis? My brain didn't even
go there."

"But they can be wrong, can't they?"

"I'd like to say they could, but they're the specialists,
Summer. All we can do right now is hope for a miracle."

Tears began to stream down her cheeks. "Oh God…"

"Are you sure you don't want to talk to the doctor
yourself? He's right here."

"Honestly, I don't think I can process all of this and
actually think of an intelligent question to ask. I'm…I'm
shocked. This wasn't something I was ever expecting to hear." She turned and looked toward the door
where Gabriella had gone. "I'd better go and check on
Gabriella. Will you be heading to the hotel soon?"

"As soon as Dad comes down, we're leaving. We
let the town car go earlier, so we called the service and
they're sending another to come and get us." He paused
and Summer heard him thanking the doctor for staying
and then saying good-bye to him. Once back on the line,
she could hear the weariness in his voice.

"Is there anything I can do?" she asked.

"No. I think we all just need a good night's rest and
some time to let all of this sink in." He yawned loudly.
"My head is spinning and my stomach is growling. I
hope the food at the hotel is decent. We talked about
stopping somewhere, but we're all just so damn tired
that we thought it best just to go right there and order
room service."

She gave him the rundown on the menu. It seemed
like a good distraction. "We ordered ours earlier and
everything was very good. Although, if you're feeling

the way I was earlier, anything will taste good to you right now."

"You got that right," he said with a slight chuckle. "Listen, kiddo, I'm going to go. If you want, one of us will call you when we get checked in. Ryder and I are sharing a room and Dad and Uncle William have one together, too. I have no idea how close they'll be to yours."

"Call me when you get settled in, but then just focus on getting some rest. I didn't think I'd be able to sleep, but once my head hit the pillow, I was out."

"I can almost feel it now," he joked.

"Have you spoken to Selena? Is she doing okay?"

"Yeah. I hate being away from her and not knowing exactly when I'll get back, but I know she's doing okay. She's with Mom and Aunt Monica and Casey, so she's got plenty of people around her."

"Well, when you talk to her later, send her my love."

"You got it, Summer. I'll talk to you soon."

They hung up and Summer hesitated before climbing from the bed. She stood and stretched. "I'd really like to get off this emotional roller coaster," she mumbled as she walked across the room to knock on the bathroom door. "Gabs? You okay?" The door opened slowly and Summer could tell her friend had been crying. "Want to talk about it?"

Gabriella shook her head. "What James said just took me by surprise. I'm sorry for being such a drama queen." She hastily wiped her tears and walked back out into the room. "Are they heading back now?" Her tone was business as usual, but Summer knew it was a defense mechanism.

"I told James to call when they're settled, just so

we know what rooms they're in. They're all going to order dinner in their rooms and call it a night." Summer headed back over to her bed and flopped down on it and thought it wasn't such a bad idea—just calling it a night. The clock told her that it was already after ten, but after her long nap, she wasn't overly tired. Dammit. She was already dressed in a pair of flannel boxers and a T-shirt; it wasn't like she could go anywhere.

Not that she wanted to.

Reaching for the TV remote, she figured the best way to kill time was to find something to watch. While she channel surfed, Gabriella called down to the front desk and alerted them to the Montgomerys' impending arrival. She wanted their rooms freshened and some form of food to be waiting for them. Summer was thoroughly impressed. The woman was amazing—in tears one minute, quick and efficient the next.

"It's pretty cool watching you crack the whip and seeing everyone scurrying around to do your bidding," Summer joked when Gabriella hung up the phone.

"What are you talking about?"

"The way you spoke to the people at the front desk? That was a thing of beauty. I'm sure there are people running around right now preparing fruit and cheese platters, dusting the rooms, and fluffing the pillows." She sat up and smiled. "Had I been thinking clearly when we left the hospital, I would have had you wield that kind of power for us earlier."

"You would have been asleep before you even noticed or appreciated it."

Summer made a face at her. "And how do you know none of them will do the same?"

"Oh, I already know they aren't going to notice," Gabriella said as she sat down and tried to tell what Summer was watching on the television. "But I'll feel better knowing that it was done."

"Silent and deadly. I like it. You're kind of like a ninja."

Gabriella rolled her eyes. "Um...no." She stared at the screen and watched as people ran around a kitchen decorating massive cakes. She glanced over at Summer. "I never would have pegged you as a reality TV person."

Summer shrugged. "I wanted something mindless to watch. No real drama, nothing that was going to make me think. I want my mind to just go blank—or numb—so I'll be able to sleep again."

"I am not going to have any trouble there. Another hour or two and I will be out for the night."

"I envy you. It normally takes me hours to relax enough to shut my brain down to go to sleep, and even then I need to take something like melatonin."

"Or Ethan Reed," she teased.

"Ha, ha, very funny."

"So are you telling me you didn't sleep like a baby when you were with him? He didn't exhaust you until you didn't have the strength to move?" The blush on Summer's face said it all.

"Well, that's neither here nor there," Summer said. "All I know is that tonight is going to be a melatonin night." Dammit.

––∿––

By eleven thirty, all the Montgomery men had checked in with Summer. They were on the floor above hers and were all looking forward to a full night's rest to prepare them for another long day at the hospital. When she hung up with Ryder and turned her phone off, she was seriously ready for bed.

"I can see what you mean about these shows," Gabriella said. "Just a couple of hours of this and I feel like I've lost several dozen points from my IQ...and my vocabulary."

"It's not that bad," Summer said and then yawned. "But you see...it did the trick. You're feeling sleepy, aren't you?"

"Yes, but it had nothing to do with the show and everything to do with the fact that I haven't had a decent night's rest in almost a week. I miss my own bed." She was pulling the blankets down on her bed and crawling in when there was a knock at the door.

"Oh for crying out loud," Summer muttered. She wasn't in the bed yet, so it only made sense for her to see who was knocking. "I just talked to all of them. What could they want?" She pulled open the door and froze.

Ethan.

"Hey," he said quietly, his hands braced on either side of the doorjamb. "How are you doing?"

How was she doing? How was she *doing*?? She wanted to scream at him that she was miserable and upset and angry and scared and worried and... She silenced her inner tirade and simply looked at him. No, she didn't just look; she drank in the sight of him. He was perfection to her. He always had been and he always would be. It wasn't fair. Why couldn't she have just gotten him out of her system? Why couldn't one night of wild sex have been enough to make her move on? Or for that matter, why couldn't a week's worth of wild sex have been enough? Why was it that she wanted him now more than ever? Even after the way he had crushed her earlier? True, he didn't really know she was there, but the fact remained.

"Fine," she finally forced herself to say. "I was just getting ready to go to sleep."

Ethan nodded. "You left so abruptly earlier. I was worried about you."

"Oh, were you?" she asked sarcastically. "I don't see why. *Summer and I don't really talk. I was playing peacemaker between the two of them. I didn't take her seriously,*" she said mockingly. "Sound familiar?"

He hung his head. "Dammit, Summer! That wasn't what I meant. I was just trying to—"

"Um, excuse me," Gabriella called from inside the room. "While I am sure this riveting drama would entertain me a lot more than the last two hours of reality TV, I think the rest of the occupants of this floor would rather not have to listen to it. So either the two of you come in and hash this out—quickly—or go to Ethan's room."

They both stood and stared at her for a long moment. Ethan stepped back and looked at Summer expectantly. "I believe we're done," she finally said and got a mild sense of satisfaction when Ethan paled.

"Five minutes, Summer. Just give me five minutes to explain."

"Explain what, Ethan? That we had a quick fling? Believe me, I got it. Loud and clear."

"It's not that!" he snapped. "This whole situation—"

"Is being broadcast for the entire sixth floor!"

Gabriella called out. "Seriously, Summer, just go down the hall to his room with him and be done with it."

Indecision warred within her. To go or not to go. She didn't want to hear what Ethan had to say; none of it was going to make her feel any better. And unfortunately, she seemed to have a habit of throwing herself at him when they were alone, and even as pissed off as she was right now, she couldn't help but notice the way that his hair was rumpled and his jawline was shadowed. She had no doubt it would be rough and scratchy against her skin.

Dammit. Her nipples hardened at the mere thought of his jaw rubbing up against her, and now she had to cross her arms to try to disguise it. Ethan's eyes followed her movements and she saw the heat flare in his dark eyes and knew that it was too late; he already knew the effect he had on her.

"Fine," she huffed. "Five minutes. But I'm telling you now that nothing you say is going to matter. You made your position perfectly clear earlier."

"Good night, Gabriella," Ethan called pleasantly into the room.

"Good night, Ethan," she replied with a smile and when the door closed, she added, "and Summer."

With Summer's hand firmly in his, Ethan dragged her down the hall and into his room. She pulled free and stalked across the room and stood by the window. He closed the door and leaned against it and just watched her. The short flannel boxers, the soft, clingy T-shirt, and her long, tan legs... She made quite a picture. Her blond hair was loose and hanging down her back, and he knew she'd let it dry naturally because it wasn't styled the way she normally wore it. Her face was devoid of makeup, she was mad as hell, and she was the sexiest, most desirable woman he had ever seen.

Quietly, he walked across the room to her. When he reached her, he placed his hands on her shoulders to get her to face him, but she stepped away before he even had the chance. His stomach clenched. Had he screwed things up so badly that she wouldn't let him touch her even in the most casual sense? "Summer?"

She turned toward him but her expression was blank. "Go ahead. Say what you have to say so I can go back to my room."

He wanted to yell that he wanted *this* to be her room. Their room. He hated coming back here by himself after spending the better part of a week sharing a hotel room with her. It was lonely as hell to be there without her after such an emotionally draining day. Normally the solitude didn't bother him, but after having so much time with her over the last week, Ethan was starting to get used to it. Beyond used to it—he wanted it, he craved it, and now wasn't sure he'd be able to live without it.

Taking a step toward her, he watched as she took a step back. They continued like that until her back was against the wall and he was toe-to-toe with her. "I panicked today," he said, his voice edged with regret. "This whole thing with us, with your family…with Zach, has me in knots. I don't know what to do or say to anyone. Everyone is upset enough and I thought that by keeping this"—he motioned between the two of them—"private for now, I was doing what was best." He stared into her face—her beautiful face so etched in his memory that whenever he closed his eyes, she was there—and smiled. Reverently, he reached up and skimmed a hand down her cheek and watched as her eyes slowly closed.

"I never wanted to hurt you. Ever. I just don't know what to do." His honest admission seemed to have the desired effect. Summer's eyes opened and she looked up at him. Ethan could tell her every thought, her every emotion because they mirrored his. He wanted her; he needed her, and the desire was like a force of nature that couldn't be stopped. "Tell me what to do, Summer," he pleaded.

Closing the small gap between them, Summer reached up and wrapped her arms around his shoulders, anchored one slim hand up into his hair, and pulled his head down toward hers. "Kiss me," she whispered.

The minute his lips touched hers, the first thing he thought was, *I am never going to get enough of her*. The way she clung to him, the way her breath caught when he touched her—it was everything. Pushing her back against the wall, he pressed his body into hers. She was so soft, so curvy, and as his hands ran down from her face to her shoulders to her hips to her bottom, he let himself stop and appreciate all of the ways she was different from him.

"Wrap your legs around me," he said gruffly against her neck as he squeezed her bottom and lifted her. Summer cried out at the contact but he quickly muffled the sound by claiming her mouth again. Again and again he slanted his mouth over hers as their tongues mated and danced. It could have been minutes; it could have been hours—Ethan wasn't sure. All he knew was while he was enjoying kissing her, holding her, feeling her, it wasn't enough.

"Stay with me," he begged as he gently rocked against her. "Stay with me tonight. Please."

Summer would have agreed to anything he said. Almost. As he rocked with a little more force, a little more pressure, she moaned. "I...I shouldn't," she said breathlessly. "I need...I need to..."

"What?" he whispered as he nipped at her earlobe. "What do you need, sweetheart?" His tongue gently laved at the spot he'd just bitten. He felt her shiver and knew she was close. He did it one more time and then dove back in for another hot kiss. "Tell me. Tell me, Summer. What do you need?" She was reaching for him, for his lips, but he held himself back. He needed to hear what she was thinking, what she wanted from him.

"I need you, Ethan," she finally said. Ethan instantly rewarded her with another kiss as he carried her across the room to his bed.

"You have me, Summer," he promised as he laid her down on top of the blankets.

"Promise?" she asked shyly.

His body covered hers as he rained kisses all over her face—her lips, her cheeks, her eyelids—and then worked his way down to her jawline, her throat, and lower. Hastily, he worked her T-shirt up and over her head and then stared in awe at the naked perfection before him. Reaching up with shaking hands, he cupped her breasts.

"Promise."

She sighed his name as he began to touch her.

She cried out his name as he teased her.

She purred his name as he pleased her.

Over and over again.

As the clock turned from p.m. to a.m., Summer felt at peace. Her body was completely exhausted, and as he pulled her in close and tucked her into his side, she smiled. Gabriella's words from earlier played back in her head, and she realized that they were true—when she was with Ethan, there was no need for any sleep aid. He rocked her to sleep better than anything she had ever known.

———

It was still dark in the room when Summer rolled over and looked at the clock. She knew she couldn't stay here in Ethan's bed forever. Although it was exactly what she wanted to do. But the sun was going to be up soon and if she didn't force herself to get moving, they were going to be found out. As much as she wanted to stop keeping secrets, she certainly didn't want everyone to find out about her and Ethan by seeing her creeping out of his room half-naked.

That would certainly not go over well.

Carefully, she wiggled out of his embrace and immediately missed his warmth. She was just about to slip out from under the blankets when she felt him stir behind her. "Where are you going?" Ethan's voice was no more than a whisper as he reached out and gently pulled her back beside him. Summer didn't put up much of a fight.

"I need to get back to my room," she whispered as she rolled over in his arms to face him. Unable to help herself, she kissed his chest, his throat, and his jaw until she felt herself melting against him.

"Don't go."

It would be so simple just to stay, she thought. To

relax against Ethan and grab a couple more hours of much-needed sleep.

"I don't want anyone to see me sneaking back into my room."

She moaned as he began to let his mouth travel in mirror image of where hers had just been.

"No one will see you," he said between kisses. "They're not even on the same floor." Not giving her a chance to argue, Ethan covered her lips with his own and kissed her until he felt her go pliant beneath him. When first one long, lean leg wrapped around him and then the other, he knew the topic was officially closed.

"Now I really have to go," Summer said as she pulled her T-shirt on over her head and did her best to fix her hair. It was almost eight o'clock and she knew not only would Gabriella be up, but her family would start calling any minute to see about breakfast and getting to the hospital.

Ethan walked up behind her and turned her in his arms. "I really wish you didn't have to." There was regret there in his voice and in his eyes. "I hate this, Summer. You have to know I do."

Sighing, she leaned into him and wrapped her arms around his waist and hugged him. "I know. And I do too." She looked up into his sleepy face and gave him a sad smile. "I just wish things could be different."

He saw she was looking at him with a hint of expectation, so he said the only thing he could. "It won't be forever."

Happiness bubbled up inside of her. It wasn't a

declaration of love, but to Summer, it was pretty darn close. What Ethan was saying without actually saying it was they were more than a fling, more than a way to kill the time. She hugged him a little tighter before pulling away with a sincere smile on her face. "I better get back. I'm sure Gabriella is wondering where I am."

He arched a brow at her. "Seriously? She all but threw you out the door with me last night. She knows exactly where you are." He pulled her back in for a searing kiss before letting her go. Walking her to the door, he pulled it open. "I guess I'll meet up with you along with everyone else."

"I hope they haven't started calling my cell phone already; otherwise, poor Gabriella must be out of excuses for where I am." Facing him, Summer stood up on her tiptoes and kissed him. "I'll see you in a little bit." She was halfway out the door when Ethan reached out and pulled her back.

"Just one more," he said before lowering his mouth to hers. Her kisses were addictive and he had no idea when they'd have another opportunity to be alone like this. When he finally lifted his head, he smiled at the dazed look on Summer's face. "I couldn't help myself."

A blush crept up her cheeks. "I don't want you to help yourself." She spun around and fairly floated down the hall. She didn't have her room key, so she had to knock and wait for Gabriella to answer. Once the door opened and she stepped inside, she gave Ethan a flirty smile and a wave before closing the door behind her.

Ethan stood there for a full minute, already missing her. Turning, he walked back into his own room and closed the door.

And neither of them noticed James Montgomery standing not ten feet away from them with a scowl known to bring strong men to their knees.

Chapter 11

"I HATE THAT HE'S SO STILL," SUMMER SAID SOFTLY. "I'm not used to it. Every memory of Zach in my entire life is of him in motion. He's always on the move." Gabriella sat quietly beside her. "I wish they'd let him wake up. I need to see his eyes open and for him to give me a goofy grin—or scowl at me. I'd even settle for that."

It had been like that for three long days. The seven of them took turns going into the ICU to sit with Zach for the few precious moments they were allowed. The doctors still had him under heavy sedation, so every morning they would arrive full of hope, and they would leave each night exhausted and full of despair.

On the fourth morning, as they were piling into the hotel van, which had been graciously transporting them back and forth, Ryder finally snapped. "I don't know how much more of this I can take," he said as he took his seat and ran a hand through his hair. "I mean, I understand the reasoning behind keeping Zach sedated, but I don't like it. I think we need to put some pressure on the doctors to start letting him wake up so we really know what we're dealing with."

"Ryder," William said patiently as he took his own seat, "we don't want to do anything to hamper your brother's recovery. If the doctors think it's in Zach's best interest to stay sedated, then we have to accept it."

Ryder turned to James for support. "Bro, come on, back me up here." But James wasn't looking at him; he was glaring at Ethan. He had been doing it a lot lately. "James?"

Whipping his head around, James turned to Ryder. "What?"

"I was just saying we need to push the doctors into letting Zach start to wake up. What do you think?"

James looked around the vehicle to see who seemed on board with the idea and who didn't. He had no idea there was even a conversation going on around him; his focus had been on Ethan and how he was going to get him alone so he could kill him.

The image of Summer coming out of Ethan's room four days ago was burned in his brain. It didn't take a genius to know she had been in there all night. Even if he hadn't caught them kissing out in the hall, her rumpled hair and clothes said it all. If James knew anything about his sister, it was that she was fairly pristine with her appearance and nothing could get her to walk around the hallway in her pajamas.

Just thinking about it still made him mad as hell. He knew he had to do something about it soon. At some point today, he was going to have to confront Ethan and tell him he'd better keep his hands off Summer if he wanted to live.

"James!" Ryder said again.

"What, dammit?" Then he remembered the question. "I don't know. The doctors seem pretty adamant about keeping Zach sedated for his own good. I don't like it either, I honestly don't, but if he's going to wake up and be in pain, then I'd rather they keep him asleep."

That didn't do much to appease Ryder. Once the van was on its way, Ryder kept his mouth shut and watched the scenery go by. He made a mental note to get James alone later and see what the hell his problem was with Ethan.

In the front of the van, Summer, Ethan, and Gabriella sat together. It seemed to be the only time they could do so without curious looks from the rest of the family. Gabriella and Summer would chat about seemingly random topics, but down out of everyone's view, Ethan would hold Summer's hand. It felt a tad bit juvenile, but it was like their own little way of rebelling against the constrictions they currently put up with.

During the day they played at being casual acquaintances, but every night for the past three nights, Summer would wish Gabriella a good evening and tiptoe across the hall to Ethan's room so she could be with him—in his arms, in his bed. So far, no one was the wiser. She still felt guilty using her brother's condition as a distraction for her secret endeavors, but at the same time, she just wanted to be with Ethan, and this was the only way it was going to happen.

They arrived at the hospital and rode the elevator up to the tenth floor and were surprised to be greeted by Zach's lead doctor. "Good morning!" Dr. Peters said brightly. "I wanted to meet you here because I have some good news."

Everyone's eyes went wide and hopeful. Was it possible? "Earlier today, we started to cut back on the meds we were administering to Zach to keep him sedated. He's starting to respond to some of the tests we've been doing, and I'm hopeful he'll become fully awake later today."

They all began talking at once and were making quite the ruckus, so Dr. Peters cut them off by saying, "Why don't we go down to the waiting area and have a seat and I'll be glad to answer all of your questions? The neurologist is in with Zach right now, and I'll ask one of the nurses to bring him down the hall to us when he's done, okay?" While everyone headed to the waiting area, Dr. Peters went to the nurses' station and relayed his request. He smiled when he arrived at the waiting room and found the entire group silent and waiting.

If only they'd been this agreeable all along!

He sat down and went through the details of how they were stopping the Diprivan IV and how by doing that, it would allow Zach to begin to wake up. "Once he's fully awake, we'll be able to do some more tests and be able to speak to him about what he's actually feeling—or not feeling."

A collective gasp stilled the room for a moment.

"So you think there's going to be some paralysis?" Robert asked solemnly.

"It is a possibility. From everything we've seen on all his scans so far, however, any paralysis will most likely be temporary. Nothing is severed or damaged to the point of lasting damage. How long the paralysis may last, however, is not something we can predict. Some patients with similar types of spinal damage may experience it for a couple of days, but I have seen cases where it has lasted for weeks or months. I don't want to give you—or Zach— false hope. He's had some serious trauma to his entire body, and the most important thing is to keep him calm."

Without conscious thought, Summer reached over and grabbed Ethan's hand while she listened to Dr.

Peters talk about the tests they were going to be doing and how he saw Zach's recovery process going from this point on. Everyone was so focused on listening, no one would have noticed anyway, but when Summer realized it, she tried to pull her hand away.

But Ethan held on. And then turned to her and smiled.

She had no idea how things were going to go for her brother, but right now she felt that everything was going to be all right for her.

When Dr. Peters was done speaking, a second doctor joined them. He looked as if he were barely old enough to be out of medical school, but once he started speaking about Zach's case, Summer realized Dr. Walter Blake was clearly a man who'd been in this field for a long time. And just happened to have good genes. He was a specialist in spinal cord injuries, and as he talked about his credentials, Summer, along with the rest of the family, felt confident they wouldn't need to call anyone else in for Zach.

Between the two doctors, Zach was in good hands. The rest, it would seem, was up to the patient himself.

"I know you're all anxious to go in and see him, but I'm going to ask that you give us a couple of hours with him. We want to evaluate him when he wakes up, and possibly move him from the ICU unit to a private room." Dr. Peters looked at Robert. "After our conversation that first day, I took the liberty of making sure one was made ready for your son."

"Thank you."

"I know it's still somewhat early, but may we suggest going back to your hotel for an early lunch, relax if you can, and we'll meet back here at two o'clock. Okay?"

What choice is there? Summer thought to herself.
Taking turns, they each thanked Dr. Peters and Dr.
Blake as they left. It was a quiet ride down in the
elevator. When they saw the hotel van was waiting outside the door, everyone stopped and looked
at Gabriella.

She shrugged. "I could tell where they were going
with all of this, so I texted the driver and asked him to
please come back." When they all continued to stare at
her, she added, "It's no big deal. Really."

Summer walked over and hugged her friend. "How is
it even possible for you to be so on top of everything?"
She pulled back. "Seriously. How do you manage to
keep track of what everyone needs?"

She smiled and winked. "It's just what I do." She
thanked the driver as he opened the door and helped her
step up into the van.

Behind them, Ryder, Ethan, and James all exchanged
looks. "She is one scary organized woman," Ryder said.

"You have no idea," Ethan said with a chuckle.

Ethan was glad for the break from the hospital, but he
was alone and couldn't spend the time with Summer.
She and Gabriella had gone to their room—she
said she wanted to call and check on her puppy—
meaning he could either hang out alone or with one of
the Montgomerys.

Both Robert and William talked about making calls
to their wives, the office, and whatnot, and Ryder mentioned calling his wife to check on the baby. James had
been suspiciously quiet.

Judging by the way James had been glaring at him earlier, Ethan chose the alone route.

Ethan sat down at the desk in his room and frowned. What the hell could James be pissed at? They had all been cordial to one another—talking business and about family and Zach—and as much as Ethan searched his memory, nothing came to mind that raised a red flag about why James would have a gripe with him.

No one knew about the time he and Summer were spending together. Or about their time at the lodge. Or at the springs. As far as he was concerned, they were flying under the radar. Ethan hated the sneaking around. Every night when Summer quietly knocked on his door, he was waiting with anticipation, but every morning when she crept out before dawn, he was filled with regret.

At any other time, it might have been fun to play these kinds of games. Maybe with another woman. But with Summer, it tied Ethan up in knots. He wanted to be able to tell everyone where they stood, how he felt about her; hell, he wanted to shout it to the world that he was in love with Summer Montgomery. Unfortunately, now was definitely not the time to throw this at her family. The Montgomery men tended to be extremely protective of Summer and never approved of the men she became involved with.

He had a hunch they'd feel the same way about him.

No wonder she had moved so far away from everyone. He was surprised she even wanted to stay on the same continent. New York wasn't far enough away, and he recalled Zach telling him more than once how he or one of his brothers had gone up north to intimidate some jackass they didn't deem worthy of their sister.

No doubt he'd join the masses in the "men intimidated

by the Montgomerys" category, no matter how much the Montgomerys all claimed to like him.

Sure, Ethan knew he and Zach had been friends for years, and for the most part he was considered family, but he also knew, where Summer was concerned, no one was going to be good enough for her.

Not even him.

He warred within himself over what was cowardly and what was being respectful. By not telling her family about them—and being cowardly—he was actually being respectful. There was no need to add more fuel to the emotional fire raging over Zach. But as time went on, it just weighed heavier and heavier on his mind. Something was going to have to give. And soon.

Slouching down in the chair, he ran a weary hand through his hair and sighed. "Leave it to me to get myself into the world's most impossible situation." He cursed himself. Cursed the fact that he couldn't leave well enough alone. Why had he gone back to the springs when the plane wasn't ready that fateful day? Why had he approached her on the boat?

And why the hell did he keep claiming her as his night after night after night?

He thought of James again and thought about maybe going to talk to him. "Sure, and why not just hand him the gun to shoot me with." *There's no way James or anyone can know what's going on,* Ethan thought. The only one in the group who knew was Gabriella, and she would never betray Summer. She may have had issues with him a time or two, but she would never throw Summer under the bus. Especially to her family. Not now. Not ever.

James had been gone from the family fold for a long time. Hell, even when they were younger, Ethan couldn't remember James being around much. Could James be nursing an issue with Ethan from back then? But really, would he still hold some grudge all these years later? They had seen each other on several occasions since James returned to North Carolina, and on all those occasions, both Selena and James had always been very friendly toward him. So what the hell was wrong now?

A loud knock sounded at the door, and Ethan had a feeling he was about to find out. Only a Montgomery man could knock that loudly.

With a muttered curse, he walked to the door like a man going to his execution. This was so not the way he wanted to spend his few free hours. Although on the bright side, maybe he'd finally get an answer out of James and that would solve one of the problems in his life. Pulling open the door, he indeed found James standing there looking thoroughly pissed.

"Give me one good reason why I shouldn't beat the crap out of you right now?" he asked through clenched teeth.

Rather than answering—or making any kind of comment—Ethan stepped aside and motioned for James to come in. He shut the door and watched as James stalked the entire perimeter of the room as if looking for something.

Or someone.

"Where is she?" James demanded.

It would be insulting to both of them for him to play dumb. Ethan wasn't sure how James had come to know about him and Summer, but it was time to face the music. "She's down the hall with Gabriella. In their room."

In the blink of an eye, James was nose-to-nose with him. "Nice. So you drag her over here and sleep with her all night and then toss her out in the morning?" He grabbed Ethan by the shirtfront and gave him a good shake. "I should kill you right now."

Maybe if Ethan had put up a fight it would have gone that way. Instead, he hung his head. "You're right. You probably should and do us all a favor," he said in a low voice.

Some of the anger left James at Ethan's words. He shoved him away with disgust and then began to pace the room. "What the hell, Ethan? How long has this been going on?" Before Ethan could answer, James held up a hand. "Please tell me it was before you got here to Alaska because if I find out you took advantage of her while she was upset over Zach, I really will have to kill you."

With a sigh, Ethan sat down on the bed and bent forward to place his head in his hands. "It was before Alaska. It was right before we left for the climb."

James stood still and listened, unsure if that answer were any better. "Did Zach know?"

Ethan shook his head. "Summer had disappeared a couple of days before we were supposed to leave. Zach was freaked out and pissed off, and I knew if he went after her, it wouldn't go well for either of them. I offered to go."

There were still too many questions for James's liking. "So then…what? You're a couple now? Or are you just screwing around?" His tone was harsh, and the look on Ethan's face spoke volumes.

Standing, Ethan faced James, his hands clenched at his sides. "You want the truth? I don't know what we're doing. And do you want to know why? Because of you. And Ryder. And Zach. And your father. I mean, for crying out loud, I've seen the way all of you have intimidated the men Summer's dated! She's afraid to say anything and so am I! Do you think I want to be in this position? Do you think I like sneaking around?"

"I don't know, Ethan. Do you?"

Ethan took a step forward. "I hate it. I hate it more than you can ever imagine. But right now? With everything that's going on with Zach? Do you honestly think now is the right time to throw this out there?"

James studied him for a minute. "It's a convenient excuse." Ethan's eyes narrowed at James's words. "Seems to me like you've got quite a nice setup going on. You get to sleep with Summer without having to deal with having any real responsibility. Now I don't know how you view it, but I'm telling you right here, right now, you're treating my sister like some dirty little secret. And I don't like it."

His words, his stance, they all told Ethan it wouldn't take much to provoke James into a physical confrontation, and that wasn't what he wanted to do. "So what do you suggest we do, huh? You want to hit me? Is that it?" Ethan prepared himself for it. "Go ahead. If that's what's going to make you feel better, then bring it." It probably wasn't smart to provoke him, but Ethan figured they might as well get it over with.

James studied him for a long moment. His jaw clenched just as tightly as his fists were at his side. "I want more than to just hit you," he said honestly. "I want to beat the shit out of you. I don't think you're good enough for my sister, and do you know why? Because you're not man enough to come out and admit that you're involved with her. You're hiding like a coward, and I hate cowards."

The fist hit his face before Ethan knew it was coming. He stumbled back until he hit the wall. On instinct, he immediately straightened and was prepared to return the favor.

Then he thought better of it. One of them had to think clearly.

"So what's the solution to this, James?" he asked, his hands held up in surrender. "Because like it or not, whether it's me or some other guy, your sister is going to get involved with someone. She's going to fall in love, get married, and have kids. It seems to me like everyone is supposed to accept that prospect for you and your brothers but there's a separate set of rules for Summer!"

Even as he said the words, the thought of somebody else falling in love and having a future with Summer filled him with rage. So much so he felt the need to hammer the point home. "You took off for years and had your life. No one even had the opportunity to question your relationships because no one was there to see them! But even when Summer was living in New York, she still had to deal with all of you going and checking on her and trying to run her life. What do you expect? That she was going to stay celibate forever? Become a nun? How is that fair?"

"You don't know what you're talking about," James said. "Now you're going to try to put the blame on her family? We are only trying to do what's best for Summer! We don't want to see her get hurt—or used—by someone like you!"

"Like me?" Ethan yelled. "You're kidding, right? It seems to me that everyone liked me just fine when Zach and I became friends. I was welcomed into the family and asked to join the company. You think I'm freaking fantastic when I'm closing deals and making money. Hell, I'm even considered a great guy when I travel all over the world with Zach and do these crazy adventures with him. But now suddenly, I'm not good enough? Explain that one to me. Please. I'm dying to know how I'm such a great guy in a thousand different ways except this one."

"Dammit, Ethan," James growled as he sat down on the chair by the window, "she's my baby sister." He raked a hand through his hair. "I know you're an only child and you don't get it, but there's just something about the whole relationship that's not always rational. I look at Summer and I don't see a grown woman. I see the little girl in pigtails I used to have to carry around."

"But she's not a little girl anymore," Ethan reminded him.

"I know, I know… Selena was reminding me of that last night when I talked to her, but it doesn't change anything. I don't want to see Summer get hurt. Ever."

"Everyone gets hurt, James. Sometimes you can't avoid it."

James glared at him. "Are you *planning* on hurting her?"

"No." Ethan feared he already had but decided to keep it to himself. "I never wanted to hurt her. I don't ever want to hurt her. This came out of nowhere and took on a life of its own. We didn't plan on it, but we also don't want to stop it."

"Shit," he muttered. "I still don't like it, Ethan. I don't like thinking that you're sneaking around and making her feel like you're ashamed of her."

"That's not what I'm doing!"

"Yeah, you are. You're not willing to fess up and tell anyone what's going on, so to me, that says you know what you're doing is wrong."

"Dammit, have you been listening to me at all?" Ethan said, unable to hide his frustration. "It's not like that! We're trying not to upset anyone!"

"Anyone? Or you? Because it seems to me you're the one with the most at stake here."

"Oh, really? Are you telling me if we all went down to lunch and I turned to the group and said, 'Oh, by the way, Summer and I are sleeping together. We have a relationship and we're looking to see where it goes. Who's ready to go and see Zach now?' that nothing would happen? Do you honestly believe they are only going to direct their anger, opinions, and disappointment at me? No one is going to say a word to Summer? Seriously?"

"I hadn't thought of that," James ceded miserably.

"Do you really think she needs that right now? Do you know she still feels guilty about Zach's accident? That she's been blaming herself for it?"

"What? Why?"

"Because of her campaign to try to get him not to go. She feels like she distracted him and he fell because of it. Then your father compounded her fears when he called and pretty much accused her of endangering Zach's life." Now it was Ethan's turn to pace. "You were gone for a long time, James. You have no right to waltz back in now and start being the concerned big brother again. I know she's your sister and you love her, but there were a lot of times when she really needed you and you weren't there." It was a low blow and Ethan was aware of it, but sometimes you had to play it that way.

"I was the one with her when she got the news about Zach," Ethan continued. "And I was the one who held her while she cried and struggled with the role she thought she played in the whole thing."

"I had no idea."

"Of course you didn't. She's trying to be strong here in front of you and Ryder and her father, but behind closed doors, she's cried. A lot. Before the climb? She was a one-woman force to be reckoned with. She was so passionate about trying to get Zach to see things her way—all the while trying to learn a new job, in a new city—and not once did she ever crack." He paused. "She's not a child anymore. She's got a lot on her plate. And we won't even go into whatever happened in New York. Do you really want to add to all that?"

"Aren't you?" James snapped. "I may have been gone for a long time, but that doesn't mean I didn't keep in touch. I may not have physically been there, but I did keep up with what was going on. She would call and we would talk. I may not have wanted anything to do with my father, but it had nothing to do with my relationship with my siblings. They knew they could call me anytime. I wasn't the best at initiating those calls, but I always knew what was going on."

"I don't doubt that, James, I really don't. All I'm saying is you haven't spent a lot of time with her to truly know the woman Summer has grown into."

"I was hoping to change that once I got settled back in North Carolina. I had no idea she was going to up and move to Portland."

"No one did. Her arrival came as a bit of a shock to all of us."

"At the time, my father and uncle thought it was for the best. They felt like maybe she needed a change of scenery and the chance to test the waters with the family business."

"Zach was not happy about it at all. To be honest, they fought almost daily. I still don't get why he's so hard on her. She wasn't doing anything wrong; she's a hard worker and a fast learner. She did what she was told and never complained. I think he just resented her being there. And then Summer started to get vocal about the climb, and it was hard for them even to be in the same room together."

"If I know my brother, it's a lot to do with what I was saying earlier. In our eyes, Summer's always going to be our little sister, the baby of the family."

"But that's not fair," Ethan said.

"That doesn't change it. Unfortunately." James stood and looked down at the city below through the window. "Zach likes his independence and running the Portland office with little family interference. By sending Summer there, he had to deal with her—with family—and probably felt like they either sent her in to spy on him or he was going to be stuck babysitting her."

"When she took off before the climb, and when I

found her, she said she just wanted to stop being a distraction to Zach," Ethan said. "She knew if she stayed, she'd be pestering him right up until he got on the plane. She thought leaving was the better solution." Ethan thought of the sadness on her face the day he first saw her at the springs. "She so desperately wanted him to listen to her, to take her seriously. I think that's all she wants from all of you."

"Geez, Ethan… That's not something that's going to happen overnight, if it even happens at all. And in our defense, Summer doesn't have the greatest track record. You can't blame us for acting the way we do when she's always kind of been a little irresponsible and flighty."

"She's changed," Ethan said. "Not to say she's not going to wake up one day and decide she wants to take up salsa dancing or wood carving, but it's just who she is and we're supposed to love her for it, not condemn her."

"Do you?" James asked bluntly.

"Do I what?"

"Love her."

Shit. "That's not something I'm going to discuss with you when I haven't even discussed it with her."

James chuckled. "If you can't admit it to me, then I have my answer. And it leads me to believe that you're just screwing around."

Ethan rolled his eyes. "You have nothing, dammit! You're not a cop anymore and this isn't a damn interrogation—no matter what you might think. What goes on between me and Summer is between me and Summer. Not you. Not your family."

"So what are you saying, Ethan? What do you think is going to happen from here?"

That was the million-dollar question. "Honestly?"

James nodded.

"I know I don't have any right to ask, but I am asking you not to say anything to anyone about this right now. You may not agree, but I'm trying to protect your sister from having any more guilt or lectures thrust upon her. I don't want anyone upsetting her. I certainly don't want to see her cry again."

James huffed and stepped away from the window. "That's asking an awful lot. I don't know if I can just sit back and watch the two of you carrying on behind everyone's backs. It's not right."

"Why?" Ethan demanded. "Why is this not right? It's none of anyone's business!"

"She's my sister! Geez, it's like we are going around in circles here, man, and I'm getting a little tired of it!"

"Just…just give us a little more time, okay? Let's get through getting Zach settled and figuring out how it's all going to work. At some point, everyone's going to have to go home. Ryder is anxious to get back to Casey and the baby; I know you're anxious to get back to Selena… There are so many other things going on right now that everyone is trying to deal with, why add this?"

James didn't have an answer. "All right. I'm not going to say anything to anyone, but believe me, Ethan, I'm watching you."

"If you don't mind me asking, how did you even find out? We've been very careful."

"I was coming down here to see if she wanted to have breakfast with me and saw her coming out of your room half-naked." He made a sound of disgust. "I'm not going to lie to you, I wanted to kill you."

"Shit. We didn't even see you."

"If *I* stumbled upon you, you can be sure it could happen again with my father, Ryder, or even my uncle. If you're hell-bent on keeping this thing a secret, you're going to have to be more careful." He cursed. "I can't even believe I just said that."

"Does this mean that we have your blessing?"

James glared at him. "Don't push your luck. I wouldn't go that far. Let's just say I'm…observing." He paced back and forth a couple of times in an attempt to get his thoughts straight. "Make no mistake, Ethan, if I think for even one second you're screwing up and making her look or feel like she's some hooker you picked up, it won't end well for you. I know you don't think I gave a damn about Summer all the years I was gone, but you're wrong. And now that I'm back, I plan on making sure she's happy."

"That's all I want for her," Ethan said solemnly.

"We've known each other a long time, Ethan," James warned. "But that won't mean shit if you hurt my sister."

"Duly noted."

With nothing left to say, James walked to the door. With his hand on the knob, he faced Ethan one last time. "Let me ask you something."

"Anything."

"If this situation with Zach hadn't happened, would you still be keeping this a secret?"

It was a hell of a question. "I don't know. If it hadn't been for the climb, Summer and I wouldn't have had the time alone together. I'm not sure if either of us would have done anything or acted on the way we felt about each other."

James continued to look at him sternly. "I appreciate your honesty. We all knew she had a crush on you when she was a kid, but I guess I thought—and I'm sure everyone else did—she outgrew it. Guess we were wrong." He shook his head. "Don't tell Summer we had this conversation. If she's as fragile right now as you say she is, I don't want to be the cause of upsetting her more." Ethan nodded and watched as James left the room, closing the door behind him.

"Well, one down, only about another dozen or so Montgomerys to go." Ethan collapsed on his bed.

Chapter 12

IF ETHAN THOUGHT IT WAS HARD KEEPING THINGS private with Summer before, it was downright painful now. Knowing that James knew, and not being able to tell Summer was its own form of torture.

They all went back to the hospital that afternoon, and Ethan felt the weight of James's stare. He had to hand it to the man: if he'd used this kind of tactic when he had been a cop, Ethan was sure many a suspect confessed to whatever wrongful deed they'd committed. Summer was oblivious to it all—mainly because she was so nervous about seeing Zach.

"What if he's still mad at me?" she asked softly from her seat in the back of the van. "What if he blames me for this?"

Ethan didn't know what to say and luckily Gabriella spoke up. "Summer, we've been over this. Zach knew the risks going into it. The tour company went over every possible scenario with the guys during their training. I know you and Zach weren't getting along before he left, but I highly doubt he can find a way to pin this on you."

Summer wasn't convinced. "Oh, please... Most days at the office he found ways to blame me for stuff that went wrong in departments I hadn't even worked in yet."

Ethan listened and frowned. Summer was right; it

was something he and Zach had discussed right before he left for the climb.

James was listening too. He didn't want to believe some of the things Ethan had said to him earlier, but as he heard Summer talking, his heart broke a little for her. What the hell had Zach been thinking? Why had he been so hard on her? Shifting in his seat, James turned toward Summer. "Hey," he said, "I don't want to hear you talking like that. Zach isn't going to be mad at you, and if he is, we've all got your back."

She gave a tremulous smile. "I appreciate it, more than you know. Unfortunately, it wouldn't be fair to argue with him right now. After all, he's hardly in a position to defend himself against all of us." She sighed. "If he's upset with me—or worse—then I'll take it. I understand. I really do. Now isn't the time to fight with him. He's got to be scared and angry and in a lot of pain."

To say that James was impressed would be an understatement. Maybe Ethan was right. Again. His sister had matured a lot. The Summer who James remembered was spoiled, more than a little self-centered, and would have done her best to prove she didn't do anything wrong, no matter how the cards were stacked against her. But listening to her now and hearing that not only was she willing to accept the blame, but she was willing to do so even if it were misplaced—well, that spoke volumes. Maybe she wasn't a kid anymore. Maybe she could handle herself. And maybe, just maybe, she could make her own decisions.

Even on the subject of the men she chose to be involved with.

Or man.

Or Ethan.

When the hell was this voyage of self-discovery going to end?

Deciding to get out of his own head, James said to Summer, "We won't fight with him, but we will try to guide him toward the truth."

"But we don't even know the truth yet. Has anyone talked to Mike Rivera? Do we have any more information on what exactly went wrong? We've all been so consumed sitting vigil with Zach and waiting for some sign of his recovery that—I know I can only speak for myself—I forgot to even ask how this happened."

Ethan pulled his phone out of his pocket. "I'm on it." He slid to the far corner of the bench seat and began to talk in hushed tones.

Summer didn't want to listen. She was afraid of what she was going to hear. Her brother still held her hand and she gave his a gentle squeeze. "Thank you."

He looked at her quizzically. "For what?"

"For just being you." She smiled. A genuine, serene smile.

She humbled him. He had a feeling that she wouldn't be thanking him if she knew what had transpired between himself and Ethan earlier. She would probably be more than a little furious with him. Maybe it was a good thing they were keeping it quiet. "I just don't want to hear you beating yourself up, kiddo."

She chuckled. "I'm not a kid anymore, big brother. I think you need to find another nickname for me."

He smiled. Yes, he could see that. It just sucked that it took this situation—and Ethan—to make him see it.

—◦◦◦—

No one was certain what to expect when Dr. Peters led them into Zach's private room—there was anxiety and anticipation on many levels. Summer stayed toward the back of the group, choosing to hide behind Ethan, and waited to see how her brother was going to react toward all of them.

"What's she doing here?" Zach snapped, and Summer's heart sank.

Robert Montgomery stepped close to his son. "Who?"

"Her." He pointed to Gabriella. "What the hell is she doing here?"

Summer had to give her friend credit; if Zach's words or tone hurt her, you'd never have known it. "She's been here since we got word of your accident," Robert said, his tone gentler than he had ever used. "She flew up here with Ethan and Summer."

"And so…what? The company is just running itself?"

"Last I checked, I don't run the company," Gabriella said, her tone dripping sarcasm, and it was enough to shut Zach up.

After that, everyone moved cautiously toward the patient and got their first real look at him. He did his best to answer all of their questions about how he was feeling but quickly became annoyed with the whole thing. Dr. Peters saw it and stepped in.

"I know you're all excited to see Zach and to finally be able to talk to him, but we don't want to wear him out. He's got a long recovery ahead of him." He looked around the room. "Why don't some of you go and grab some coffee and maybe hang out in the waiting area and then switch off with one another, okay?"

Gabriella exited the room first.

William walked over to his nephew and smiled. "It's good to see you awake." He placed a gentle hand on Zach's good shoulder before turning and following Gabriella. Robert stayed where he was. There was no way he was leaving his son just quite yet.

Ethan walked up to the bed and looked down at Zach with a wry grin. "You always were an attention hog."

Zach chuckled. "Yeah, but I must be losing my touch if these are the extremes I have to go to." They laughed at that.

"I'll be back later, man. Do you want anything?"

"To not be in a hospital bed in a freaking near-full body cast would be a good start. Any chance you can help me out?"

Ethan shook his head and held up his hands helplessly with a grin. "I skipped that lesson in the Boy Scouts. You're on your own there."

"Yeah, yeah…that's what they all say." Their easy banter went a long way toward easing everyone's minds. Repeating William's actions, Ethan placed a reassuring hand on Zach's shoulder and walked away.

Summer followed him out the door, her throat clogged with emotion. As much as she wanted to walk over to Zach, to see him up close and touch him, she was so scared that he would turn cold on her just like he had to Gabriella. She wasn't ready to face that yet.

Out in the waiting room, she found her uncle talking to Gabriella quietly in the corner. Summer had no idea why her brother had reacted that way to seeing his assistant, but she knew it had to have hurt Gabriella's feelings. She didn't want to interrupt their conversation though. Turning around, she walked straight into Ethan. "Oh! Sorry. I didn't realize you were right there."

His hands had come up to steady her. "Are you okay? You came out of Zach's room right behind me. Did you even talk to him?"

She shook her head, shame overwhelming her. "Did you hear the way he spoke to her?" She nodded her head in Gabriella's direction. "He has no reason whatsoever to be upset with her and yet he spoke like he hated her. After listening to the two of you bantering back and forth, I didn't want to ruin his good mood." She looked up at him and blushed. "Actually, I didn't want to ruin my mood. If I can avoid him for a little while...if I can just watch him and see he's okay, then maybe..." A tear rolled down her cheek. "Maybe he'll have some time to forgive me."

Unable to stand her sadness and self-doubt any longer, Ethan took her by the hand and led her over to one of the sofas.

"I spoke to Mike." He waited for any kind of reaction from her. When her eyes only seemed to appear more anxious, he continued. "Everyone is situated at different hospitals so that's why he hadn't called. He needed to make the rounds and talk to his guides first, and then to the climbers. He would have come and talked to Zach, but he heard Zach was sedated."

"Was Zach the most injured?"

Ethan shook his head. "There are three others who are in similar condition. Injuries range from cuts and bruises to mild hypothermia, to broken bones and concussions and...spinal injuries."

"Oh God..."

"Summer," he said as he took both of her hands in his and tugged her gently to get her attention. "The storm came out of nowhere, Mike said. They were at a particularly steep part of the mountain with very narrow walking space. It was mountain on one side and a steep drop on the other. Everyone was tied together and they were moving along when a strong gust of wind hit and one of the team members lost their footing and slipped. They were hanging on by a thread and were going to fall for sure when Zach jumped into action to help them. Another gust hit and it became like a chain reaction." He waited for that information to settle in. "It wasn't your fault, Summer. Zach was trying to save someone who was in need, and the weather turned against them. He's got nothing to be angry with you about."

The words filled her with hope. It wasn't her fault! She didn't distract him and cause her brother to make a foolish mistake that, in turn, caused his injuries! She wanted to jump up and high-five someone; she wanted to squeal with joy! She wanted to… "Wait," she said suddenly as all of the joy seemed to slip away. "But he was angry with me before he even left. What if he's still hanging on to that anger?"

Ethan rolled his eyes. "Why are you looking for trouble? I told you he and I talked before he left and he came to realize how hard he'd been on you. Can't you just have a little faith? A little hope he's going to be happy to see you?"

"If I had to go by previous experience…"

"Then don't go by previous experience," he teased, and unable to help himself, he leaned in close and placed a gentle kiss on her forehead. "Forget about what happened before the climb. Let's look at this as a clean slate and hopefully Zach will too. Okay?"

She nodded and then looked across the room to where her uncle and Gabriella were still standing. "I just feel so bad for her. And believe me, I know exactly how she feels."

"Yeah, I'm not sure what that was about, and I'm not sure we'll find out anytime soon." Ethan looked at his watch. "I don't know how long your dad and brothers are going to be in there with him. Do you want anything? Something to drink? A snack?"

Summer shook her head. "I'm going to go over and see how Gabs is doing. Maybe you can talk to Uncle William and get his take on the whole thing." The one Montgomery—other than Summer—Ethan didn't mind talking to. He readily agreed.

Divide and conquer. It was a good tactic, and Summer hoped they'd be victorious in figuring out what was going on. She hated to admit it, but she was beyond relieved she had been spared Zach's wrath. But she felt bad it was at Gabriella's expense.

"Want to grab some fresh air?" Summer asked Gabriella.

Gabriella seemed to welcome the distraction, and with a murmured thanks to William, the two of them headed toward the elevators.

They rode down in silence and walked to the cafeteria for some hot chocolate.

And to their bench outside the hospital entrance.

"William saw Ethan kiss you," Gabriella said once they were seated.

"What? When?"

"Just now. Up in the waiting room."

Crap. "What did he say?"

"Nothing at first. He just sort of raised his eyebrows and smirked."

"Oh great," Summer groaned.

"I told him you were upset because you thought Zach was going to blame you for the accident and Ethan was probably just trying to make you feel better. Like a surrogate big brother."

"Do you think he bought it?"

Gabriella turned toward her with a bland expression. "Are you kidding me? You know what your uncle's hobby is, right?"

"The whole matchmaking thing?" Gabriella nodded. "Oh, please…he did that with his own sons. He's not trying to do that anymore—especially not with us."

"Are you sure about that? I've heard him taking credit for getting Ryder and Casey back together as well as James and Selena. You think he's not watching you and Ethan and getting ideas?"

As much as Summer wanted to blow off the idea, it did have merit. If her uncle got on board with setting her up with Ethan, then she'd have a family ally on her side. Hmm…

"I suppose worse things could happen," Summer said dismissively and took a sip of her hot chocolate.

"Yeah, like your brother could snap at you and make you feel like a complete outcast in front of everyone."

"My brother is a jerk. I'm so sorry, Gabs. I don't know what he was thinking."

"That I'm not supposed to be here. That I'm just an employee and should be sitting at my desk like a good girl. That I shouldn't have a life or any interests outside of work."

Okay, where did this come from? Summer had to wonder. "He's probably just overwhelmed and he knows he can count on you to keep things running smoothly when he's not around."

Gabriella shrugged. "Maybe. He just didn't have to be so hateful about it."

"Are you kidding me? Are you just meeting my brother? Have you forgotten all of the hateful things he said to me since I arrived in Portland?"

"That's different. He doesn't hate you; he just felt like your family was trying to keep tabs on him by making him babysit you."

"You know, I really hate that everyone keeps saying that, like I'm some sort of child who needs to be looked after."

"It doesn't matter how old you are, Summer. To them, you'll always be their baby sister. It's kind of sweet."

"Sure. When it's not insulting."

They sat in amicable silence for a long time until Summer's phone beeped. Pulling it out of her purse, she saw she had a text from Ryder. Putting her phone back, she took one last sip of her drink and stood. "Time to face the music."

Gabriella looked at her quizzically. "Excuse me?"

"We've been summoned up to his lordship's room. Looks like we both get to hold court with him."

"It's like being called into the principal's office. Only worse." She stood and together they walked back into the building.

"At least we get to do it together, right?" Summer said hopefully, but Gabriella walked silently beside her.

And all the way up in the elevator.

And down the hall.

They bypassed the waiting area and stood in front of the door to Zach's room. "Okay, this is ridiculous," Summer said as she turned to face Gabriella. "We don't need to be afraid of him. We need to have compassion and understanding because he's hurt and in pain. So let's just go in there and visit with him like he didn't just act like a complete ass to you and hasn't acted like one to me for the last month or so. Deal?"

The only acknowledgment was a quick nod of Gabriella's head as she pushed open the door. Summer was two steps behind her and came to an abrupt halt when she realized they were well and truly alone with Zach. Neither wanted to move any farther into the room for fear of what he was going to say.

As if sensing their wariness, Zach rolled his eyes. "Seriously? I can barely move a muscle on my own. I think you're safe to come closer than ten feet away." Summer moved first, and as soon as she got next to the bed, she burst into tears and leaned down to gently hug him. His one good arm came up around her and hugged her. He felt the sobs wrack her body and knew he was responsible for them. "Hey, squirt, come on. Don't cry," he said softly.

Summer lifted her head and looked at him as if he were crazy. He hadn't used any form of endearment for her in a long time. Years, actually.

"I'm sorry. I've been a real bastard to you since you showed up in Portland, and that wasn't fair to you. I don't have an excuse for my behavior." He tried to shrug, but it caused him to jerk with pain. "Dammit. I didn't realize how hard on you I was being. Ethan got me to think about that, and all I can say is it wasn't anything you did, Summer; it was all me. Can you forgive me?"

In a million years she had never thought this would be the conversation they'd be having right now. She straightened and wiped away her tears. "Of course I forgive you, you big jerk," she said with a watery smile. "You're my brother and I love you. I couldn't stand to think that you hated me or you didn't want me around."

He chuckled and then winced. And cursed. "I still don't think Montgomerys is your future, but I'm glad you're here. And there. In Portland," he stammered. "You know what I mean. We all just want you to be happy, and I don't want you to feel pressured to stay in Portland or at the company. You need to do what makes you happy. And I'm sure it's something a little more... creative, shall we say, than what we do."

She immediately wanted to argue with him, to remind him she didn't need to be doing something creative because it didn't define her. But now wasn't the time. He was making the effort to be a good guy, and she wasn't going to ruin the moment. They could discuss her future with the company another time.

Pulling up a chair beside him, she asked how he was feeling and found that she was just enjoying listening to the sound of his voice. This was the brother she remembered; this was the brother she enjoyed spending time with. The man she had been working with did not resemble this in any way, shape, or form. She listened to him talk about the physical pain he was feeling, and her heart broke as he spoke about the fall itself. What he had gone through was nothing short of terrifying, and Summer had never been more grateful for anything in her life than Zach being able to sit here now—even though he was a bit battered and broken—and talk about it. She had no idea what she would have done if they'd lost him.

When he had exhausted his story, he looked beyond Summer to Gabriella. She had stayed rooted to the spot two feet inside the room the entire time Zach and Summer had talked and reconciled. His eyes narrowed for a moment. "Who's handling things back at the office?" he said curtly.

"Bob Davis is running the day-to-day operations. Ethan calls him at least three times a day to check in."

"And who is covering your work?"

"My assistant Carolyn. With you out of the office, her workload isn't quite as intense. She handled the rescheduling of appointments and is keeping everything else up-to-date so I won't be behind when I get home. If you'll remember, it was your decision for me to take my vacation time while you were away. I'm not missing anything important. I talk to her almost daily, so getting up to speed won't be a problem when I get back."

"You should probably look into doing that. Going home," he said for clarification.

Gabriella stood a little taller as she walked closer to his bed. "I probably should. Now that we've confirmed that you're alive and on the mend, there's no reason for me to be here."

"There never was," he said with a hard edge to his voice. "You would have been more useful back in Portland, making sure everything is running the way it needs to. Bob is a good guy and he has a good work ethic, but he doesn't know everything there is to know about running the company."

"Neither do I," Gabriella retorted. "After all, I'm just the hired help too."

Zach quirked a brow at her tone. "You work with me every day. You know what needs to be done before I even have to say it. That's why you need to be back there."

Without another word, Gabriella nodded, turned on her heel, and walked out the door. Summer sat with her jaw practically on the floor. Geez, if she thought Zach had been hard on her before, it was nothing compared to what she'd just witnessed. She looked over at him and saw he was staring at the closed door. Clearing her throat, she carefully said, "What was that about?"

As if coming out of a trance, Zach turned to her. "What?"

"With Gabriella. You were a little hard on her. She was very concerned about you, and having her here with all of us was extremely helpful. She handled all of the transportation and hotel reservations. I don't know how she keeps everything straight in her mind, but she is scary organized."

"Yeah," he said wearily. He yawned and badly wanted to stretch, but the casts and pins and bandages prevented it.

Summer stood and leaned down and placed a kiss on his cheek. "You should rest."

"I've been resting for days. I want to get out of this damn bed."

She laughed. "I was wondering how long it would be before you started complaining. We should have placed bets."

"You try having to stay in this position for any period of time and tell me you wouldn't be chomping at the bit to get out of it."

"You've got me there." She smiled down at him and wished there was something she could do to comfort him. The door opened behind them and Ethan walked in. He was placing his phone in his pocket, and Summer smirked at him. "How many times have you been told you're not allowed to use your cell phone in here?"

He made a face at her. "It was a work emergency. Sue me."

"Emergency?" Zach asked, perking up. "What's going on?"

Ethan realized his mistake immediately. They were supposed to be keeping Zach calm and here he was talking about work. Real smooth. "It's…it's nothing. Really. Bob's got it all under control." Zach shot him a look of disbelief, and Ethan began to squirm under his scrutiny. "What?"

"Look, I may have hit my head when I fell, but I'm not a moron. Something's wrong. What is it?"

Walking across the room, Ethan stood next to the bed and figured he'd better just tell Zach what was going on or risk agitating him more. "Morrison wants to pull out of contract negotiations."

"What?" Zach roared and then cursed when he

couldn't move. "Why? This was supposed to be a done deal!"

"Word's gotten out about your accident and how you'll be out of commission for a while, and Morrison's feeling squirrelly. Bob reassured him nothing was going to change, and you'd be back at the helm in no time, but our competitors are already swooping in and trying to lure customers away."

"Son of a bitch," Zach muttered. "Are you going to talk to Morrison?"

"I've just left him about half a dozen messages. It seems he doesn't want to talk. He's agreed to meet with Bob before completely pulling out, but I don't think it's going to do any good."

"Then you've got to go and meet with him," Zach said firmly. "Go back to the hotel, pack, and make sure he doesn't leave."

"I can't," Ethan protested.

"Why the hell not?"

Why did Zach always feel the need to complicate everything and argue? Ethan wondered. "Look, don't get pissed but…your father was standing right there when I got the call and he wants to arrange a conference call with Morrison from here. This way we can all talk to him and try to calm him down. It seems like one of his biggest gripes is he wants to deal with a Montgomery specifically. I can go there, but I'm not a Montgomery."

"I'll go," Summer said diplomatically. "You all stay here and I'll go back to Portland and sit with him and hold his hand if need be while he talks to you." There were any number of reactions she was expecting— thankfulness, relief, gratitude—but what she got was laughter. And she wasn't sure who was laughing more—her brother or Ethan. "What's so funny?"

Zach looked at her like she had sprouted a second head and then turned to Ethan. "Do you believe her? One month in the company playing Debbie-Do-Gooder and she thinks sitting down with a corporate giant like Morrison is her thing!" He laughed until he was almost crying in pain.

Ethan shook his head and tried to rein in his laughter. He placed a hand on Summer's arm and patted it. "Summer, you're out of your league here. A guy like Morrison is not someone you can handle. You can't bake him cookies or teach his daughter to dance. He'll take one look at you and definitely run from us."

She was fuming. Not only were they unwilling to even consider taking her seriously, but they were out-and-out making fun of her for it. Summer might not know a lot about the corporate world—or love, apparently—but she knew it shouldn't be like this.

An idea began to form in her mind. As she glared at the two men beside her, she decided to play it cool. "I guess you're right. You know me, I tend to jump in without thinking." She put her all into a fake laugh and was relieved when they seemed to believe her. "I'm sure he would have appreciated the cookies, but I know that's not the image you want for Montgomerys. Sorry." Her smile was bright and her tone was light and breezy. She glanced at her watch before leaning over and kissing Zach on the forehead.

"I'll let you two big shots talk business. I'm going to go and check on Gabriella. I'll see you both later!" With a smile and a wave, she flounced out the door and ducked into the first room she could find and dialed Gabriella's number. Luckily she answered right away. "Where are you ?"

"Downstairs waiting for a cab."

"Don't leave without me. I'm on my way down."

"Wait, why?"

"I'll explain on the way." She disconnected and slinked out of the room and down the hall without any of her family members seeing her. Her heart was hammering in her chest, and she didn't take an easy breath until she was on the main floor and racing toward the exit.

She stepped outside just as Gabriella's cab was pulling up. Stepping up beside her, Summer looked up at Gabriella's confused face. "You and I are about to show these jackasses what we're made of."

She didn't need to know the details. All Gabriella knew was whatever Summer had planned, she was one hundred percent on board.

Chapter 13

"I'M NOT SURE WE SHOULD HAVE TAKEN THE COMPANY jet," Gabriella said two hours later as the plane lifted off the runway.

"Oh, hush. It was just sitting there not being used, and Mark knows he has to come right back after we land in Portland. After he gets some sleep, of course."

"Of course," Gabriella parroted, although she still wasn't sure what they were doing was right. She shifted in her seat until she was facing Summer. "So tell me again how this is all going to work?"

"I think it's cute how you remember every little thing everyone else tells you, and you're choosing now to have memory issues."

"Okay, let's just say I think it's not going to go as smoothly as you do."

"Oh, ye of little faith," Summer said with a confident smile. "Here's the deal—you've already called Bob and told him Ethan and my father cannot be disturbed because they are in meetings with Zach's doctors, right?" Gabriella nodded. "Okay, once Mark gives us the green light, we are going to call Bob and tell him I am on my way back to Portland and to set up a meeting with this Morrison guy. Bob will be none the wiser because—let's face it—he's kind of out of his element already. He's going to be so grateful someone is coming to take over this mess that he's not going to question which Montgomery is there to do it."

"Yes, but can you do this?" Gabriella asked cautiously. "I mean, I know you are an extremely talented woman, Summer, and you've yet to find anything in the company you can't do but...let's be realistic. Zach has been throwing you table scraps. He hasn't let you get your hands on anything major yet. What if you go through all of this and Morrison still walks away?"

"What if we go through all of this and Morrison stays?" she countered.

There always was that possibility, but Gabriella still had her doubts. "You know your entire family—and Ethan—are going to freak out when they realize what you've done, right?"

"They're lucky I didn't freak out in the hospital. I mean, it's one thing if they all think I'm some sort of brainless twit; it's another to pretty much say it right to my face."

Hard to argue that logic.

Mark's voice came over the intercom to tell them they had reached cruising altitude and were free to use their phones and electronic devices. Summer looked anxiously at Gabriella. "Do you want to call the office or should I?"

"I'll do it. It will seem more official if it comes from me," Gabriella said. "No offense."

"None taken. Are you kidding me? If they get the call from the company president's executive assistant, I'm sure he'll take it seriously. You're an evil genius." She smiled conspiratorially. "By the time we're done, I think we will both be owed apologies. From everyone."

Gabriella had a feeling the great Zachary Montgomery didn't apologize to mere employees. Family, yes. Employees, no. With a steadying breath, she pulled out her phone. "And we're sure about this? You really have no idea what the exact problem is with Morrison."

"Listen," Summer began, "I know everyone looks at my kooky résumé and thinks that I'm only into fluff jobs. What they all choose to ignore is my psychology major in college, my year of veterinary school—"

"Last I checked, Morrison was a human."

"Not funny," Summer chimed. "What I'm saying is I had to take a lot of business and sociology and psych classes. I know a lot about dealing with people, and besides that, I am a people person. You've seen the way I've been with everyone in the office. I know how to listen, decipher what's wrong, and get a solution. With guys like Morrison—from the little I gleaned from Ethan and Zach's conversation—a lot of times it's about ego. He's upset Zach is unavailable, and now he feels like he's not important enough to warrant time with the president of the company." She rolled her eyes. "So stupid, really. It may only take a few minutes of making this guy feel like there is no one in the world more important than he is to make him not only change his mind, but agree to do even more business with Montgomerys."

Gabriella frowned. "It can't be that easy."

"Why not? Men always make everything more difficult than it needs to be. Trust me. I have three brothers and about a hundred male cousins. I know what I'm talking about. And even if I didn't, just dealing with Ethan the last couple of weeks is enough to prove my point."

"You know you're going to have to deal with him

eventually, Summer. I know you're upset and running was the way you felt you needed to go, but I'm sure he's going to be upset too."

"Well, then he can join the club. I'm upset he laughed at me. I'm upset he didn't defend me. I'm upset he wouldn't go near me whenever my father or brothers were around. I'm upset it was okay to sneak me in and out of his room! He can take his pick."

"Okay, okay, down girl." Gabriella laughed. "I'm on your side. I was just pointing out the obvious. How long do you think it will take for them to realize that we're gone?"

Summer looked at her watch. "Well, they all know you left the hospital and I went to go check on you, so they're not going to question anything. They may call the hotel when they're heading to dinner to see if we want to join them, but if we don't answer, they'll think we're pouting." Leaning back against her seat, she considered her options. "Or we could answer and make it seem like we're out on our own, maybe going to see a movie…something that will plausibly have us out of the hotel until late."

"That's fine until Ethan's sitting in his room waiting for his nightly booty call. When you're a no-show, and he thinks that we're out on the town, he's going to think something happened to us and get everyone all freaked out."

"Hmm…I hadn't thought of that," she muttered. "Okay, so then we go with the silent treatment and they'll think we're pouting. By the time they leave the hospital tonight and get back to the hotel, they'll come to the room and when we don't answer, they'll possibly contact the front desk and concierge and then they'll find out we've checked out."

"And it will be too late for them to do anything because we'll already be back in Portland," Gabriella concluded. "It will be too late for Mark to get back there tonight, and if we play this right, we can have a meeting with Morrison first thing in the morning and be done with it before Ethan or your father can get back." She glanced at Summer and smiled. "If this actually works, it will be a stroke of genius."

"If this actually works, I should firmly secure my place in this family and have everyone stop treating me like I'm a child."

Gabriella waved her off. "Not going to happen. You are the baby of the family and the only girl."

"Great."

"But," she added hopefully, "now they'll see you can also take care of yourself."

"That's the dream."

Standing, Gabriella went to the galley and got them each a beverage. She came back and handed a can of soda to Summer. "And where do you think this will all land with Ethan?"

"I wish I knew," Summer said. "As much as I want to be with him, I don't think I can be with someone who doesn't defend me. Who doesn't believe in me."

"Maybe he was just doing it for Zach's sake."

Summer shook her head. "That would make it even worse. I know he defended me before to my brother; right before the climb I know Ethan did his best to make Zach understand where I was coming from. No, today was different. It was hurtful."

Gabriella nudged Summer's knee. "Hey," she said softly. "You know he's in an awkward position with your family. Maybe you just need to cut him a little slack on this."

"No," Summer replied just as softly. "If Ethan was really serious about me, about us, about our future, he would have been a little bit kinder with his words—and actions. It breaks my heart because it tells me he's not the man I thought he was."

"Do you love him?"

Sadness filled Summer's eyes as she nodded her head. "Always. I always have and I'm sure I always will. But I need someone who is going to put me first and to hell with the consequences." She shrugged. "I know my family would have given us a hard time, but it would have happened and then everyone would have moved on. Ethan is so stuck on playing it safe and not upsetting anyone that he never took into account how he was hurting me." She paused and took a steadying breath.

Unable to help herself, Gabriella put her drink down and pulled Summer into her embrace. "I am so sorry, sweetie. I really thought the two of you were going to get it together. When Ethan pestered me to tell him where you had gone off to when you went to the springs, I was secretly hoping the two of you would hook up."

Summer pulled back. "You were?"

She nodded. "It was so obvious you were both into each other. And I knew if it weren't for your brother, you would have acted on it. I thought, with a little nudge in the right direction, you'd finally get the chance to explore the chemistry you had." She pulled Summer back in and hugged her tight. "I'm so sorry."

"Me too."

After a few minutes, they broke apart and got comfortable in their seats. Gabriella remembered she still had a call to make. "I better get Bob on the phone and get him busy. If we want this to go according to plan, he'll need to get Morrison into the office first thing in the morning. I'll tell him to get all of the information you're going to need organized and have it faxed over to your place. Do you have a fax machine there?"

"No. Ask him to scan it and email it to me. This way I'll have it on the computer, and if he gets it out fast enough, I may even be able to start looking at it while we're here on the plane, on my phone."

"Good idea." Gabriella sat up straight in her seat and then did what she did best. In her most authoritative executive-assistant tone, she barked out her orders to poor Bob Davis and made sure to remind him it was up to him to make this happen—or Zach would not be pleased. She actually felt a little guilty for doing it, but she had worked for Zach long enough to know exactly how to speak to some of the executives to get them to do what was needed.

Once she hung up with Bob, she placed a second call. Summer looked over at her quizzically. "Even though you are a woman on a mission, you are going to want your puppy home with you tonight."

"Oh my goodness! Yes! Thank you for thinking of that!"

Gabriella smiled. "Hey, it's—"

"What you do," Summer finished for her. "I know, I know, and I am so thankful for it." She curled her feet up under her and faced Gabriella. "I hate that I had to leave

Maylene for so long. Do you think she's going to even remember me? She's just a baby!"

"Um, Summer, she's a puppy, not a human. And I'm sure she'll remember you. She may be a little bit spiteful for a few days once you get her home, but then the two of you will bounce right back into your old routine."

"Spiteful, huh?" She frowned. "I hadn't thought of that."

"If I were you, I'd be hiding my shoes."

Summer's eyes widened.

"And your pillows."

That didn't sound good.

"And pretty much anything that means anything to you."

"I guess we'll have to go back to kennel training for a little while, until I'm settled in back home," Summer said.

"So you're planning on staying in Portland? Even after all of this?"

Summer shrugged. "I don't know. It's all too much to think about. I want to stay; I really do like it there. But if things don't work between me and Ethan, I don't think I can. Then I'll probably head back to North Carolina and maybe see about working for James or Ryder or one of my cousins."

"I would hate to see you go, Summer. You're my best friend," Gabriella said quietly. "Actually, you're the only real friend I have."

It was hard to see a woman who seemed so confident and so outgoing admit she was alone. Of all the people in Portland who mattered to Summer, Gabriella was the one she would miss the most. She'd miss her brother, but she knew she'd still see him and talk to him all the time. She would definitely miss Ethan, but she knew in time it would be for the best.

No, she would genuinely miss Gabriella the most because she was a true friend and ally. If it hadn't been for her, Summer didn't know how she would have survived any of this. "You could always come with me," she suggested. "I'm sure you've had enough of my brother, and maybe you could use a fresh start too."

"Don't tempt me. After his behavior earlier, he's lucky I didn't break the rest of his bones."

Summer laughed. "Nah. The way to go would have been to break his jaw so he couldn't speak. It would have gotten the message across better than anything else."

Now Gabriella was laughing too. "I'll have to remember that for next time."

"Guys," James said as he walked into his brother's hospital room, "I think we have a problem." Zach, Robert, William, and Ethan all turned and looked at him expectantly.

"What's the matter?" Robert asked.

"I can't get either Summer or Gabriella on the phone."

Robert waved him off. "Oh, they're just a little upset. They probably went off to get their nails done or their hair done or they've gone shopping. Nothing to worry about. Apparently your brother here upset them both pretty good,"

James couldn't quite put his finger on it, but he didn't

think it was quite that simple. "Then I could see them not answering the phone for him, but why won't they take my calls?"

"Guilty by association," Zach said from his bed with a chuckle. His pain medication was kicking in, and everything was mildly amusing to him.

Everyone laughed and for a moment, it was okay to forget the girls were upset because it was a relief to see Zach doing all right and returning to his normal self. When everyone quieted down, James said, "Well, I was going to see if they wanted to meet us for dinner so we could let Zach get some sleep."

"We'll try again in a little while," Ryder said. "Hell, we'll keep calling them from all of our phones. They're bound to get annoyed eventually and answer just so we'll leave them alone. Are we sure their phones are on?"

"They didn't go directly to voice mail." James paused and thought for a moment. "Maybe I'll call Selena and ask her to call."

"Oh, for crying out loud," Robert huffed. "Sometimes you still think too much like a cop. They're pissed off right now. You know how women get. Just let them have their time to pout. If they don't join us for dinner, then don't worry about it. By tomorrow, everything will be fine and back to normal. They'll join us for breakfast, Gabriella will do her daily check-in with the office and get us an update, and—"

"Gabriella needs to be back at the office," Zach snapped. "I don't want her here. Don't bring her to breakfast, don't have her making calls. Send her back to Portland where she belongs. At her desk." Four pairs of stunned eyes looked back at him. Zach was looking at the IV in his hand and wasn't aware of all of the glances being exchanged around him.

Ethan cleared his throat. "I'll…um…I'll talk to her in the morning." Zach nodded slowly at his words. "Listen, buddy, why don't you get some sleep? This has been a long day for you, I'm sure. We're gonna go, and we'll plan on seeing you in the morning, okay?"

"Without Gabriella, right?" Zach asked, his eyes beginning to droop, his voice slurring.

Why argue? Ethan thought. "Without Gabriella. Sure." He reached out and patted Zach's good shoulder and wished him a good night before stepping away from the bed. He walked to the door and watched as the others did the same, and then they all walked out of the room single file.

Out in the hall, they all sort of stopped and looked at one another. "What the hell was that about?" Ryder asked. "Gabriella has been his assistant for years. Since when has he been so hostile toward her?"

Ethan shook his head. "I have no idea. I only noticed something was off a couple of days before he left for the climb. He snapped at her and she snapped back. It wasn't anything dramatic enough for him to still be in a snit over."

"What was it about?" William asked.

"Zach wanted to know where Summer was, and Gabriella refused to tell him." He stopped and thought about it. "Actually, it was more like Zach wanted her to get Summer on the phone, and she refused. She said that it was a family problem, not a work one, and she wasn't going to get involved."

"Makes sense," William said.

"Not to Zach," Ethan said as they all began to walk toward the elevator. "In his mind, when he asks—or tells—her to do something, she should do it. He's got a little bit of tyrant in him, and he really didn't like her telling him no."

No one commented and when they stepped into the elevator, Ethan figured the subject was over.

"Do you think she'll leave?" William asked.

"Alaska or Montgomerys?"

William chuckled. "Take your pick."

"She doesn't scare easily. I've watched her handle Zach for years, and his foul moods never had her walking toward the door." He leaned against the elevator wall. "I think she'll probably head back to Portland. There's no point in her being here anymore anyway. We know Zach is safe and he's getting medical attention. If he is openly hostile toward her, she won't want to stick around and risk hindering his recovery. As for leaving Montgomerys? I don't see it happening. She's a company girl, and I think she likes the challenge of working with someone like Zach—no matter how much he ticks her off."

"Maybe now that he's going to be incapacitated for a while he'll learn to appreciate her a little more," William said slyly.

"Oh no," Ryder mumbled.

"What? What's the matter?" James asked.

"I can just see the wheels in his head turning now." He nodded toward his uncle. "Don't even go there. Zach isn't going to fall in line with your matchmaking schemes, so just forget about it."

"I don't know what you're talking about," William said, feigning innocence.

"Oh, please. We all know exactly what you're think-ing. You're thinking Zach and Gabriella will work out as a couple—especially in the right circumstances." Ryder snorted with laughter. "If you think that's going to happen, then you really don't know Zach. If he were interested in Gabriella, he would have acted on it by now. And if you're itching to play matchmaker so badly, work on Ethan here. He's been sullen and pouty and damn-near sighing with loneliness."

"Hey!" Ethan interrupted, and James made a choked sound in the corner.

"He may not be blood related, but he's practically family. Find someone for *him*!" Ryder said.

William shook his head and chuckled at how cute and clever his nephews all thought they were. If only they knew. "First of all, I would not even dream of setting Gabriella up with Zach. All I'm saying is maybe a little time apart will repair their working relationship." He shrugged. "I think Zach is going to need somebody who is outdoorsy and adventurous just like he is. And from what I can tell, that is not Gabriella." He made a face as if even the thought of the two of them together was offensive. "Besides, Zach is going to be busy getting better and getting rehabilitated for a good six months or so. He's safe from anything I might have planned."

"Well, good," Ryder said, seemingly relieved. "The last thing he needs right now is you springing potential wives on him."

"You make it sound like it's a bad thing, and yet you and James and my boys are all happily married now. Thanks to me."

They all laughed. "You keep saying that, old man,"

Ryder said with a laugh, "but I keep telling you Casey and I were already on the right path. You had nothing to do with it. Same with James and Selena."

"And as for our boy Ethan here," William said with a twinkle in his eye, "I'll have to think on that one. I have a feeling all of the pouting and sighing you've noticed means he's already found someone. And doesn't quite know it yet."

Robert and Ryder laughed. Ethan broke out in a sweat while James glared at him. "I think you'll just have to deal with the fact that this branch of the Montgomerys isn't as easy to manipulate as yours, Uncle William," Ryder said.

William smiled serenely as the elevator doors opened on the main floor. "Whatever you say," he said pleasantly and stepped out into the lobby.

It was after eleven and Ethan was getting worried. He knew Summer had been upset earlier when she'd left Zach's room. It didn't take a rocket scientist to figure it out. Maybe he shouldn't have laughed; maybe he should have just kept his damn mouth shut and let her hash it out with her brother rather than saying anything at all. But who could really blame him? The idea of Summer going to fix a multimillion-dollar deal with someone like Morrison was almost too comical even to consider.

He looked at the clock again. She was normally here by now. He went to sit down on the bed. Okay, so maybe she was more than a little upset and she was punishing him with the cold shoulder. Not that he didn't deserve it.

The thought of spending the night alone, however, was completely unappealing.

Should he go and apologize? Should he take the chance of being discovered and walk across the hall and try to make things right? Ethan thought about how long he'd been back in the room and realized he'd been listening for any signs of life from across the hall and hadn't heard a sound. Not that he could normally hear anything, but if the girls had gone out as Robert had suggested, maybe he would have heard their return.

With a sigh, he reached for the TV remote and turned it on. Maybe he should just let it be for tonight. With any luck, things would look clearer in the morning, and he could figure out a way to talk to Gabriella and convince her it was for the best for her to go back to Portland and then convince Summer he didn't mean to act like such a jerk earlier.

He wasn't sure which one was going to be the harder sell.

He was tired. Tired of trying to make everyone happy except himself. Ethan tossed the remote aside, stacked his hands behind his head, and stared at the ceiling. Life had gotten too damn complicated and he wasn't sure what he had to do to get it back on track. He thought he was going in the right direction when he stood his ground with Zach and backed out of going on the climb.

And then he found Summer in Alaska.

So the Montgomerys were going to be upset about him and Summer? So what! He'd known them long enough to know it didn't take much to get them worked up, but also that they didn't hold grudges for long. So what was he worrying so much about? Why was he taking the coward's way out and making excuses?

And as for trying to protect Summer, hadn't he witnessed her bravery when she stood up to her father just a few days ago? At first he had been shocked that she was being so vocal and defiant, and then he could do nothing but stand there in awe of her.

Time and time again, Summer had proven to be strong, confident…brave. Ethan thought he had those qualities too, but the last few weeks had shown him how wrong he was. What good was it to think you were all of those things if, when it came time to actually prove it, you clammed up and took the easy way out? Self-loathing filled him. This was not the man he wanted to be—not the man he had been raised to be.

With a renewed sense of purpose, Ethan knew what he had to do. He would let matters settle for tonight but come tomorrow, things were going to be different. Tomorrow he would get up and be the man he always thought he was—the man he should be—and not worry about what everyone else was thinking or what they wanted.

He wanted to be with Summer.

He was in love with Summer, and he was tired of hiding that fact and lying to everyone—including himself.

When morning came and it was time to walk down to breakfast, he was going to walk into that dining room hand in hand with her and deal with whatever the consequences were—no matter what anyone had to say. Ethan Reed was many things. And he refused to list "being a coward" as one of them.

And he was tired of not claiming the woman he loved.

He was almost too excited to sleep. Right now he wanted to go to Summer's room and bang on the door until she answered and tell her that he was in love with her and wanted to spend the rest of his life with her. He wasn't foolish enough to believe it would be that easy to win her over—he had been a colossal jackass earlier—but Ethan was confident in what they felt for one another.

If he had to beg and grovel, then he would. Hell, he'd even do it in front of Gabriella just to prove that he wasn't afraid, and then he'd do it all again tomorrow in front of her family just to reinforce his sincerity. She'd have to believe him then.

As he relaxed back on the bed, a smile crossed his face as excitement coursed through him. He'd been on many adventures in his life and he was used to the anticipation that went along with them. But this? Getting ready to finally tell Summer how he felt? He had a feeling this was the greatest adventure he had ever embarked on, and he couldn't wait to get started.

Chapter 14

THE NEXT MORNING, ETHAN SPRANG OUT OF BED WITH a sense of purpose. All night he had dreamed of this moment, and he quickly went about getting ready so he could finally look at Summer, touch Summer, and tell her he loved her.

Now, standing in the hallway, Ethan looked at the strange man standing in a bathrobe and profusely apologized. *What the hell?* Before he could ask who he was and what he was doing in Summer and Gabriella's room, the other occupant in the room—also not Summer or Gabriella—appeared and begged the man to come back to bed. The man shut the door and Ethan immediately jumped into action.

Running down the hall, he punched the down button for the elevator but immediately decided it was taking too long. Turning, he quickly sprinted to the stairwell. He was breathless by the time he reached the lobby, but he was frantic. Slamming his hands down on the concierge counter, he demanded to speak to someone in charge.

"Is there something I can help you with, Mr. Reed?" the impeccably dressed gentleman behind the counter asked with a serene smile.

"Miss Montgomery and Miss Martine? Do you know where they are?"

The man stepped over to his computer and typed for

several seconds. "It appears they checked out yesterday afternoon, sir. If you'd like, I can inquire if anyone knows where they were heading to."

Dread lay heavy in Ethan's gut. This was not good. "That won't be necessary," he said as he tried to catch his breath. How the hell was he supposed to tell Summer how he felt if she wasn't here? He needed to say it to her face, for her to see in his eyes that he was serious. He wanted a life with her.

Over his shoulder he heard voices and immediately recognized them as the Montgomerys. They were obviously heading to the dining room for breakfast. Ryder spotted him first. "Ethan? Is everything okay? You look a little out of sorts."

"Summer and Gabriella are gone," he blurted out. "They checked out yesterday afternoon. I have no idea where they are." His head dropped, and he felt defeated. Before he could say anything else, James had him by the throat up against the wall.

"You son of a bitch!" he sneered. "What did you do to her? What did you do to make her leave?"

Ryder jumped in and pulled James away. "What the hell are you talking about? What's going on?" By now Robert and William had joined them and watched as James struggled in his brother's grip. "James! Tell me what's going on!"

"Him!" he shouted and pointed at Ethan. "Summer's gone and it's his fault!"

Ryder looked over at Ethan. "Ethan? What is he talking about? Why would my sister leave because of you?"

James wouldn't let him answer. "He's been sleeping with her! Dammit, I knew I should have put a stop to it. I knew I should have kicked your ass the other day! I knew you were going to hurt her!" He pulled out of Ryder's grasp. "I never should have trusted you!"

"Wait a minute," Robert said as he came to stand in the middle of the melee. He turned to Ethan. "Is this true? Are you sleeping with my daughter?" His eyes narrowed at Ethan, and he used his most intimidating glare in hopes of scaring the truth out of him.

"I'm in love with her," Ethan said evenly. "I'm in love with your daughter, sir. I have been for a long time. We didn't want to say anything right away because of everything that was going on with Zach. We didn't want to upset anyone."

"You," James spat. "*You* didn't want to tell anyone because you knew we'd all tell you to back the hell off."

Robert ignored his son's rantings and kept his attention on Ethan. "What did you do to make her leave? Did you break things off with her?"

Ethan shook his head. "No. I would never do that." He paused. "Zach and I were discussing an issue back at the office in front of Summer, and she volunteered to go back to Portland to meet with the client." His shoulders slouched. "We, um…we kind of laughed at her. We accused her of not knowing what she was talking about and joked about her job within the company."

"I see." Robert turned to James. "And you knew about this? About this relationship between Ethan and your sister?"

James nodded. "I should have stopped it. I confronted Ethan, but I should have gone to Summer and made her see reason. Now she's off somewhere, hurting most likely, and it's all his fault."

Robert then turned to Ryder. "How about you? Did you know about this?"

Ryder shook his head and held up his hands. "This is all brand-new information to me."

Lastly, he turned to his brother and noticed the smirk on his face. "Do I even need to ask?"

William shrugged. "I plead the fifth."

"Oh, come on now. You're honestly going to stand there and not take credit for any of this? Are you telling me that you haven't been orchestrating this since we first thought to send Summer to Portland?"

"Well…maybe."

"That's what I thought." With more annoyance than anything else, Robert turned to Ethan, his glare no less intimidating than it was a minute ago. "When was the last time you spoke to Summer?"

"When she was in Zach's room yesterday. She left, saying she was going to check on Gabriella. I didn't think anything of it. She was smiling and even laughed along with us. I had no idea she was upset. Then, when she didn't answer any of our calls last night…"

"Or show up at your room," James said snidely.

Ethan sighed. "Or show up at my room, I thought maybe she was still pouting about what had happened. I didn't even consider the possibility that she had left."

"Then you have no idea where she might be?"

Ethan shook his head.

"Wait a minute, didn't Zach tell Gabriella to go back to Portland?" Ryder asked. "Maybe Summer decided to go with her. That would be my first guess."

For a long moment, Robert considered it and then closed his eyes wearily and reached up to rub his temples. "If she's as hardheaded as the rest of us, I'd say she not only went back to Portland, but she's moving ahead with meeting this client you laughed at her about." Reaching for his phone, he called his pilot to confirm his suspicions. He walked away while he talked.

Ryder stepped up to Ethan and stared him in the eye. "You've got a lot of nerve, you know that, right?"

Ethan nodded.

"If Summer is hurt, if she's upset because of you, there won't be anyplace you'll be able to hide where we won't find you."

Ethan nodded again. "If she is hurt and upset over me, then I won't hide. I'll take whatever you think I deserve because I'll deserve it all and more." His heart ached at the thought of Summer leaving because of him. "I never wanted to hurt her. I never intended things to go this far."

"Yeah, well…they did," Ryder said before turning and walking over to where his father was still speaking on the phone.

Though he was certain James was going to come back over and threaten him some more, Ethan was surprised to see him walk over to his father and brother. Ethan followed his progress across the lobby and when he turned back, William was standing right in front of him. He braced himself for the lecture.

"I hope you're not going to let them intimidate and badger you like that all the time," William remarked.

Confusion crossed Ethan's face.

"I mean, you know they're going to try to throw their weight around and make you feel inferior. Don't let them. Summer deserves more from the man she loves."

Ethan shook his head. "How can you be so sure she loves me?"

William placed a hand on Ethan's shoulder and gave it a reassuring squeeze. "Because I know my niece, and I've known for a long time she has feelings for you. I also knew that you were the perfect man for her. Don't let me down." Then he removed his hand and walked away.

What the…?

It took a minute for Ethan to snap out of it and walk over to the rest of the group. Robert was putting his phone away. "Well, just as we suspected, Mark flew Summer and Gabriella back to Portland yesterday and then was given instructions to get a good night's sleep before heading back here to us." He gave a mirthless laugh. "I'm not sure if that was Summer or Gabriella's doing. Either way, he's getting ready to leave Portland within the hour. Let's go grab some breakfast before heading over to see Zach." He paused and asked his sons and brother to get them a table in the restaurant and then looked directly at Ethan when they were alone. "You and I will be flying back to Portland this afternoon and hopefully keeping Summer from making a bigger mess of this Morrison deal than it already is."

And just like that, they were fine.

"Yes, sir," he said and watched as Robert walked away to join the others at their table.

Ethan had agonized and worried for weeks, and in the end there was nothing more to it. Disappointment filled him—not because there weren't more fights or arguments, but because he had let himself believe differently. Because he'd expected the worst, he'd wasted precious time with her and ultimately had pushed

Summer away. There was no way he could ever forgive himself for his cowardly behavior. But if Summer were willing to listen to him and give him another chance, Ethan vowed to make sure he never gave her reason to doubt him ever again.

———⁓———

Zach took the news of Ethan and Summer's relationship the worst. Even more so than James. He tried to jump out of the bed to throttle Ethan, and if it hadn't clearly been so painful for him, it would have been comical.

"You son of a bitch!" he shouted. "All this time you've been playing go-between for me and Summer and you were sleeping with her! I trusted you! I trusted you with her! What the hell's the matter with you? I should kill you!"

"Zach," Robert warned.

"No!" he shouted. "This is what you do to a friend? You take advantage of his sister? You use her? And you do it all behind my back?" He fell back against the pillows on his bed and grimaced with pain. "She's why you didn't go on the climb, isn't she? All those bullshit reasons you gave me were lies. You stayed behind so you could screw my sister!"

"That's not true!" Ethan yelled back. "My reasons for not going on the climb were true. Everything I said to you that day was the truth. But if you're asking me if Summer and I were already involved, then yes. We were. I tried, man, I really tried not to let anything happen between us. And I put you first, Zach. I hurt Summer because I was putting my friendship with you first."

"Don't you dare try to put any of this mess on me," Zach spat, seething. "You know you're not good enough for her. Hell, no one is! You just proved it by sneaking around behind all of our backs."

"If I came to you and told you that I wanted to date your sister, you're telling me you would have said yes?"

"Hell no! And I would have kicked your ass for even asking! You should have stayed away from her!"

"I couldn't! Don't you get it?"

Zach growled with frustration. "You just...you shouldn't have snuck around. We should have known."

"It was nobody's damn business! Do you tell everyone in your family who you're sleeping with? Do you have to get everyone's approval before getting involved with someone?"

"It's not the same thing!"

"The hell it's not!" Looking around the room, Ethan decided the only way to get his point across was to show that he wasn't the only one to make a stupid decision in his life. "Did you ever tell Ryder you slept with Cheryl Mackie the summer we all took up surfing?"

"Dude!" Ryder interrupted. "What the hell?"

Zach ignored him.

"Or did you ever tell your father it was you who took Mindy O'Brien skinny-dipping and that's why her father backed out of those contract negotiations?"

"Zach?" Robert asked. "Is that true?"

Zach glared at Ethan before turning to his father. "That was ten years ago. Seriously? You're going to give me crap for it now?"

"It was a big contract! How could you have been so irresponsible?"

"I can't believe we're even talking about this," Zach mumbled.

"But you see my point?" Ethan asked. "We've all been there. We've all gotten involved with people when we knew we shouldn't and yet we couldn't help ourselves. The only difference here is that I *love* Summer. I want a life with her, a future." He looked around the room, at all of the Montgomerys he had been so scared to have to deal with. "I'm going to have a future with her. As soon as we get back to Portland, if I have to beg her to forgive me, then I'll do it. For far too long I let my fear of this exact moment keep me from telling her how I felt. Well, I'm not afraid anymore. There isn't anything any one of you can say to stop me."

For a long moment he stood there and silently dared anyone to try.

"What if I tell you if you pursue this relationship with my sister, you're fired?" Zach asked with a low and deadly tone.

Ethan stepped close to the bed and stared his friend down. "Then I'd say good luck finding another vice president. There's nothing you can threaten me with. There's nothing you can do or say to change the way I feel for her. I'm just hoping I'm not too late and Summer still feels the same way about me."

"And if she doesn't?" Zach asked.

That was definitely not something Ethan wanted to have to contend with. "Then I'll change her mind."

"What if I forbid it?" Robert asked from the other side of Zach's bed.

"Then I'd have to respectfully tell you to mind your own business," he said confidently. "Summer's a grown woman, not a child, and she is free to make her own decisions. If she turns me down, if she's decided she can't forgive me and I can't change her mind, then I will gracefully bow out and walk away. Away from her, and away from Montgomerys. But not forever. I'll never give up on her, sir. You can forbid it all you want, but I love your daughter more than anyone else possibly can, and I'm going to spend the rest of my life proving it."

Robert looked at the rest of his family. "Anyone got anything to say about that?" When there was no response, he said, "Good. Now let's get down to business."

For a moment, all Ethan could do was stare. Was that really it?

Robert cleared his throat. "William, I'd like you to stay here with Ryder and James to talk to the doctors and see when it will be possible to get Zach moved." He turned to Ethan. "You and I need to get back to the hotel to pack and get to the airport. It seems to me like you have a potential appointment with a client to intervene in."

After a round of handshakes and words of good luck, Ethan and Robert exited the room. Once the door was closed, William sat down and looked at his three nephews and grinned broadly. "Well, well, well…" Cheerfully, he crossed his ankles as he relaxed in the chair. "Anyone have anything else to say about my matchmaking abilities?"

They were smart enough to keep their mouths shut.

"Did you get any sleep last night?" Gabriella asked the next morning as she rode up in the elevator with Summer.

"Between the thousands of pages to read on this

Morrison guy and Maylene wanting to play, I think I managed to get about thirteen minutes' worth."

"Hmph…that's thirteen more than I got."

"Why? You're not the one who has everything to lose here. If I screw this up and Morrison ends up walking anyway, everyone is going to be pissed at me. And not in their usual 'Oh, it's just Summer' way. It's going to be huge." She leaned against the wall of the elevator. "You'll be praised as a hero because you left when Zach told you to and came back here to make sure that everything was running smoothly."

Gabriella gave her a sour look. "I didn't leave because Zach told me," she said defiantly. "Obviously, my being there was causing him some stress."

"And why is that, exactly?" Summer asked with a smirk.

"Beats me. We argued before he left for the climb because I refused to get you on the phone for him. I told him it was a family matter, not a business matter."

Summer's eyes went huge. "Seriously? And what did he do?"

"I don't know. I left for lunch."

"No!" Summer said with a laugh.

"I'm not proud of it, but…I also kind of am. It was a glorious exit." She couldn't stop the huge smile that crossed her face. "In my mind, his head pretty much exploded."

"Oh, I can totally picture it! He must have stood there, all red in the face and stammering and not knowing what to do! Too bad there weren't any witnesses."

"Ethan was there, but I'm sure he just played peacemaker like he normally does and calmed Zach down."

At the mention of Ethan's name, Summer's smile faded. "Hey," Gabriella said softly, "I'm sorry. I didn't mean to bring him up and upset you. Have you heard from him?"

"He left a couple of messages on my phone, but I haven't listened to them. I can't. Not yet. I have to get through this meeting with Morrison first. If I hear Ethan's voice, it will definitely shrink my confidence in what I'm trying to do."

"Why?"

"Because no matter what he says, I'm going to hear him laughing at me with Zach. I'm trying to push that from my mind and remember I am totally capable of doing this. I am not some brainless twit who was only given a token job within the company. I want to earn my place here and show my father and my brothers how wrong they've been about me."

"I believe in you, Summer," Gabriella said as the elevator doors opened. "You've totally got this."

"From your lips to God's ears," she muttered as they walked out into the lobby of the Montgomerys offices.

"Please…everything is going exactly as you'd hoped. Morrison doesn't stand a chance."

They opened the wide glass doors and walked in and were greeted by a frowning Bob Davis. "Ladies, I'm afraid we have a problem."

It was three o'clock in the afternoon and Summer was sweating bullets. Her original plan was for a first-thing-in-the-morning meeting with Alan Morrison, but it appeared he wasn't going to be easily swayed. Even though he had agreed to a nine a.m. meeting, he called and postponed it until three fifteen.

Summer was no idiot; the man wanted to show he was the one in control. The only problem with that was, with such a lengthy delay, her father and Ethan and whoever else wanted to join in could be here at any time and blow this whole thing up in her face. Although her nerves were starting to get the best of her, she managed to make the most of this extra time to hone her presentation and to do even more research on Alan Morrison and his company, so she could talk to the man on his level and appear to know exactly where he was coming from.

Sitting alone in the conference room, she said a silent prayer that whoever was going to come back from Alaska today would be delayed long enough to let her get through this meeting. She knew exactly when Mark left to head back to Denali, and she had no doubt his passengers would already be waiting for him at the airport so the turnaround time would be swift.

Dammit.

The door to the room opened and Gabriella stuck her head in. "It's showtime." She paused and looked at Summer. "You're going to be great. I believe in you."

Summer felt oddly calm. She thought she'd be sick to her stomach as soon as her clients arrived, but now she calmly stood and smoothed her skirt. "Please send them in." She took a steadying breath and stood by her chair at the head of the table until she heard them coming. Then, as if she had been doing this for years, she walked confidently to the door and extended her hand with a smile. "Mr. Morrison, it is a pleasure to meet you."

—ⱽⱽ—

Ethan held his breath as the helicopter landed on the rooftop pad of the building. "I still can't believe you pulled this off," he said as he and Robert waited for the pilot's signal that they could get out.

"Gabriella isn't the only assistant who can pull a rabbit out of her hat at the last minute. Janet has been with me for almost twenty years. When something needs to get done, she does it. She's not as crafty as Gabriella, I'll give you that, but in situations like this, she does me proud." When Robert had called his assistant to tell her his change of plans and what he needed, he had been surprised when she'd come up with the idea of taking a helicopter from the airport to the office. He'd simply asked her to make sure a car was waiting, but Janet said if he wanted to get through downtown Portland at that time of the day, a helicopter was the way to go. As he glanced down at the building four o'clock traffic, he had to agree.

The pilot gave the thumbs-up, and Ethan and Robert quickly took off their headsets and disembarked from the aircraft. Together they walked through the doors and into the building. At the top of the stairs, Ethan stopped. "What are we going to do, Robert? Go in there with guns blazing? I mean, we didn't really discuss this."

Robert stopped and gave pause. "Honestly, I was so consumed with getting here that I really didn't focus on what exactly we were going to be walking into. For all we know, Summer could have had her meeting with Morrison already."

"Are we sure she didn't?"

Robert nodded. "I managed to get Bob Davis to talk a little bit this morning. I didn't come off as being upset; I played it like it was all my idea for Summer to come here and handle this. He mentioned the meeting had been postponed until later in the day, but he couldn't give me an exact time. I guess we need to go down there and evaluate what kind of damage control we might need to do." He looked at Ethan. "What about you? Do you know what you're going to say to Summer?"

He shook his head. "I'll know when I see her. If I can just look at her, I'll be able to see in her eyes how upset she is."

It did Robert's heart good to hear Ethan talk like this. If ever there was a man he thought capable of taking care of his daughter, it was Ethan. He didn't want to like it at first, but as the idea began to settle and take hold, he knew William was right. Ethan Reed was exactly the perfect man for Summer. He only hoped they weren't too late. "Then let's stop chatting up here like a couple of schoolgirls and get down there."

They descended the stairs and came to the eighteenth floor of the office building, which housed the Portland branch of the Montgomerys offices. They strode through the glass doors and the lobby and noticed that several people had stopped working. Without a word or a glance, Robert continued on to the conference room. Out of the corner of his eye, Ethan saw Gabriella pale at her desk. She went to stand, but Ethan held out a hand to stop her, never breaking stride.

The door to the conference room was slightly ajar, and Robert held Ethan back before he could walk through.

He signaled for them to listen to what was being said on the other side of the door.

"So you see, Alan," Summer said in her sweetest voice, "with this projection, you will triple your investment in a little more than two years. Now I don't know about you, but that's not something I'd be willing to walk away from."

Silence. Ethan wanted to walk through the door and see what the hell she was talking about. In all of the dealings with Morrison, they'd never discussed that kind of return. What had she done?

Inside the conference room, Summer held her breath. She was taking a huge risk here. She couldn't quite get a read on the man.

"This is a very different deal from what your brother and I discussed," Alan Morrison said evenly. "Or from my discussions with Ethan Reed."

"After reviewing your files and doing a little research into your company, I knew the deal you were working on was not nearly worthy of a man of your stature. I don't believe in making a client feel small, Alan. I think there is a lot of potential here for both of our companies, and working together is going to do wonders for us both."

She had schmoozed and dazzled him with her flattery, but in the end, this was a business deal, and batting her lashes and smiling was only going to get her so far.

Alan Morrison let out a loud laugh and Summer's heart sank. She'd blown it. Dammit.

He stood. "Summer," Morrison said as he walked over to her seat and held out a hand to help her up, "you are one hell of a woman." He enthusiastically shook her hand. "I don't know where your family has been hiding you, but I'm sure as hell glad they chose now to have you come out and join the ranks. In all of my dealings with Montgomerys, I was beginning to feel a little boxed in; no one wanted to look at the big picture. But you did. You did your homework and it means a lot to me." He released her hand and took a step back to look at the projection up on the wall and smiled.

"I knew we were capable of something like this, but Zach wouldn't listen," Morrison continued. "And I knew if Zach wouldn't listen, no one else below him would either. That's why when I heard of his accident, I decided to cut my losses and walk away. I didn't want to deal with some junior executive. I wanted to be heard. I vowed I would make your brother listen to my ideas before we signed on the dotted line. Looking at what you've presented here, it's like you saw in my head exactly what I wanted to do." He placed his hands in his pocket and continued to smile at her.

"Alan, I am so pleased that you're pleased," Summer said brightly. "That was my goal. I wanted you to see that you are a valued client and we are anxious to do business with you. I know Zach is going to be happy we were able to sit down and move forward with this deal and that you're going to stay on with us." She reached for the contracts and a pen and saw him hesitate.

"I don't mean to seem ungrateful, because I am," he said carefully. "But I still have an issue or two here."

She wanted to crumble to the floor. What could she have missed? There was no telling when her father or Ethan or both of them were going to come crashing through the door. If she could just get Alan Morrison to sign the contracts, she'd feel a lot more confident.

Casually, she sat herself back down in her chair and moved the contracts to the side and smiled serenely up at him. "Tell me what we can do to make you happy here, Alan."

Ignoring his earlier seat, he pulled up a chair right beside her. "How do I know that once Zach is healed and back here in the office, he's not going to try to rene-gotiate these terms? How do I know he's not going to say you weren't authorized to make this deal?"

At that moment, Robert and Ethan walked confi-dently through the door. Robert's hand was outstretched as he walked toward them. "Alan Morrison? I'm Robert Montgomery."

Alan looked from Summer to her father and back again. "Your father?" he asked, and Summer nodded, slowly rising to her feet. "It's a pleasure to meet you, Robert. You've got one hell of a daughter here."

"Yes, I know," he said proudly. "That's why we sent her here to work with you. With Zach being temporarily incapacitated, we knew Summer would be able to meet with you and work through the negotiations."

Summer beamed with the praise but couldn't help focusing on Ethan. Just the sight of him took her breath away. If they hadn't been in the middle of this meeting, she'd have been tempted to throw herself into his arms and tell him how she'd missed him. And she had. Even as angry and disappointed as she was with him, being without him last night had felt wrong. Funny how just a few short weeks had changed so much.

He was staring back at her with an intensity she

couldn't quite read—was he angry or as relieved to see her as she was to see him? She glanced at her father and Morrison and gauged whether she could walk right over to kiss Ethan senseless without either of them noticing. She chose not to try it.

"This means a lot to me," Alan said loudly, and Summer turned just in time to see him reach for the contracts and sit down to sign them. She almost jumped up and cheered. They all stood and watched as the legal teams jumped in and had everyone, including Summer, sign in the appropriate place. At last, everyone in the room was standing and shaking hands and offering congratulations.

It seemed to take forever to get Morrison and his people out the door, and as Summer walked by Gabriella's desk, she gave her a huge smile and a thumbs-up. Once everyone was gone, Summer headed toward Zach's office—she had used it as her own this morning—and sat down to wait for the confrontation she knew was coming. It didn't take long for her father and Ethan to join her. Robert closed the door behind him.

He sat down in one of the large upholstered chairs facing Zach's desk and stared at his daughter—a smile on his face. "That was quite a chance you took today, young lady."

She nodded. "So it was." She met his even stare with a small smile of her own.

"How did you know he'd go for it? What made you so sure you'd be able to come here and convince him to stay?"

"You've been sending me reports and updates on all

things Montgomerys since I turned twenty-one. I've learned a lot over the years between reading the reports and my own life experiences and education. The idea that you didn't think me competent enough to do this is like you thinking I can't read."

He barked out a laugh. "You are my daughter, that is for sure."

"Was that ever in doubt?"

He shook his head. "No…no it wasn't. What I meant is, you chose such a different path from your brothers, I just naturally assumed business wasn't your thing." He studied her and then bowed his head a little. "A mistake I'm not likely to make again. I'm very proud of you, Summer. You did an amazing thing here today."

She couldn't help but beam and blush at his praise. "Thank you. All I ever wanted was a chance. I just want to be taken seriously."

"Well, I don't think it will be an issue ever again. You've more than proven yourself. You tell me the position you want here, and it's yours."

She was tempted to say she wanted the vice presidency—Ethan's job—but held her tongue. "I'll have to give it some thought."

"Good. I want you to. You just made the company about ten million dollars. Not bad for your first real day on the job," Robert said with a grin. "Now, if you'll excuse me, I believe I will call your brother and check in and let him know everything's all right." He stood and left the room but not before noticing neither Summer nor Ethan seemed aware of him. He quietly closed the door behind him.

Ethan studied the woman he loved, and words eluded

him. What could he possibly say to make up for all of the things he'd done? It was obvious she didn't need him—not the way he'd once thought she did. Summer Montgomery wasn't a weak woman; she was the strongest one he had ever met. The way she not only stood up to her family, but also made such a grand stand to prove them all wrong—and have it work so magnificently— left him a little in awe of her.

"Aren't you going to get up and leave too?" she asked, quirking a brow at him. "After all, what will people think if you're left alone in a room with me?"

To anyone else she sounded confident, but he knew her well enough to hear the hint of vulnerability in her voice. He stood and walked around the desk until he was beside her, looking down into her beautiful, yet confused, face. "People will think that I'm in here groveling to the woman I love."

Summer's eyes went wide at his words and a whispered "What?" came out before she could stop it.

Kneeling down beside her, Ethan took one of her hands. "I love you, Summer. I'm so sorry for the way I acted in Zach's room yesterday. That was completely uncalled for. You didn't deserve it and I know it was wrong."

She looked at him and saw the sincerity in his eyes. "You really hurt me, Ethan."

He squeezed her hand. "I know, I know, sweetheart, and I'm sorry. More than you know. But I want to make it up to you. I want to spend the rest of my life making it up to you."

Now she was really confused. Was he saying what she thought he was saying? "What about my family?"

He told her about the confrontation he'd had with all of them earlier that morning. "I think your brothers are going to give me a hard time for a while, but your father and your uncle took it better than I could have expected. I'm sorry I didn't stand up for us sooner, Summer. I'm sorry if I made you feel like I was ashamed of what we were doing."

"You were afraid," she pointed out.

He nodded. "I know. And I'm so ashamed of myself because of it." He cupped her cheek in his hand and smiled when she nestled into it. "You took me by surprise, Summer. When I came to the springs to find you to make sure you were okay, never in a million years did I suspect you were attracted to me. I certainly never expected to kiss you." He rested his forehead against hers. "Or to make love to you."

She sighed. "I've always been attracted to you, Ethan," she said quietly. "You just never noticed."

"Tell me I'm not too late, Summer," he pleaded. "Tell me I didn't screw this up so badly that we can't move forward from here."

It would be so easy to agree with him—to simply say she was fine and they were fine and everything was going to be all right. But for the first time in a long time, Summer felt like she was just beginning to know herself. For years she had gone wherever her whims took her and tried new things and careers just because she could. Closing a deal like she just had with Morrison was an eye-opening experience. She felt empowered. Confronting her family and seeing the sky didn't fall was a revelation. How much more was she capable of now?

Carefully, she pulled away from Ethan until his hand dropped away and confusion now marred his features. "I don't know if I can, Ethan," she said honestly. "You really hurt me. All of my worst fears about my family? You proved them all true to me. You didn't believe in me, and what was worse, you sided with them over me." She straightened in her seat and did her best to steady her racing heart and say what she had to say.

"I need time, Ethan. Time to figure out what I want to do with my life." She looked around Zach's office. "I don't think I want to be here. I don't want to be in a place where I know I'll constantly have to prove myself over and over and over again. It's exhausting."

"You won't!" he cried, panic lacing his voice. "You've done it, Summer. Ten times over you've done it. No one is going to doubt you ever again."

She smiled sadly at him as they both stood. "Zach has a long recovery ahead of him. And this is his company. He never wanted me here, and no matter what he may think right now, I don't want to interfere. The two of you have worked so well together and made this office a success."

"But so have you, Summer. You did more in one day than we've sometimes done in months."

"Thank you for saying so," she said shyly. "But...I don't think this is where I belong. It's not where I'm meant to be."

He reached out and grasped her hands in his and refused to let go even when she tried to pull away. "It *is* where you're meant to be," he said anxiously. "With me. Here. There's a reason you were sent here, Summer. It was our time. It was for us. Don't go. Please."

Tears began to well in her eyes. "I don't regret this time together, Ethan. How could I? It was everything I ever wanted."

"Then don't go. It doesn't have to end. Tell me what I have to do to make this right. What can I say to convince you not to leave?" His heart was breaking. He never thought she'd actually turn him down this quickly. He thought he might really have to persuade her, but he didn't imagine things going quite like this. He was drowning and he couldn't seem to stay afloat.

"This isn't about you," Summer said. "It's about me. I'm finally seeing what I'm capable of, and I'm tired of living in the shadows of my brothers."

"You can still do that here, Summer. You don't have to stay with the company; you can still live here and figure out what you want." He pulled her close, until they were toe-to-toe. "Don't leave me," he begged quietly.

She wanted to lean into him, to feel his strong arms around her and have him tell her everything was going to be all right. Unfortunately, she also knew it was just going to be that much more difficult down the road when she still needed the time to figure out what she wanted to do with her life.

Did she still want Ethan?

Yes, more than her next breath.

Could she continue to live here in Portland?

Absolutely.

So why was she leaving?

Because he was a distraction. A sexy one, but a distraction nonetheless. Her family had sent her to Portland to give her a chance to find out what she wanted to do with her life. Well, she had experienced a lot, but she was no closer to finding the answer. Portland was Zach's home; he'd lived there for years and he loved it. Summer had lived up and down the East Coast, but no matter where she went, North Carolina was her home. It was where she always went back to.

And there was her answer.

Doing her best to step back, she gently pried her hands from Ethan's. "I think I'm going to head back east."

"To stay with your parents?" he asked.

She shook her head. "No. I think it's time I found a place of my own there. I love my family and I love spending time with them, but they'll never stop looking at me as the baby of the family if I keep acting like one."

"You don't. I think you managed to change everyone's way of thinking today. No one thinks that, Summer."

"Up until about forty-five minutes ago, they did."

She's really going to do this, Ethan thought. She was really going to leave. He wanted to beg, he wanted to get down on his knees and grovel and then take her home with him, but as he looked into her eyes, he knew. This was important to her. For far too long, people had been dictating her life and she was ready to take a stand. How could he deny her that opportunity?

"When will you leave?" His voice cracked on the last word.

She took a steadying breath. "I'll need to wrap up a few things here with my condo and make arrangements to get my things moved. Say good-bye to friends." The look in Ethan's eyes was killing her. "A week, tops."

"I wish there was something I could say to change your mind, Summer."

"I really need to do this."

"I know." He had to leave. He needed to run before he made a fool out of himself. Unable to help himself, he reached out one last time and stroked a hand down her cheek and then placed a gentle kiss there. "Be happy," he said softly before turning and leaving the room.

Summer waited until the door closed before collapsing down in her chair and crying.

Chapter 15

"THIS ISN'T FAIR."

"I know."

"Are you sure you won't change your mind?"

"I'm sure."

Gabriella looked around the condo filled with boxes. They sat on the floor with a pizza and a bottle of wine between them. Summer held Maylene in her lap. They were both wearing tiaras. "It's a good look for the both of you."

Summer chuckled. "It makes us feel pretty, doesn't it, baby?" she cooed to the pug, which, in turn, licked her face excitedly.

"What am I supposed to do around here without you? You were my only friend at Montgomerys."

"That's not true and you know it," Summer admonished. "People are just intimidated by you because you're a supermodel."

She snorted with laughter at that one. "Right. If I'm such a damn supermodel, tell me why I haven't had a date in like…forever."

"You just haven't found someone worthy of your awesomeness." Summer leaned back against a box and took another sip of her wine. "You will and you'll know when it's right." Summer had thought she'd known when it was right, but it was just an illusion. A temporary, heartbreaking illusion. She sighed and then gasped when Gabriella took the wineglass from her hand. "Hey!"

"We said no sad thoughts tonight, remember?" Gabriella said with mock sternness, and Summer nodded. "So tell me about your plans. The moving truck is coming in the morning and you're flying home—via the family jet—tomorrow afternoon. Right?"

"Yup," she said, forcing herself to sound cheery. "My sister-in-law Casey found me a cute little place near the beach to rent until my place is built."

"I still can't believe you worked it out so fast."

"Hey, sometimes it helps to play the Montgomery card."

"Still…it's just not right."

"Aidan Shaughnessy said he'd be more than happy to work with me on the project. I told him exactly what I wanted and where I wanted it, and he already had a piece of land in mind."

"Convenient."

Summer made a face at her. "He knows the area like the back of his hand. He's doing the work on James and Selena's place, and if I can get the plans nailed down quickly, he said he could probably find a way to work it into his schedule right afterward."

"So what did you have to do to bribe him? Go on a date?"

Summer laughed. "I haven't seen Aidan in years. He was always a super nice guy, but he was friends with James and older and…"

"So? Ethan is Zach's friend and he's even older," she reminded.

"We said we weren't going there tonight."

"Oh. Right. Sorry. Continue with your story of luck us mere mortals aren't privy to."

"Shut up," she said and took her wineglass back. "Anyway, I doubt it will all work out as smoothly as we think, but just knowing the ball is in motion makes me feel a lot better."

"You could have built a house here, you know."

"Beach," Summer reminded her. "I wanted a house on the Carolina coast."

Gabriella rolled her eyes. "Picky, picky, picky. Nothing says you can't make it a vacation home instead."

Ignoring the suggestion, Summer shifted until she was sitting Indian style. "You can come visit, you know. My brother can't force you to work nonstop without vacations. Just come and spend them with me."

"Please, he's probably already talked to payroll and human resources to dock my pay for the time I was in Alaska—even though a large portion of it was spent doing work for his stupid company."

Summer couldn't help but chuckle. "Sounds about right."

"But seriously, once you get back home, are you going to start dating? Do you think this Aidan guy is a potential boyfriend? What does he look like?"

"Oh my God," Summer said with exasperation. "I'm not looking to date anyone. I need to get my head together. Believe me, dating is the last thing on my mind."

"Because you're in love with Ethan."

"Of course because I'm in love with Ethan!" Summer yelled back and then gasped. Maylene jumped from her arms, and one hand flew to her mouth.

"What?" Gabriella said. "What's the matter?"

"I love him! I love Ethan!"

"Yeah, yeah, old news."

"I didn't tell him!"

"When?"

"The other day. In Zach's office. He told me he loved me and I didn't say it back!"

"So? What difference would it have made? You were still planning on leaving. Telling Ethan you love him wasn't going to change that, was it?"

Summer's eyes were wide. "No…but…"

Gabriella scooted over and put her arm around her. "Look, don't torture yourself. You made your feelings for him very clear while you were involved. I'm sure he knows you love him. You just need some time."

She rested her head on Gabriella's shoulder. "Maybe."

Refusing to look hopeful, Gabriella slowly raised her head. "What are you saying?"

"I miss him. I miss him so much it hurts. I cry myself to sleep every night and I wake up feeling horrible. If I'm doing the right thing, why does it feel so wrong?"

"If you figure out the answer to that one, let me know."

"Oh, Gabs…what if…?"

Hope crossed Gabriella's face. "What?"

Summer shook her head. "Nothing. It's… it's nothing."

"Ugh. Let me ask you something. Are you really happy to be leaving?"

"I don't know. I thought I was. I know it's something that I wanted to do but…"

"But?"

"I thought he'd stop me," she said sadly. "I didn't

think that he'd just go along with it and let me go. I thought Ethan would at least try to talk me out of it."

"Maybe he's just trying to give you what you asked for."

"Maybe."

Gabriella groaned again. "Okay, let me ask you another question."

"Yes, you're totally bringing me down here."

"Ha, ha. But not the question. What do you want Ethan to do? I mean, what could he have possibly done differently?"

Summer thought about it for a minute. "Well…he could have showed up here and tried to stop me."

"And that wouldn't have pissed you off?"

"Oh, it would have. But it also would have shown me that he really cares."

"Seriously? That's what would show it? What's wrong with you?"

"Or he could go all caveman on me and haul me over his shoulder and…and…keep me from leaving."

"You've read too many sappy romance novels."

"Nothing wrong with that. Who doesn't want one of those alpha males carrying them off?"

"Um…a lot of people." She made a *tsking* sound. "I never would have pegged you for going all girly over caveman tactics."

"Well, there was this one time…"

"La-la-la-la-la-la!" Gabriella sang loudly, plugging her fingers in her ears. "I keep telling you that I do *not* need to hear about you and Ethan's…escapades. Caveman or otherwise!"

Laughing, Summer held up her hands in defeat.

"Fine. Don't listen. All I'm saying is that I just wish he would have taken the decision out of my hands."

"You can't have your cake and eat it too, Summer. You said you were tired of people making your decisions for you, and now you're saying that you want Ethan to make your decisions for you. Which is it?"

Before she could answer, Summer's phone rang. With a sigh, she stood and went to answer it. "Zach!" she said with a smile. "I can't believe you're actually calling me. I didn't think you were allowed to."

"I've got multiple broken bones, Summer, but my fingers still work," he said dryly.

"Ha, ha, very funny. I just thought it would be too hard for you to do anyway. How are you? How are you feeling?"

"Like I fell off a mountain," he said and then paused. "Listen, I wanted to call sooner, but they're so hell-bent on putting me through tests and scanners and whatnot that I haven't had a minute to myself."

"What are the doctors saying? What kinds of tests?" she asked, worry for him overwhelming her.

"I don't want to talk about them right now, Summer. I'm calling to talk about you."

"Me? What about me?"

"I heard about your meeting with Morrison."

"Oh."

"Yeah…oh. I can't believe you did that." He didn't sound angry, but he didn't sound pleased either.

"I tried telling you I could do it, but—"

"I know, I know…"

"Anyway, it all worked out, right?" she asked hopefully.

"Yes it did. Thank you."

Summer pulled the phone away from her ear and looked at it as if she were hearing things. Her brother was actually thanking her? Maybe his head injury was worse than they thought. She needed a moment to compose herself.

"So…um…yeah, it did. Bob Davis is going to work with him until you're back on your feet. I think he's going to do a good job."

"You would have done better, squirt," he said, and Summer could hear the smile in his voice. "I really wish you'd reconsider and stay."

That made her smile. "You say that now, but once you get back, you'd probably hate having me here."

"I was hard on you, Summer, I know it. I don't even know why. But when you could have let me down and lost a big client, you went to bat for me. I don't deserve your kindness and I'm sorry for not being nicer to you before…well, you know."

"We're family, Zach. I never want to see you fail. Ever. Even when you're being a jerk," she teased.

"We could have worked well together. Now I see that you're not a pushover, I could have groomed you to a top executive level. Like a mini-me."

"Thanks, but I'm good."

He was quiet for a long moment. "So what are you going to do now? I mean, once you get back home? Do you have a job lined up?"

"I don't know. I talked to Casey, and her business partner is struggling with balancing their wedding planning schedule, and motherhood, and Casey is struggling with it too, so I think I'm going to meet with the two of them when I get back. See if maybe there's a place for me with them."

"Ah…so working for the family without actually working for the family. Nice."

"It seemed like a good compromise."

"I'm sorry if I made you feel like you couldn't stay in Portland. I know that Ethan—"

"North Carolina was always my home," she interrupted, unwilling to discuss her relationship with Ethan with her brother. "Portland is very nice, and I certainly wouldn't mind coming back to visit, but I always imagined living back on the Carolina coast."

"I know and I'm sure you're going to be happy, but still, I'm going to miss you."

His admission humbled her. "I'm going to miss you too. And as soon as you're allowed to leave Alaska and come back here to recuperate, I promise to fly out and check on you. You'll be so tired of seeing me that you'll be glad I didn't stay."

"Never. I would never feel that way again, Summer. I was an idiot for not taking advantage of the time we had together—when it was just me and you. I don't know how long it will be before everyone is done hovering over me and making me feel even more useless than I already do."

"You're not useless, Zach. You've had a serious accident. We're all just so relieved you're alive. You have to expect a certain amount of hovering." She wanted to sound reassuring but the inner little sister continued, "You know as soon you give Mom the green light to come and stay, you'll have to pry her off with a crowbar."

He groaned. "Don't remind me. I can't believe she's not here already."

"Dad was pretty firm with her. He said it would be much more beneficial to you if she waited until you were home. That's when you're really going to need someone to hover."

"Ugh."

"She actually wanted to fly you back east to recuperate. Be thankful she didn't get her way then."

"You're telling me." Summer heard voices in the background and figured it was time for Zach to go. He got back on the line and confirmed it. "I'm off for another round of tests. Take care of yourself, Summer, and call me when you get home."

"I will. Don't give the doctors such a hard time. They're only trying to help you."

"Yeah, yeah, yeah," he said. "I love you, squirt."

"Love you too," she said and felt like she was on the verge of tears. Again. "Dammit." Placing the phone down, she slid to the floor next to Gabriella.

Pulling Summer close again, Gabriella said, "Yeah. I know."

The next morning, Summer opened the door, expecting it to be the movers. Instead, she found Gabriella standing there looking tall and glamorous, holding a tray with two Starbucks cups and a bag she could only hope contained muffins.

"You're not supposed to be here," Summer said, still surprised.

"Why yes, I will come in. Thank you," Gabriella

said with a smile as she stepped around her. Walking directly to the kitchen, she placed the drink tray and the bag down before unwrapping her silk scarf from around her neck. Maylene was dancing and barking around her ankles, and she bent down to pet the puppy on the head. "Who's a pretty girl? Huh? Who's a pretty girl?"

Summer walked over to peek in the bag and smiled before remembering she was supposed to be annoyed. "We said our good-byes last night and it was horrible. Why are we going to torture ourselves again?" The puppy pranced over to Summer now and danced on her hind legs in hopes of getting in on the action.

"Because you shouldn't be here alone." And there it was in a nutshell.

Summer leaned on the counter, her face in her hands. "I really thought I would have heard from him by now." Something in her voice signaled to Maylene that now was not a good time to play. She sat down regally at Summer's feet and watched.

There was no question as to who "him" was. "I know you did."

"And now I'm leaving," she sighed and reached into the bag and grabbed a muffin.

Gabriella snatched the muffin from her hands.

"Hey!"

"This is exactly what I said to you last night. You need to get off the damn fence, Summer," she said with a little more annoyance than she had intended. "Besides, the blueberry one is mine. There's a chocolate chip one in there for you."

"I'm not on the fence," Summer said defiantly, grabbing the elusive muffin. "I just...I just thought..." She placed it none too gently on the counter. "How could he proclaim his love for me, and tell me how sorry he is and he'll do anything to convince me to stay, and then just let me leave?"

"I honestly think for such an intelligent family, you Montgomerys are so clueless sometimes."

"What is that supposed to mean?"

Gabriella sighed and placed her own muffin down before getting their cups out of the cardboard tray and handing Summer hers. "Did it ever occur to you *that* was his grand gesture?"

"What? Letting me leave? How is that a grand gesture?"

"Again, clueless." And to make her suffer, Gabriella made a big show of taking a bite of her blueberry muffin and then a long sip of her latte. When she was satisfied that Summer's head looked like it was about to explode, she placed her cup down, wiped her mouth daintily with a napkin, and explained, "He didn't want you to go. He told you that flat-out, right?" Summer nodded. "But you, in your infinite wisdom, decided you needed to go back east and get your head together. Am I correct?" Again, Summer nodded. "You and I both know that if he wanted to, he could have convinced you to stay. It probably wouldn't have taken much on his part either. But did he? Did he try to manipulate you? No. He's giving you the space you said you need. Why? Because he loves you."

The muffin was like sawdust in her mouth. If it weren't for the fact that it was chocolate and so bad for the dog, she would have thrown it to the floor. "You really think so?"

"I've had to sit at my desk and watch him at work every day since then, Summer. He's a mess."

"Really?" she squeaked, knowing it was foolish to be happy that Ethan was miserable because of her, but she couldn't help herself.

"You haven't been fifteen in a long time. Please don't go back there now," Gabriella said and took another sip of her drink. "The way I see it, you have two options."

"I'm listening."

"One, go on with your plans. Go back to North Carolina and get yourself situated. Take a little time to get your head together so you won't have any doubts about how you feel about Ethan and about your future with him."

Summer considered it and then glanced at Gabriella. "And what's plan B?"

"Plan B is get off your butt and go tell him right now that you're sorry and you love him and you don't really want to go back to North Carolina. Not permanently and not without him."

Both plans had merit in Summer's eyes, but before she could choose, there was a loud knock at the door. She looked anxiously at Gabriella. "What do I do?"

She shook her head. "The decision has to come from you. It's what you've wanted all along, isn't it? The freedom to make your own decisions without everyone else telling you what to do?"

Another knock. "I hate it when you're right." Another knock. "Oh God. I have to let them in. They're here to take all my stuff back to North Carolina!"

"You can always tell them you changed your mind," Gabriella suggested, her eyes twinkling.

Another knock. All her life, Summer had been impulsive. It came naturally to her. Thinking and planning and waiting were so not her thing. For the most part it worked for her, but with something as important as this, as important as her future, she wasn't willing to take that risk. Her eyes said it all as she looked at Gabriella before walking to the door.

"Sorry to keep you waiting," she said to the two men standing there. "Everything's right through here." She led them around and pointed everything out to them before heading back to the kitchen.

"So you're going."

"I'm going."

"Well…damn," Gabriella said, crossing her arms and leaning against the countertop. "I really thought the muffins were going to change your mind."

"I did too. But just for a minute. I don't want anyone accusing me of jumping in and being impulsive. When things go wrong, it's the first thing I hear."

"You'd never hear it from me."

Summer smiled. "I know. You're such a good friend." She walked over and hugged her fiercely. "You have no idea how much I'm going to miss you."

"I do know, because it's the same for me." Behind them, the men started moving the furniture and boxes out, and Summer and Gabriella silently finished their breakfasts.

A couple of hours later, the place was completely empty. Summer did a final walk through with Maylene in her arms. They had only lived there a short time together, but it still felt bittersweet. "Our next place will have a yard for you," she said to the puppy and kissed her little head. She received a snort in return.

"Are you going to be okay?" Gabriella asked, standing in the doorway of the bedroom, watching her friend walk around.

"Eventually," Summer said sadly. "I knew this wasn't going to be my forever place, but a lot happened here and I'm sad to leave it."

There were a million things Gabriella wanted to say. She knew Summer was in pain and this was a very emotional time for her. So rather than lecture and offer suggestions, she opted simply to offer her support.

Walking into the room, she took the puppy from her arms. "C'mon. You're supposed to meet Mark in an hour." She looked around the room. "Are you taking anything on the plane with you?"

Summer nodded to the corner of the room where a single suitcase stood. "Just that. I left the majority of my clothes back at my parents' place. I'm probably going to crash there for a day or two. Visit my mom. Hopefully I'll get to see Casey and the baby, and Selena too." She took another look around. "It'll be good." Maybe if she said it enough, she'd actually start to believe it.

"Okay, then. Let's get this show on the road. Do you want me to drive you to the airport?"

Summer shook her head. "I really need for this to be good-bye." She looked sadly up at her friend. "Because if you're at the airport with me, I'm not going to want to get on the plane."

"Good," she said with a nod. "Because chances are if I got you in my car, I wouldn't take you to the airport. I'd pull a Thelma and Louise and keep driving until you saw reason." They both laughed.

Then they both cried a little.

And then they walked out of the condo and out to their cars.

"What are you going to do with your car?" Gabriella asked.

"I've made arrangements with the dealer to come and pick it up at the airport. He'll sell it for me."

"Oh. That's good." They stood and looked at one another for a long time. The moving truck had pulled away and it was fairly quiet. "I'm not saying good-bye."

"Me either."

"I'm going to come and visit."

"You better."

"Be happy, Summer," Gabriella said and turned quickly to get into her car. Summer stood frozen in place. Those had been the exact words Ethan said to her before he left.

Be happy. It seemed like such a simple thing, and yet Summer had to wonder if it was even going to be possible. In her head she knew she was doing the responsible thing. But her heart was saying something completely different. Maybe once she was home and surrounded by her mother and her sisters-in-law, they'd help her to find the right perspective.

Maybe.

Securing Maylene in her kennel in the backseat, she climbed in and took one last look at the condo where she'd lived when her life had changed so much. It wasn't that long ago when she'd moved in and felt completely full of hope. And now here she was leaving it and feeling more or less hopeless.

"Sitting here and staring at it isn't going to change

anything," she said softly and started the car. The clock showed she was due to meet Mark in a little less than forty minutes. The drive to the airport was going to take at least thirty. With a final look, she said good-bye to her little home and pulled away.

<hr />

"What do you mean the plane's not here?" Summer said with more than a hint of frustration. "It's not possible. I spoke to the pilot earlier and confirmed our flight. Was there some sort of problem?"

The attendant behind the counter typed something into the computer before turning her attention back to Summer. "I don't see that this flight was even scheduled, Miss Montgomery. Are you sure it's for today?"

She wanted to bang her head against the counter. "Yes, I'm sure it's for today. I'm moving across the country so I know I didn't get the dates wrong." She began to search frantically through her purse for her phone to try to call Mark. Clearly there was some sort of misunderstanding.

"You'll need to step to the side to make your call, ma'am," the attendant said. "There are people waiting behind you."

Summer glared at the woman and swung her purse over her shoulder before reaching down to pick up Maylene's kennel, all the while mumbling about how rude people were and how she was going to kill Mark when she got him on the line.

Kennel in hand, phone at her ear, Summer turned and immediately slammed into someone. "Oh, sorry," she said softly without bothering to look up.

"Can I give you a hand with some of this?" a deep, masculine voice asked.

Her head shot up and she found herself face-to-face with Ethan. "What…what are you doing here?" she asked lamely.

"I would think that's obvious," he said, staring down at her.

"Obvious?"

He nodded. "You're supposed to leave today, aren't you?"

She nodded.

"Well, I'm here to stop you." His words were said so simply, so lightly, Summer thought she misunderstood him.

"Stop me?" she parroted again and realized she was beginning to sound like a complete idiot. "I don't… How?"

"I'm the reason Mark isn't here." He actually sounded proud of himself. "There was a client who needed to be picked up, so we sent him to take care of it."

"Oh." Her whole body was trembling. She was nervous, anxious, and more than a little excited. For a week she had dreamed of Ethan showing up and carrying her away. He was here but so far there was very little carrying. They stepped aside to let the next person in line get to the counter. She gently placed Maylene's kennel on the ground and then straightened and crossed her arms over her chest. "I can just find a commercial flight then," she challenged.

Ethan stepped in close. Really close. "No." Her eyebrows rose at his one-word response but she remained silent. "Not gonna happen, Summer."

Well, if he wasn't going to throw her over his shoulder and carry her off, then she was starting to get annoyed. "Oh, really? You can't possibly buy up all of the open tickets that would get me back to North Carolina. Eventually, you'll have to let me go."

"Never," he said quietly, calmly. "I'll never let you go. I never should have walked away when you told me you were leaving. I thought I was doing the right thing. I wanted to give you what you said you wanted, but in the process, it was killing me." He reached out and cupped her face in his hands. "I love you. I've had to wait a long time to be able to say that and now that I can, I want to say it every day. All the time. If you'll let me."

Everything inside of her softened and she swayed toward him. "I love you too," she said and felt as if a giant weight had been lifted off her. "I should have said it the other day in Zach's office. Hell, I should have said it back at the springs. I was just as scared as you were, Ethan. But I'm not scared of it anymore. The only thing that scares me is living without you."

And then he did swoop in and scoop her up in his arms, lifting her off the ground and spinning her around before he stopped and looked deep into her eyes. "Say it again."

"I love you."

Placing her on her feet, Ethan pulled her tightly into his embrace, then leaned down and pressed his lips to hers. He gently nipped and licked at her lips until she sighed and opened for him. Summer was so lost in the sensation, she didn't notice the action going on around her, as Maylene was whisked away by a porter. Her arms came up around his shoulders and she pressed up

against him. Over and over again he slanted his mouth
over hers, letting their tongues duel one another until she
thought she'd lose her mind.

Quick as lightning, he stooped down and picked
Summer up, tossed her over his shoulder, and began to
stalk to the exit. "Ethan!" she squealed. "Put me down!"

"Not a chance," he said and continued walking,
paying no attention to the odd looks they were getting
from the people around them.

"I can't believe you're acting like a caveman in the
middle of the airport!"

"I thought you liked it when I acted like a caveman,"
he teased and let out a little growl to add to the moment.

"Ethan," she said with a laugh. "My luggage…my…
my dog! Oh my gosh! Where's Maylene?"

"In the car."

"Wait…what?" Summer tried to look over her
shoulder at him, but Ethan's gaze was fixed on the
door and getting them out of the airport. She was
going to question him more, but they were suddenly
outside and he was lowering her to the ground next to
a black limousine. She looked from the car to Ethan
and back again.

And smiled.

"Pretty confident, weren't you?"

He shrugged. "Hopeful. I was hopeful. Now, are you
going to get in, or do I need to carry you in myself?"

She giggled. She honestly and truly giggled like a
young girl and was almost mortified by the sound.
Her hand flew to her mouth and she said, "I'm going,
I'm going."

He leaned in close and nuzzled her neck. "That's a

shame because I was looking for another reason to get my hands on you."

"Well, let's get in the car and close the privacy glass and then your hands can do whatever they want." His gaze heated and he managed to keep his hands to himself until they were in the car and the door was closed. "Oh, wait!" she said when he reached for her.

"Now what?"

"All of my stuff. It's all on its way to North Carolina already. I know it's supposed to take a few days but—"

"It's not a problem," he interrupted.

"I'm sure my mom will sign for it and all but—"

"I'm telling you it's not a problem."

"I'll have to call her and let her know when it will be there."

"Summer!" he snapped playfully. "Would you be quiet for just one minute and listen to me?" Her mouth instantly shut and she looked at him with big eyes. "Your things aren't going to North Carolina." Her brow furrowed as she continued to look at him. "I took care of that too. That truck is currently unloading all of your things at my place."

If she didn't love him so much, she might have been angry at his high-handedness. Instead, she launched herself across the seat at him until she was fully on top of him and he was reclined against the seat. "Like I said, pretty confident, weren't you?"

Ethan's hand reached around and anchored itself in her long blond hair. "Yeah." That was it. He was done talking. She was here with him, and he wasn't going to let her go. Ever. Gently, he guided her face down until their lips met and then he kissed her with all of the pent-up longing and frustration he had felt for the last week. She melted against him, and Ethan knew this wasn't the place for what was going through his mind but he couldn't find it in himself to care.

As carefully as could, he reversed their positions until he was the one on top. Lifting his head, he looked down into her passion-dazed face and smiled. "When we get home, I'm shutting off all the phones and locking all the doors. We'll call everyone tomorrow. We have a lot of lost time to make up for."

"But they're expecting me back home. My mother is supposed to pick me up from the airport."

He shook his head. "Gabriella already called her and let her know about the change in plans."

Summer looked up at him and smiled; her love for him was obvious to see. "You've been pretty busy, haven't you?"

"I'm efficient. I believe that's the word we're going for here. I'm extremely efficient."

"Uh-huh," she said and lifted her head to place kisses along his jaw. "So basically, no one is expecting to hear from us until tomorrow."

"Well, I'm sure they would have preferred to hear from you today—to make sure you're all right and that I didn't do anything to force you to stay…"

"Oh, but you did," she teased and then used her tongue to torment his earlobe. He groaned in response. "You were pretty forceful back there in the airport."

"Yeah, well…desperate times called for desperate measures," he said with a low growl as she continued to work her way along his jaw, his throat, and his ear.

"Were you?" she whispered. "Desperate?"

His resolve broke. She was teasing and tormenting him, but he'd reached the end of his rope. He lifted his body up slightly and looked down at her with a dark and fierce expression. "Would you like to see how desperate I was?"

She shivered with excitement. "Please."

He ran a hand from her shoulder to her knee and back again. "Anything for you," he said as he lowered his body to hers.

———

It was after nine that night and they were lying in Ethan's bed. "Welcome home, Summer," he said and kissed her temple.

She, however, was still trying to catch her breath. Since they'd arrived at his house almost eight hours ago, they had managed to christen almost every room. He saved the bedroom for last on his house tour. Rather than speak, she turned her head and placed a light kiss on his chest.

"Stop that," he said with a weary chuckle. "That's how this all started the last time." Truth be known, he never wanted her to stop. She was here, she was his, and for the first time in his life, Ethan was looking forward to a little less adventure and a whole lot more settling down.

Together they shifted and got more comfortable under the blankets. "Do I need to take Maylene out?" he asked.

Summer peeked across the room to where they had set up the puppy's bed earlier. "She's sound asleep. Let's let her be for now." She snuggled closer to him. "Thank you."

"For what? She's just a puppy. This space is new to her and I want to make sure she's all right."

She smiled against his chest. "Not that. I mean for everything. For not letting me leave. For canceling my flight and commandeering my movers." She lifted her head and looked at him. "Thank you for loving me enough not to let me leave."

With a soft kiss to the top of her head, Ethan relaxed even more. "Thank you for wanting to come home with me."

Home. It had a nice ring to it, Summer thought. And she couldn't think of a more perfect place for it than right here in Ethan's arms.

Epilogue

THE TIMING WASN'T IDEAL, BUT IT COULDN'T BE helped. As Summer rushed around the house gathering her things, she checked her watch for the hundredth time. "Darn it," she muttered. "I'm going to be late."

Ethan strode into the room as he adjusted his tie. "You okay?"

"Just late as usual."

"So? Just call Mark and tell him you're running a few minutes behind. He'll understand."

She knew he would, but at the same time, it frustrated her that she was so completely out of sorts lately. Between settling in and getting her things set up in Ethan's home while still moving forward with designing a vacation home for them back in North Carolina, she was exhausted. "I just hate to make him wait."

"It's fifteen minutes, sweetheart. Not hours."

"I suppose." She pulled on her shoes and then stood up. "I just wish you were able to go with me."

He walked over and kissed her until he felt her relax. "I wish I could too, but with Zach coming home next week, and trying to get his place ready for him to recuperate, I just can't get away."

It had been almost a month since Summer had moved in, and while she had been looking forward to working with Casey on her business, she came to realize how much she was needed here until Zach came home.

They had discussed the possibility of splitting their time between the East and West Coasts, but until they got Zach settled, it wasn't something they could solidify.

"I'm going to do my best to be back here before he gets home. I think we've got it coordinated so Mark will fly me back here and then head right on to Alaska to pick up Zach and the medical team."

"Do you really think that's going to last?" Ethan asked as he poured himself a cup of coffee.

"What do you mean?"

"Do you think for a minute your brother is going to tolerate having all those strangers in his house for any length of time?"

"Well, he's going to have to if he wants to do his rehabilitation and everything at home rather than in an actual rehab center."

"I don't know… I don't think this is going to go smoothly."

"Where Zach is concerned, it rarely does," she said with a sigh. She didn't want to leave, but it was Selena's baby shower and she desperately wanted to be there. Plus, it would give her the opportunity to discuss business with Casey and see if there was anything she could do long distance to help with the day-to-day operations of their wedding planning business.

As if reading her mind, Ethan placed his mug down and asked, "So you have plans to meet with Casey?"

She nodded.

"Any chance you're up for discussing an actual event?"

Summer thought about it for a minute. "I'm guessing she has several events on the calendar. With any luck, I'll be able to observe her in action while I'm there. Otherwise, I'll have to pencil in another trip so I can see what they actually do."

"Clueless," Ethan muttered with a laugh.

"Excuse me?"

He stepped in close to her. "What I'm saying is, do you think you might want to talk to her about a wedding? Not someone else's. An actual…wedding. Like…ours."

Her mouth formed a perfect *O* as she looked up at him. "Are you serious?"

Right then and there, he reached into his pocket and dropped down to one knee. "Summer Montgomery, I love you. I cannot imagine my life without you in it. I want us to build a home, a life, a family together. Will you marry me?"

Never in a million years had Summer imagined Ethan proposing so soon, and yet it seemed as though she had been waiting forever. "Yes," she said as the first tear rolled down her face. "Yes, I'll marry you!"

Ethan stood and slipped the ring on her finger before leaning down and kissing her. He hadn't planned on proposing to her this morning, but when he thought about her trip and all of the possibilities, he knew the timing would be perfect. He lifted his head and looked down into her eyes. "I want you to start planning your dream wedding," he said softly. "I want you to have everything you want to make your dreams come true."

She reached up and cupped his cheek. "They already have because I have you."

Other than her agreeing to be his wife, those were the sweetest words Ethan Reed had ever heard.

READ ON FOR A SNEAK PEEK AT

Made for Us

BOOK 1 IN SAMANTHA CHASE'S BRAND-NEW SERIES
THE SHAUGHNESSY BROTHERS

———

LATE ON A FRIDAY NIGHT, AIDAN SHAUGHNESSY SAT alone in his apartment. He was tired but his brain wouldn't shut down enough for him to go to sleep. He was restless. His skin felt too tight for his body. And for the life of him, he didn't know what to do about it.

Earlier at dinner his sister had accused him of being too nitpicky—but that was hardly new, and didn't seem enough to keep him awake. *Meticulous* was a word that was often thrown around when people talked about him. It didn't bother him. Much. Meticulous could be a good thing, if his brothers didn't add "anal-retentive control freak" to it all the damn time.

He rested his head on the back of the sofa and let out a long sigh. If he allowed himself to stop being the big brother for a minute and just be a bystander, he could admit Darcy wasn't asking for anything out of the ordinary. He knew she was itching to spread her wings. But there was no way in hell he or any of his brothers were going to let her go off to some faraway college on her own. She'd just have to learn to deal with it. But he supposed there were some things they could compromise on.

Looking at the clock on the wall, he saw it was after midnight. He should be getting ready for bed.

Instead, he grabbed his cell phone and pulled up Hugh's number. Although Aidan couldn't remember exactly where his brother was this month, he knew it was somewhere on the West Coast, and three hours earlier.

"If you're calling me this late on a Friday night it can't be good," Hugh said as he answered the phone.

Aidan chuckled. "Maybe I just wanted to hear your cheery voice."

"Yeah, right," Hugh said with his own laugh. "Seriously, everything okay? This is late for you, old man."

The comment burned more than it should. He was responsible, so what? Why did everyone have to make it sound like there was something wrong with him? "It's not that late," Aidan grumbled. "I just…" He paused. "Something's going on with Darcy."

"Oh, shit," Hugh muttered. "That is all on you and Dad, bro. There is no way I'm dealing with a teenage girl. She scares the hell out of me."

This time Aidan's laugh was hearty. "For crying out loud, Hugh, she's a child. And she's our sister!"

"What is it this time?"

"It's mostly the same song and dance but she's getting more…vocal about it. At dinner tonight she kind of yelled at me and Dad about the whole college thing."

Hugh sighed loudly. "Listen, Darcy is going to be pissed because, well, she's Darcy. She's a female and she likes to argue. Aidan, look…it's Friday night. I've got a resort filled to capacity…"

"I'm thinking of letting her work for me a couple of days a week after school."

"That's brave, man. Very brave. And she's good with that? I would have thought she'd take issue with having to work for family."

"I haven't mentioned it to her yet. I just thought of it right before I called you. What do you think?"

"Like I said, you're brave."

"Bravery has nothing to do with it. It's just that …"

"She doesn't need to work," Hugh interrupted. "Dad takes care of everything for her. Why can't she just be grateful and…go shopping or something?"

"I agree with you, but maybe she wants to feel like she's contributing."

"To what?"

"To her family," Aidan said. "With all of us moved out, now it's just her and Dad at home."

"And you."

Aidan sighed and pinched the bridge of his nose. "I don't live with them. I have a place of my own and…"

"And you still spend a whole lot of time at home," Hugh said carefully. "It's not a bad thing, Aidan. I think it's great you're close by in case either of them needs you, but don't you ever want more?"

How had the subject suddenly turned to him? This wasn't about him; this was about Darcy. Ignoring Hugh's question, Aidan went back to his original train of thought. "If she has a job, maybe it'll pacify her about the whole college thing, and I can still keep an eye on her."

"And working for her brother is going to accomplish that?"

"It's a start."

"Fine. Go ahead and ask her, but do me a favor."

"What?"

"Have someone record it. I want to see her reaction." He laughed. "Look man, do what you think is best. Let me know what you need from me and I'll do it. You're the responsible one in the family. You always seem to know exactly what to do and say to smooth things over. If you think offering Darcy a job in your office is the answer, then do it."

"But…?" Aidan knew there was more.

"But…" Hugh began, "maybe it's time for you to stop smoothing things over for everyone else and start doing something for yourself."

"What are you talking about?"

"Dude, it's midnight on a Friday freaking night and you're on the phone with your *brother*. And that's after you went and had dinner with your father and sister. For God's sake, go out! Go on a date! When was the last time you were even with a woman?"

"None of your damn business," Aidan snapped.

"That long, huh?" Hugh chuckled. "Okay, fine. Don't tell me. I can pretty much guess." He stopped and collected his thoughts. "Just…think about it, okay?"

"About what?"

"And you call me a dumbass," Hugh said with exasperation. "Think about *yourself*, damn it! Think about doing something on a Friday night that isn't family-related. Think about going out with a beautiful woman and wining and dining her and spending the night with her nails raking down your damn back."

Aidan hadn't thought about it that way but he had a feeling he would be now. "Fine. I'll think about it."

"Hey, and Aidan?"

"What?" he said grumpily.

"You can call me any damn time you want. Seriously."

A small smile broke on Aidan's face. "Thanks, man. I appreciate it."

"Keep me posted on the whole Darcy situation."

Aidan agreed and they hung up. He was no closer to any decisions on anything. The only thing that had changed was that he definitely had an itch that needed to be scratched.

Chapter 2

"Reason number nine hundred and forty-seven why my life sucks. This job. At least this job today." Zoe Dalton slouched down in her office chair and looked at the pile of messages in front of her. She'd been an interior designer for years, but she'd just moved to the East Coast the month before and working for well-known designer Martha Tate was quickly grating on her nerves.

A flurry of activity outside her door made her look up and her boss appeared as if Zoe'd conjured her up by force of griping.

"Zoe," Martha said breathlessly as she stepped into the office and sat down at the desk, "I'm going to need you to take over on the Shaughnessy job."

From what Zoe had heard in the previous weeks, the Shaughnessy project was a huge undertaking. There were a lot of houses going up in a brand-new community, and at least half a dozen model homes needed to be decorated. "Why? What happened to Sarah?" Zoe asked.

Martha waved her off. "She went rogue and the client is majorly pissed."

"Went rogue?"

"She ignored the design plans the client requested," Martha said reproachfully. "This was a fairly straightforward job; everything was clearly specified per Mr. Shaughnessy's directions."

"So I have to go in and do damage control, is that it?"

Her boss nodded. "And…redo everything Sarah did. And make sure the next five houses are done *exactly* as requested."

Seemed like a no-brainer. Zoe shrugged and smiled. "I'm on it."

Martha looked visibly relieved. "Good…good. You have a meeting with Mr. Shaughnessy in an hour. Sarah's collecting all her files, along with all her personal belongings, and you'll have them to go through in a few minutes."

"Her personal belongings?"

"Her files. She's fired," Martha said.

Maybe this job *wasn't* a no-brainer. She was going to have to tread very carefully from this point forward.

She nodded and straightened in her seat. "Okay, I'll go and meet with Mr. Shaughnessy at ten and then I have an eleven o'clock with…"

"Oh, no, no, no, Zoe," Martha interrupted. "You aren't meeting with anyone else today. You'll have to cancel."

"But—"

"You have to give this project one hundred percent of your attention."

"But—"

"You can't expect someone like Aidan Shaughnessy to wait on you and your schedule. I know you haven't been here very long, but the Shaughnessys are a very important family in the community and this account is huge for us. Sarah can fill you in about them. You're going to need to be available not only to fix Sarah's mistakes but to make sure absolutely nothing else goes wrong with the rest of the houses. You need to be on this 24/7."

Zoe was not one to raise her voice but right now it was the only way to get her boss to stop interrupting her. "Hold on!" she said. "I have at least six other active projects I'm working on. I've put a lot of time and effort into developing relationships with these clients. I can't just toss them aside, Martha!"

"Already taken care of," Martha said dismissively. "I've reassigned all of your projects. If you'll just go through your messages, I'll be sure to pass them on to the designers who are taking them over."

Zoe's head felt ready to explode. Back in Arizona, she'd had her own firm and had been her own boss. Zoe had known there were going to be some compromises when she went to work for someone else, but this was worse than she'd expected. The decision to move had been an emotional one and she had hoped for a more positive transition. This was not something she was willing to take lying down.

"Look, Martha, I'm sure Mr. Shaughnessy is a reasonable businessman…" she began diplomatically and was surprised when Martha actually snorted sarcastically. Zoe raised her eyebrows but continued. "Surely he can understand that while Sarah made a…mistake… we will do everything to rectify it without compromising our other clients." There. That sounded reasonable, didn't it?

Leaning forward in her seat, Martha gave Zoe a pitying look. "Zoe, trust me. If it were any other client, I would let you keep your other projects. But this is a… special…case. This is going to demand much more of your time than you think. If, by some miracle, you get things going to the point where I'm not hearing from him several times a week, I'll consider letting you take on other projects again. Until I can be sure of it, though, he's your one and only client."

"What if I promise not to let my other projects interfere with the Shaughnessy job?"

Martha shook her head. "Trust me; you can't keep that promise."

Zoe sat back in resignation.

"You've had your own business, Zoe, so I know you've had your share of difficult clients, right?"

Zoe nodded.

"And that's why I'm putting you on this job. Think of your most difficult client and multiply by say...ten."

Music of doom began playing in Zoe's head. "Well, I wasn't scared before, but now..."

"We'll talk about this after your meeting." Standing, Martha put an end to the discussion by walking out of the room.

Just when she had thought her day couldn't get any worse. Zoe immediately suspected she was going to hate Aidan Shaughnessy.

The next fifteen minutes were like an out-of-body experience for Zoe. People came and went from her office to get files and messages and collect what they could on her former clients. Zoe felt like she was watching the whole thing happen in slow motion; it was as though she wasn't even there. And just when she thought the worst was over, Sarah walked in and dropped a massive box on the floor in front of Zoe's desk.

"Good luck with *that* one," she said snidely and walked right back out.

"Sarah! Wait!" Zoe cried, scrambling out from behind

her desk. Luckily, Sarah halted in the hallway. "Can I talk to you for a minute? Please?" Zoe could see that her former coworker would as soon spit in her face as talk, but Sarah reluctantly walked back into Zoe's office.

"Thank you," Zoe said, quietly closing the door. She offered Sarah a seat but the woman continued to stand with her arms crossed, ready to flee. "I know the last thing you want to do is help me with any of this, but could you please just let me know what I'm getting into?" Zoe was practically begging.

Sarah relaxed her stance. "I've known Aidan Shaughnessy all my life, and he is an arrogant, condescending jackass. *That's* what you're getting yourself into."

Not quite what she was hoping for, but it was a start. "Okay, I got that part. But what about the job itself? I know there are five houses left and..."

"Six," Sarah corrected. "He's going to make you completely redo that first house. I wouldn't be surprised if he's gotten the entire thing stripped down to bare walls already."

Zoe's stomach lurched. She swallowed hard and sat down in her chair. "Okay, six houses. What makes them difficult?"

Sarah finally took a seat. "It's not the houses that make the job difficult, Zoe, it's the man. Just...be careful."

This was getting worse by the minute. "How so?"

"Look, you're new to the area so you're probably not aware of it but...the Shaughnessys are like the Kennedys around here. They've been here forever. There are a lot of them and they're all successful."

"Define successful."

Sarah settled more comfortably in her seat and gave her words some thought. "Let's see…Hugh, the second oldest, owns a bunch of luxury resorts pretty much all over the world. His newest one is in Napa—he bought a vineyard and built a five-star resort on it. It's huge with the celebrity crowd right now. Most of his other resorts are on islands—his next one is going up in Australia, I think—and he does destination weddings and that sort of thing."

"Wow." Zoe was impressed but not to the point of a comparison to the Kennedys.

"Then there's Quinn. I graduated with him. He was a star athlete in high school and we all thought he was going to go play major league baseball but he took up race car driving. He doesn't do it anymore—one crash too many, I think—and now he has a chain of custom auto body shops up and down the East Coast."

"So they're overachievers," Zoe said conversationally. "So what?"

"It's not just those two." Sarah smirked. "Next we have Riley."

"Wait a minute," Zoe interrupted. "Are you talking about Riley Shaughnessy…*the* Riley Shaughnessy?"

"I am," Sarah said.

"The rock star?" Zoe said, as if it needed clarification.

"Yes. Riley's been singing since he was old enough to talk, but he's very down to earth on top of being incredibly talented. No one makes that big a deal of it anymore when he comes back to visit—to the locals, he's just Riley. Folks are protective of him. When he comes home, they do what they can to make sure the tourist fans don't get too out of hand."

"I had no idea this was such a touristy place," Zoe said. When she'd decided to relocate, all she knew was she wanted to live on the beach. Growing up in Arizona was all fine and well, but Zoe had dreamed of a time when she could wake up, walk out her back door, and put her toes in the sand. Finding the job with Martha had seemed like a godsend.

Until now.

"Okay, so it's an overachieving family," she finally said.

"Still not done," Sarah said. "Did you know that Riley has a twin brother?"

Zoe shook her head, surprised. Everyone knew the rock star, but Zoe had never heard of a twin.

"Owen and Riley are fraternal but they still look a lot alike. I always thought Owen was the sweetest of the bunch by far, but he's also the shyest."

"And what does he do?" Zoe was almost afraid to ask.

"Owen is an astrophysicist. He's absolutely brilliant."

Of course he is, Zoe thought.

"He got picked on a bit because he was so nerdy and quiet compared to his brothers—especially his outgoing twin—but now he goes all over the world teaching at universities." Sarah let out a sigh. "And then there's Darcy."

"Oh, you mean there's actually a female in that bunch?" Zoe asked.

"The one and only. She's got it the hardest."

"Why?"

"Are you kidding me?" Sarah said. "She's got five older brothers and everyone in this town knows her family, along with everything about her life. She's seventeen years old. How much do you think she gets away with?"

Zoe was an only child so she couldn't imagine what it was like having even one overachieving sibling, let alone five. "Poor kid," Zoe said. "What about Aidan? Where does he fall in the lineup?"

"He's the oldest," Sarah said, suddenly tense again. "Maybe that's why he's such a control freak and such a pain in the ass to work with."

"I'm sure he's just…"

Sarah cut her off. "He's a perfectionist and he's totally unreasonable. If you don't follow his instructions to the letter, he goes right over your head. I substituted some perfectly fine paint colors—they were from last year's palette, so they were thirty percent off, and they work just fine. You'd think he'd be grateful I'd taken the initiative and found a way to save him some money. But no, it's his way or the highway. And all Martha cares about is getting him off her back. And then there's the stuff he doesn't tell you and when you figure it out on your own, it'll be all wrong. Do yourself a favor, Zoe. Brush up on your ESP skills and plan on not getting any sleep. Good luck. You're going to need it."

"I'm so sorry, Sarah." It was the only thing Zoe could think of to say. "I really appreciate all of the background."

Sarah nodded and stood. "I need to go. You have a meeting with him in less than half an hour. Better be early. He hates it when you're late. And by late, I mean on time."

Perfect, Zoe thought apprehensively.

She watched Sarah walk out of her office and then looked at the box on the floor.

"Reason number nine hundred and forty-eight why my life sucks today? Aidan Shaughnessy."

Okay, that was a lot of information, Zoe kept saying to herself on the drive over. She wasn't sure how helpful it would be in dealing with the man himself.

After perusing Sarah's project files, Zoe could see what Sarah had done with the colors and finishes on the first model home. It didn't sound so bad, but Zoe wasn't foolish enough to believe it was going to be an easy fix. As Zoe had left for her meeting, Martha had warned her again that no matter what Mr. Shaughnessy wanted done to make it right, Zoe wasn't to argue.

Zoe frowned. It wasn't as if she argued with clients. Much.

Her GPS signaled that she had arrived at her destination—ten minutes early, thank you very much—and the sight before her took her breath away. After parking the car, she slowly got out and removed her sunglasses.

"Stunning." The word was a mere whisper from her lips. She'd done her fair share of work with architects, builders, and your everyday homeowners, but never before had she seen a home that drew you in like this one.

The landscaping was immaculate; vivid colors mixed with the perfect amount of greenery. For a moment, Zoe would have sworn the plants were fake. Crouching down, she touched the leaves on some of the flowers and leaves just to make sure. The lawn felt like some sort of plush carpeting, and she itched to kick off her shoes and feel it on her bare feet. It wasn't as soft as the sand surrounding the beach house she was renting, but this was a pretty close second. She wouldn't mind walking outside to something like this every day.

The stonework on the front of the house was perfect and the color complemented the siding beautifully. All the windows were top of the line and just beckoned you to come inside. But not before stopping on the wrap-around porch and maybe spending a few minutes on the swing.

She sighed. She actually stopped and sighed.

The low white picket fence around the front yard kept it separate from the worksites around it, like an oasis in the middle of a combat zone. Standing in the middle of the lawn, you could almost overlook the chaos going on around it.

Zoe, however, knew the real battleground was inside the house.

Standing, she gave the yard one last smile before walking up to the front door. It was like walking to an execution and her feet suddenly felt filled with lead. Taking a fortifying breath, she gripped the doorknob and walked inside.

The spacious entryway led into a wide, open floor plan. The floors were real hardwood—not engineered—and the dark finish shone like polished glass. Zoe looked down to see if she could see her reflection. She was about to call out and announce her presence, but first she crouched down one more time to run her hands over the floor.

"Like silk," she said softly, loving the feel of the wood beneath her hands.

"That's what I was going for," a deep male voice said from a few feet away.

Aidan had been watching this woman since her arrival. He had been in one of the upstairs bedrooms when he saw her car pull up, and had watched in fascination as she inspected the yard. While he felt mildly guilty for causing the other decorator to lose her job, he couldn't help but be intrigued by her replacement. From what he'd observed so far, this woman was somebody who took notice of details. It wasn't hard to see the appreciation in her eyes as she looked at the house.

And he couldn't help but look at *her* with appreciation. The woman before him had fiery red curly hair and a body with the kind of curves that made a man want to…scratch an itch. *Damn it*. This was so not the time for *that* thought to come to mind. As she straightened before him, he had to admit she was even more stunning up close. Tall. In heels, she was maybe only four inches shorter than him, and that was saying something. Most women didn't come close to his six-foot-two-inch height.

Aidan's mouth went dry when she took off her sunglasses and he caught sight of the greenest eyes he had ever seen. She smiled and held out her hand in greeting. "Mr. Shaughnessy, hello," she said, her voice was just a bit husky. "I'm Zoe Dalton."

For a moment, Aidan couldn't speak. He reached out and took her hand in his, fully intending to give her a businesslike handshake, but as soon as he felt her soft skin, he pretty much forgot his own name.

You really have been without a woman for too long, he admonished himself. "Miss Dalton," he murmured, forcing himself to focus. He shook her hand a little too roughly and released it as if she'd burned him.

Zoe was equally speechless. Why had no one mentioned that this man was the sexiest thing on two legs? His rock star brother may have been nominated one of the sexiest men alive, but Riley had nothing on his older brother. Dark hair, blue eyes, and hands rough enough that Zoe wanted to feel them all over her. It was rare for a man to make Zoe feel small and delicate, but Aidan was built like a linebacker and managed to make her feel it now.

Zoe fanned herself briefly as Aidan turned and walked away.

And the view was just as spectacular from behind.

She almost groaned.

About the Author

New York Times and *USA Today* bestselling author Samantha Chase released her debut novel, *Jordan's Return*, in November 2011. Although she waited until she was in her forties to publish for the first time, writing has been a lifelong passion. Teaching creative writing to students from elementary through high school and encouraging those students to follow their writing dreams motivated Samantha to take that step as well. When she's not working on a new story, Samantha spends her time reading contemporary romances, blogging, playing Scrabble on Facebook, and spending time with her husband of more than twenty years and their two sons in North Carolina.